WHAT HAPPENS WH
NOWHERE LEFT

RUNNING

FROM

MYSELF

AMBER GILBERT

Running From Myself

This is a work of fiction. While reference may be made to actual events or existing locations, the names, characters, and incidents are either the product of the author's imagination or are used fictitiously. Any resemblance to any actual persons, living or dead, business establishments, events, or locales is entirely coincidental.

Book designed and formatted by Laura Murray at Peanut Designs www.pnutd.co.uk

Dedication

For those who feel they have nowhere left to run,
may you find the love, hope, and freedom waiting within these pages.

Contents

1

Teen Mum

The rain was streaming down the windows, the rhythmic sound comforting Saff as she watched the raindrops land on the window and followed their smooth ride down the glass. *Why did it always rain in Manchester?* She thought. The sound of the kettle reaching boiling point snapped her out of her thoughts, and she began to make Levi's bottle and a cup of tea for herself. He would be awake soon.

While the tea bag sat in the boiling water, Saff took a swig of water as she swallowed her anti-depressant and sighed, *another day of the same old.*

This wasn't the life she had imagined for herself. When she had decided to go ahead with her pregnancy at the age of seventeen years old, she hadn't thought this far ahead; that each day she would be facing this alone. She had wanted so much more for herself and her future.

When she became pregnant, she had this strange notion that at least now she would have someone who loved her unconditionally. She knew her mum loved her, although it was rarely spoken in words, rather actions but who else cared for her? A baby would, surely.

"Mama," Levi called from his room. She walked to get him, rubbing his head of black curls when she reached his cot. "Good morning my little man," she said as she picked him up and carried him across the hallway to the living room.

She settled him in her arms, and he took the bottle with his chubby little hands and began guzzling the warm milk. She looked around the living room of their little flat. The patterned wallpaper that she had bought using the decorating vouchers given to her by the council, a small portable television perched on a TV unit not much bigger than the television itself where Levi watched Teletubbies, and she watched Jerry Springer and the little wooden sofas she had been given. With her mum's help, Saff had covered the sofa seat cushions with a bright blue material and chose to have contrasting bright orange cushions placed in the corners. She had done her best to make it homely with her little money, but it still looked sparse. That did help her keep it tidy which is what she preferred; mess made her head spin. Most things in her home had been given to her or bought from the catalogue.

She closed her eyes as she remembered the catalogue, and felt her tummy do an anxious flip, the payment was overdue now along with a few other bills. How was she going to pay them? Her benefits barely covered the essentials. Her mate Katy owed her £20, which would come in handy, but it still wasn't enough to cover the bills that were piling up. She glanced sideways at the pile of letters on the windowsill, some still unopened because she knew what they said but didn't want to face them.

Levi was squirming in her arms to get down.

"Okay, okay. You can have a play for a while, then we will get dressed and go see Nana."

"Nana, Nana, Nana" Levi sang happily while playing with his toys.

Seeing Nana was the main thing they did in the week because all her friends were busy, and who wanted to hang out with a baby every day apart from Nana. It was company for Saff and would provide some relief from being the sole carer of an energetic toddler. They would hopefully stay for dinner too, saving Saff from having to buy or cook anything, another thing she hadn't thought about when she was pregnant, the dreaded dinnertime.

Later that day, Saff finished clipping Levi into his pram and turned to lock the front door of her flat.

"Hello Sapphire" Saff looked up to see her neighbour Jim who lived downstairs. "How's little Levi?" he asked as he began to walk over to where she was stood. She waited patiently, knowing he was now in his late 80s and noticing that his movements seemed to have slowed down, particularly his walking.

"Hi Jim, he's great thanks. We are just going to visit my mum. Do you need anything from the shops on my way back?"

"Oh no, I'm ok thanks," he smiled and stooped down to pinch Levi's cheek, who giggled joyfully. "I've got a microwave meal ready for later. That will do me. You get on now. Bye Levi" he waved and grinned and Levi did the same back.

Jim watched as they walked off down the street, Sapphire as he always called her, was marching as she pushed the baby's stroller. It was nice having a young family living upstairs, and he loved having Levi hobble round his garden pointing to all the flowers that his lovely Betty had planted over the years. Oh, he did miss her, she would have loved Sapphire and Levi. They never had any children of their own, it was always a regret for him, but they had tried, oh they had tried. He felt tears stinging in his eyes, he shook his head as he turned to go back through his back gate.

Oh, you silly old man, stop hankering after the past. Since Betty's passing a few years back each day was getting lonelier, and he felt his body getting slower, realising his mortality.

Sapphire and Levi refreshed him. She was a lovely young girl, with long dark hair and olive skin. She reminded him of his Betty in her younger days, what a beauty she had been. The prettiest girl he had ever seen. Yes, Sapphire often reminded him of her, and she didn't look old enough to have that baby with his head of big black curls and big brown eyes. Poor girl, bringing him up on her own and not being married. These young ones today didn't have the same values as his generation.

He knew some of the neighbours didn't like it when Sapphire had her friends over, or when they heard her music, but she was young. They needed to remember they were young once. He enjoyed hearing the laughter and music, and when it got too loud or too late, he turned his hearing aids off and went to sleep. Thinking of sleep, he yawned and looked at the time on his mantlepiece clock. It was time for his afternoon nap, he made himself comfy in his armchair, pulled up his blanket, and turned his hearing aids off.

Saff let herself into her mum's house with the key she still had.

"Nana will be home from work soon" unclipping Levi from his pram. "Let's go and get a snack while we wait."

After peeling and chopping an apple, she settled Levi in front of the TV in the living room and made herself useful. She looked around her mum's kitchen as she ran the hot water to wash the dirty dishes left on the side from breakfast. Her mum had never been great at keeping the house tidy but with four children, two of whom were still living at home, being a single parent and working a part-time job, it must be hard. It wasn't that Saff particularly enjoyed cleaning, but she enjoyed the result, she couldn't sit still if she knew there was a pile of dishes.

"Hello? Sapphire?" her mum, Kara, called just as she was draining the washing-up bowl, "I wasn't expecting you today, you've been here nearly every day this week" She picked Levi up for a cuddle and then took her coat off. "Still not got much food in?"

Saff slumped onto the sofa, "I've got to wait a few more days for my money to come in. All my mates are at work or uni mum, what am I meant to do all day? I go out of my mind sitting in the flat with Levi day in and day out now that college is finished. I'm even bored of watching Jerry Springer and Ricki Lake on TV. I thought taking a year out would be a good idea but it's hard work!"

Kara came and hugged her, "I know it's hard. Come on, let's put the kettle on and let me get sat down," she said as she walked into the kitchen to put the kettle on. "Oh, you've cleaned up Sapphire, thank you. It was a crazy rush this morning getting everyone out on time."

"You know leaving dirty dishes in the sink drives me mad mum, it's like I can hear them calling out to me. I couldn't have sat down and relaxed knowing they were there."

Sitting down with a brew when they were back in the living room, Saff quietly spoke, "Mum, could Levi stay here on Saturday night please?"

Raising her eyebrows, Kara responded, "Again, Sapphire?"

"It's not like you are going anywhere on a Saturday night, is it?" pleaded Saff.

"That's not really the point Saff and you know it. Levi is your son; you can't keep leaving him here while you go out partying."

Saff rolled her eyes; she didn't know why it was such a big deal. She was eighteen years old and wanted to go out, not be stuck in every weekend and her mum was not going anywhere so what difference would it make? She knew her mum would give in eventually; she always did when it came to Levi.

Saturday night couldn't have come quick enough. Saff jumped out of the taxi and ran to join the girls inside The Orange Grove Pub in Fallowfield.

"Hey Saff, do you want a drink?" shouted Katy as she stood at the bar, "we've got time for a few shots before the minibus gets here."

"Come on Katy, do I want a drink? Of course, I do!" she laughed, "I've already had a few glasses of wine while I was getting ready, after I dropped Levi at my mum's of course." She knew she was already feeling a little lightheaded.

"She agreed to have him then. He's such a cutie!" grinned Katy before turning and giving the waiter her order across the bar.

"Yeah, she loves having him really and I would go out of my mind if I didn't have these nights out. I just need to let loose! She's not too happy that it doesn't finish until 4am though." Saff knew she was asking too often but appreciated her mum's support.

Katy put two shot glasses in front of Saff and two in front of herself, "Let me give you that £20 back, you really helped me out with that!" handing her a crisp £20 from her purse, "Ready?" she said as she picked up a shot glass. Saff nodded and they knocked them back one after the other. Saff was already drunk before the minibus arrived at 10pm. She felt more confident when she was drunk, and a night out wasn't the same without being absolutely off your face; she could forget her life as a single teenage mum. For a while anyway.

The packed minibus pulled up outside the Wigan nightclub Maxime's. You could already hear the bouncy house music from the club upstairs. *Back to the Old School* was always the last Saturday of the month. The music was loud, the bass was thumping, and the place was buzzing. Once the group got through the bouncers on the door, they headed up the stairs to the main room. There was a large square dance floor in the centre of the room that was already starting to fill up, along the two side walls there were bars selling drinks, and towards the back of the room was a seating area and a bar serving food. The smoke swirled from the smoke machines around the room, and it carried with it the smell of cigarette smoke mixed with perfume, sweat, and alcohol.

"Let's go to the toilet and then get drinks" Katy shouted into Saff's ear. Saff nodded and followed Katy to the toilets. The floor was already covered in water and wads of wet toilet rolls.

"You go first," said Saff. Only one of the cubicles in the ladies' toilets had a door and that was hanging on for dear life. Maxime's wasn't known for being a high-end club, it was a dive with sticky carpets, but the music and atmosphere were what they came for.

"I wish Jack was here. He loves it in here" Katy shouted through the toilet door that Saff was holding shut with her foot hooked underneath it.

Saff smiled, "Aww he really does, doesn't he? Well, he will have to come with us when he gets out of jail."

The toilet flushed and Saff felt Katy tug at the door, so she moved her foot to let go. "If he behaves, he's only got a few more weeks to go. I can't wait!"

Saff waited until Katy had washed her hands, before going into the same toilet cubicle. Katy pulled the door shut with her foot and held it shut for Saff.

"I bet you can't wait to see him. I hope he realises how lucky he is that you keep standing by him every time" Saff knew Katy stayed loyal every time he went to prison and hoped that Jack appreciated it.

Katy moved her foot once she heard Saff coming out, "He says he does realise but it's not easy. I pray to God that he stays out of trouble once he's out. Now let's hurry up and get some cans of Stella and find the others" pulling Saff's arm towards the door. The music was already pounding in their ears and making them move their bodies to the beat as they walked to the bar.

As the night wore on Saff looked at her watch. 1am. She tried to stifle another yawn, wishing they would stop and hoping no one would see how tired she was. She shook her can of Stella gently, it was practically empty, and she didn't want another drink. The thought of another beer made her belly turn and she didn't have the money to switch to spirits. She knew how the rest of her friends stayed awake all night. *Ecstasy.* She had always been too scared to take them and usually just stuck to alcohol and sometimes some other amphetamine, like speed to keep her going. She suddenly noticed Tom with a bag of ecstasy tablets in his hand, he was going around the group offering them out.

"Not for you eh Saff?" laughed Tom, pushing the bag in her face, and mockingly raising his eyebrows.

"Oh, go on then" Saff shouted above the music. She took one out of the bag, took a deep breath, and swallowed an ecstasy tablet with the final swig of her can. *What harm could it do?* Her friends were doing them every week and they were fine.

Tom showed a face of pretend shock, then winked. "Enjoy yourself!"

At first, she felt no different and thought maybe they wouldn't work for her. But as she began to feel the drug take effect, the music sounded different, like she could feel it in every part of her being, deep down into her soul, every note, every beat, she felt it. The tablet gave her the energy to dance the whole night; she couldn't stop her body from moving to the music. It felt like electricity running through her body. And she felt overwhelming feelings of love for her group of friends, telling them constantly that she loved them, and hugging them. It was an incredible feeling and she wondered why she had hesitated until now. Those feelings of the very serious dangers of the drug pushed from her mind.

The next morning, Saff woke up to her phone ringing, again. She picked up the phone to see who was calling, it was her mum. 12pm. Her head was banging, and she realised she had only slept for four hours.

I probably should have just come straight home from the club and not gone back to Tom's for the after-party. Everyone else is probably still asleep because they don't have a kid to look after.

She fell back on the pillow and felt like she wanted to cry, but she knew she had to get up and go to Levi. With a heavy head, she dragged herself out of her bed. Last night had been a good night, but now the feelings of coming back down to reality returned as those familiar feelings of depression reared their ugly head.

As Saff walked round to her mum's house from her flat, she

swigged on her bottle of water, hoping to shake off this horrible feeling of dehydration, and was mindful to dodge the dog poo littered on the pavements. Her thoughts were running away with themselves, *if only I had made better choices for Levi, he doesn't deserve to be left at my mums all the time but what am I meant to do? I'm still a kid myself! He deserves better. Her thoughts went to his dad, messed up there didn't you Saff! Why can't you choose better guys? Guys that actually want to be with you. Levi deserved a dad, and I deserve to be loved. But do you? You're a mess!*

Saff rubbed her temple with her free hand, her head was really banging and thoughts like this were not helping her, but she always did this to herself, it was part of the comedown from the night before. Feelings of depression and low self-worth were magnified.

Suddenly she ducked down behind a car and swore under her breath, John, the doorstep lender she had been avoiding. He was getting out of his car, no doubt to knock on some other vulnerable person's door to sell them something they couldn't afford. Hoping he hadn't seen her she turned on her heels and quickly made her way back the way she had come. She would have to walk the long way round down Wilbraham Road now, but it was better than bumping into him. She had done well to have avoided him so far.

"Good night then?" asked her mum, as she looked Saff over thinking that she looked rough.

Saff's voice was hoarse when she replied, making her sound as rough as she looked, "Yeah, it was. Thanks for having Levi, has he been ok?"

"He's having a nap, but he's been fine. He always is." She said as she looked over at Levi fast asleep in his travel cot she had set up in the living room.

"I won't go out as much when I start uni next year Mum," Saff said sleepily, "I don't think I will be able to hack it anyway or be able to afford it. Is it ok if we stay for dinner today?" she was already closing her eyes to snuggle up on the sofa for a nap before her mum could answer.

Kara pulled a blanket over Sapphire and checked on Levi. She secretly loved having him stay, but she couldn't let Saff know or she might take advantage. Kara's youngest two went to their dad's every weekend, and her other son was with his dad for a while. He needed a male figure in his life and Kara couldn't give him that right now. So having Levi to stay was a joy. Thinking back to when Sapphire was a baby and how hard it had been, Kara felt she needed to help. She hadn't planned to bring Saff up as a single parent, she had married her dad, but it didn't work out. She had decided to walk away from the relationship, which meant Sapphire grew up without her dad, and here she was repeating the same cycle with her son. Kara wanted to help as much as she could, she wanted more for her kids. More than she had been able to achieve.

2

No Angel

The following Saturday night, Saff and Katy were in a taxi to the nightclub M-Two in Manchester.

"I've felt so rotten all week, I don't even know if these anti-depressants are doing anything," Saff said gloomily, "Levi started nursery this week, and I had to wait in the parent's room for a bit, you know to see if he would settle, and the radio was on. Hearing about the Twin Towers in America actually made me cry. Like what the heck? I don't even know anyone involved but that's how I'm feeling!" throwing her head back on the seat headrest and closing her eyes.

"I heard about that on the news and had to sit down. It was shocking so you're not on your own there, but I think you need a man. You need some loving" winked Katy.

"Well, I wouldn't say no right now. Maybe you're right. Let's see what happens tonight!" Saff perked up, leaning forward she spoke to the taxi driver. "Just here please Boss."

"Oh, look at the queue, why is it always so long?" moaned

Katy as the taxi pulled up on the side street. "Is that Gabe and his boys near the front? Gabe would do anything for my Jack, so let's get in with them."

"Hey Gabe" Katy called as they walked quickly from the taxi to the front of the queue, "is it ok if we jump in with you? The queue is crazy, and we aren't really dressed to be stood out in the cold!"

Gabe glanced them both over, thinking that they must be cold in those little dresses, but they were looking nice, especially Katy's friend.

"Yeah, that's sweet Katy. And it's Saff, right?" Saff nodded and smiled; she didn't realise he knew her name. She felt herself blushing and tried not to stare at him. He was wearing a smart double-breasted jacket, unopened and she could see how tall and athletic he was through the material of the crisp white shirt he was wearing.

"Katy when does Jack get out?" enquired Gabe.

"Only a couple of weeks now, as long as he behaves himself this time!" Katy laughed. "I was fuming when he got those extra few weeks, he just needs to keep his nose clean now. So if you speak to him, please remind him!" Gabe nodded, agreeing that he would.

Once inside the club, they got a drink from the bar, and then nipped to the toilet. Katy pulled her into the same cubicle and shut the door behind her. She pulled out a little plastic zip-lock bag, waving it at Saff.

"Shall we?" she said as she opened the bag taking one of the white pills out and swallowing it.

"Eww, I don't know how you can do that without a drink. I hate even taking paracetamols, they make me gag. Did you bring these in with you?" asked Saff as she took one for herself, swallowing it with a big gulp of her vodka and coke. She shivered as it went down.

"Na, Gabe passed them to me before at the bar. So, it would be rude not to. I think he likes you too because he asked me if you had a man. I told him no of course!" she winked and gently punched Saff's shoulder.

"Really? He is kind of cute you know, and he smelled so good. I've never really got to know him. Well, let's see what happens, eh?! Tonight might be my night after all" doing a little celebratory dance.

They ended up staying with Gabe and his boys for the rest of the night, letting them buy drinks for them. Gabe liked to dance, and they had spent a lot of the night laughing and dancing on the dancefloor to cheesy pop and R&B. Katy and Saff had taken another two ecstasy tablets each. It was like the more Saff took the drug, the less she thought about the dangers and the braver she felt.

When the club was closing, and they were making their way out, Gabe offered them a lift home. *Saves money on a taxi,* thought Saff, so they agreed.

"Drop me off first please," said Katy giving him directions to hers and winking at Saff.

"Yeah, then me Gabe. I'm shattered and I've got to be up early in the morning" yawned Jason, Gabe's friend.

"I think I'm not far from you Jason, so I could get dropped off after that if that's ok. My feet are killing me from all that dancing" said Saff as she kicked her shoes off.

Once Katy and Jason were dropped off, Gabe turned to Saff "You wanna come back to mine for a bit?" he asked.

"Yeah cool," she said, feeling anything but cool. Her tummy was doing flips, but they were happy flips. Gabe was cute and had made her feel good tonight. She was also still buzzing from the ecstasy so she didn't fancy going home to bed just yet, she wouldn't be able to get to sleep.

Over the next few weeks, Saff and Gabe spent more time together. He was either at hers or she was at his. Saff loved being in a relationship, it made her feel safe, and she longed for stability and a normal family life, which was a far cry from what she had experienced growing up. Thinking back to her childhood, growing up in the crescents in Hulme had been carefree but unpredictable. You could regularly hear music thumping from somewhere reggae, and soul, especially on a sunny day. She often thought of Hulme when she smelt the sweet scent of weed as Gabe smoked. She could remember being sat on the grass outside The Eagle Pub on a hot summer's day, sipping a cold can of coke and nibbling dry roasted peanuts with the sweet smell of weed floating in the air as her mum chatted to people sitting nearby. She would be telling them how great a community this was, and boasting about how they didn't even have to pay rent because the council had given up on the place.

The way she talked, she made it sound like squatting in this dump was the best thing ever, but Saff didn't share her enthusiasm at the time. The four, hulking concrete blocks that made up the Hulme Crescents were depressing, and most of the flats were infested with cockroaches and rats. Saff thought it was gross, but her mum loved it, as did the other adults who'd flocked there from all walks of life: the artists, the poets, the photographers, hippies, musicians, and students . . . there they were without the influences and restrictions of the outside world, they felt free; and anyone and everyone were welcome.

Looking back Saff could see the attraction but once they had moved on from there, they moved from one place to another with Saff changing schools along the way. Seeing men come and go, some she remembered fondly but others she was glad to see the back of. She didn't want to experience those things in her life, she wanted a different life to the one her mum had had. She craved family and stability. Maybe she could have this with Gabe and maybe he would treat her like she deserved to be treated.

Saff soon found out this wasn't going to be possible, as she lay in bed with Gabe one morning after a night out. Levi was with her mum. Gabe had just sat up and lit a spliff, Saff pulled back the covers to get up when he grabbed her arm and pulled her back, "Where you going?"

She pulled her arm free, and looking at him with a furrowed brow said, "I'm getting up."

He took a big draw on his spliff and shook his head, "Na, you can get up when I get up."

She looked at him confused, he didn't sound like he was saying this in a romantic loving way as you see in the movies, where a man pulls his woman back to bed for a bit of fun. He looked vexed. "You're messing, right? I need to get up."

"Do I look like I'm messing? You can get up when I get up, I said. So just sit back down."

Saff still thought he must be messing, why would he stop me from getting up? She stood up and was about to speak when he pulled her back down and slapped her across the face with the back of his hand.

"Didn't you hear me?" he growled, "I don't know who the eff you think you're talking to."

Saff reached up to touch her cheek and sat there in shock, tears stinging her eyes. *Did that really just happen? What did I do? What did I say? Maybe I did something wrong?* Saff couldn't work out what had made him so mad and what would warrant a slap. She had never been in this situation before; oh, she had seen her mum be slapped by a boyfriend and badly treated but she had not expected that for herself.

She sat there silently, her stomach turning and her heart beating fast. It hadn't been a particularly hard slap, but she was still in disbelief and unsure what to do or say. She suddenly felt unsure about everything, any feelings of stability she had previously felt, left her with that slap.

Gabe smoked the rest of his spliff, "I'm getting off." He pulled his clothes on and walked out.

Hearing the front door shut, Saff waited until she heard the gate open and close to let her know Gabe had gone, then she quickly ran down the stairs of her flat and locked the front door. *What do I do now? Do I tell someone?* Saff felt confused, not sure what to do next.

Hot tears ran down her face. She knew she had to collect Levi, as he was at her mum's again, so she wiped her tears and headed to the bathroom to try to make her face look like she hadn't just been slapped and then crying. All while trying to push what had happened out of her mind. Feeling embarrassed she decided she wasn't going to mention it to anyone. It soon dawned on Saff that she was more like her mum than she had thought.

Gabe pulled the zip up on his jacket while holding his spliff between his lips, *Why did she do that? Why couldn't she just listen to him? She had a mouth on her that girl.*

He took his spliff in his hand and sucked his teeth. Gabe liked his girls to just do as he said, he didn't need them to have an opinion or a voice. Saff had a pretty face, and she had her own place, which meant she had something going for her, but she had too many big thoughts and ideas. It might be time to try to bring her down a peg or two and shake them out of her. He took his car keys from his pocket and made his way to his car, he had things to do, and there was money to be made.

It was a couple of hours later when Gabe knocked at the door holding a bunch of flowers. Lilies, her favourite.

"These are for you," he said sweetly as he handed them to her. He hung his head as she took them from him, "I am so sorry. I don't even know what happened, what made me snap."

Saff had been thinking about the slap all day, her head was reeling from it. She had looked at it from every angle and she kept coming back to the same thought – he can't have meant to do that.

"I just wanted to spend as much time as possible with you, and you always seem to be busy. I just wanted you all to myself" Gabe continued.

He does seem sorry, and it hadn't been that hard, to be honest. Maybe I overreacted this morning. I am always busy doing stuff, maybe I should think about him more, she thought as she looked into his eyes.

Saff opened the door to invite him in as a sign she had forgiven him. As he stepped into the house, she put her hand gently on his arm, "It can't happen again you know," it came out as almost a whisper.

"I know, I know. And it WON'T happen again. I promise" he hugged her and carried on up the stairs to her flat where Levi was now happily playing. Saff watched him almost bounce up the stairs, and hoped to God it was the right decision to forgive him.

Finding herself with a free Friday night with no plans, Levi was staying at her mum's and Gabe had gone out of town clubbing with his boys, Saff ran herself a bath filled with bubbles and was looking forward to some time to herself. She sank into the hot soapy water and closed her eyes, hoping to relax. She began thinking about Gabe, he seemed to be on his best behaviour the last few weeks, being really nice and it reassured Saff that the slap must have been a one-off. But just as she was beginning to put her guard down and relax, little arguments started to creep in, arguments over nothing it seemed. Well to Saff they felt like they were over nothing but the way he spoke to her was getting worse. She had noticed he was putting her down, making snarky comments about her weight or the way she looked, and then sometime after was always very apologetic.

Saff began to think about one particular night when he had turned up around midnight. Saff had already gone to bed; she enjoyed an early night so he would have known she was already in bed. He had let himself in with the spare key she had recently given him.

Gabe came into her bedroom and turned the main light on causing Saff to wake and cover her eyes. *What was he doing?* Saff felt the quilt be pulled off her and off the bed and shivered as the cold chill of the night hit her.

Levi had fallen asleep in her bed, and he was still there, he squirmed and turned over shielding his eyes from the light. Saff had no idea what Gabe was playing at, and she had no desire to find out in front of Levi, so she scooped him up in her arms shushing him back to sleep and carried him to his bed in his room.

Once he was settled, she had returned to her room and after a time of pleading with Gabe to let her go back to sleep, he turned the light off and walked into the living room.

Saff shivered at the memory of it and opened her eyes, hoping to stop the thoughts and images. He had been sorry the following day and said he had just wanted to spend time with her.

Another memory forced its way to her mind, she had been feeling low one day and was sat with her head in her hands, having a bit of a cry on the sofa when he let himself in again.

"What's the matter with you?" he had said when he saw her, "It's always so depressing round here. Have you taken your medication today?" he jeered cockily.

She had looked up at him with red-rimmed eyes filled with tears, "Gabe, that's a horrible thing to say. Of course, I've taken them, I need them, they help me."

She remembered him looking down at her with a look of disgust, he saw people with depression as losers and lazy. "Sort your head out, you act like a right basket case sometimes. You do know that no one else would want to be with you. Sometimes I don't even know why I'm with you" sucking his teeth angrily.

"Well leave then Gabe, go please leave." Saff had felt her blood boiling at the time, why couldn't he support her? She had depression. He made her feel worse and this last year with him was starting to take its toll now. Any little thing she did seemed to set him off. It had her questioning herself all the time – *was it my fault that he got angry at me? Did I imagine it? Did I deserve it? Did I do something to press his buttons?*

This wasn't turning into the relaxing bath she had hoped for, as the water was becoming cold, and the bubbles had all melted away, she reached for the plug. She knew she was confused when it came to Gabe. Her emotions and feelings all mixed together and when he did hurt her, it was embarrassing. She didn't want to tell her friends, or her mum that he had hurt her again. He was such a nice person to everyone else, and to her in front of everyone else. And he was always so apologetic afterward, she believed his promises that he would try harder, and would get help with his anger. One thing she could never understand was despite it being him who caused her pain, it seemed the only person who could comfort her was him. She hated that about herself.

Despite thinking of some of the horrible situations she had experienced with Gabe recently, she had managed to enjoy the rest of her evening alone and a good night's sleep until Gabe woke her around 5am having just returned from his night out in Niche in Sheffield. By early afternoon they were having a brew together when one of her close friends Amy popped over.

"Thanks for letting me use your washing machine Saff, I don't even know if I can afford to get a new one right now, and if I ask Mum and Dad, they will only hold it over me head. These things always happen to me" said Amy as she lugged a big bag of laundry up the stairs of the flat to the kitchen.

Gabe was sitting in the living room building a spliff. Saff didn't smoke but knew her flat had that lingering smell of cannabis whenever Gabe was around.

"It's fine Amy, anytime. Let me show you how to load up the machine."

Once the machine was loaded, Amy went to sit on one of the chairs in the living room and Saff walked into the room behind her, she stood up by the window.

"Y'alright Gabe?" Amy asked Gabe, she had chatted nonstop since Saff had let her in, "Have they been fighting again up the road? Couple of the windows are boarded up."

"Yeah, the police have been around a couple of times this last week or so. I don't know why she keeps letting him move back in. I feel sorry for the kids."

"Aww yeah, how many they got now? Must be five or six?"

without waiting for an answer, she continued "Saff, I feel like we haven't been out for ages. Why don't we go out tonight and get a couple of bottles of wine?" Amy suggested excitedly. "I miss you and need some girly time. But who knows where the night will lead, right?"

"Sounds like a plan, but I would need to see if my mum would look after Levi again, he stayed there last night."

Suddenly, Gabe jumped up and grabbed her by her neck "You ain't going anywhere unless I say so" he snarled at her.

"Gabe, get off," Saff responded, her hand instinctively reaching up to his to move it. Saff's eyes flitted to Amy who had jumped out of her seat. Gabe had never snapped at her in front of anyone else, it was always behind closed doors.

"Gabe" Amy laughed nervously as she wondered what on earth had got into Gabe. Saff could see the veins in his neck and although his eyes were already red from smoking weed, she could see they were filled with anger "I was only messing; we aren't even going out tonight."

Gabe let go of her. She knew Amy was trying to stick up for her, but she hadn't done anything to make him snap at her like that, and she didn't want Gabe to start with Amy.

Gabe looked at Amy in disgust, and then back at Saff. He sucked his teeth and marched out of the flat, slamming the front door behind him.

Amy walked over and put a hand on her arm "Saff, are you ok? What was that? Did something happen before I got here? I've never seen him like that!" Amy's words came out quickly and rushed, she was visibly shaken.

Saff sighed, still rubbing her neck where he had gripped her, "Nothing happened. He's tired and hasn't had much sleep but to be honest, nothing ever has to happen. I've told you that Gabe is a different person when no one else is around. But that is the first time he's ever done that in front of anyone. No one believes me because he's so nice, and sometimes even I question myself."

Amy was pacing the room, "It's not right you know. He proper reminds me of that David guy I used to see, do you remember him?" she carried on not seeming to want an answer. "He used to flip out like that, but Gabe, na I never thought he was like that."

Saff stared out of the living room window, watching the trees moving gently in the wind, she could still hear Amy talking but was no longer listening to what she was saying. The fact that Gabe had attacked her like that in front of Amy scared her.

-

The following week had felt tense, Saff and Gabe hadn't spoken much, and he hadn't been over, but he had apologised over the phone. He had told her it was because he didn't want her going out, especially with Amy because he knew what she was like and didn't like the influence he thought she had on Saff. He also said he didn't like the fact that she was making plans with Saff while he was sitting there, it was disrespectful.

She had tentatively accepted his apology, but she had plans to go out that weekend. She needed to let loose and get drunk. Meeting a few friends in Queen of Hearts in Fallowfield would do the trick and Gabe couldn't make those decisions for her. She was looking forward to seeing Katy, gutted that Amy and Zoe couldn't come. Someone had slashed all of Amy's car tyres, so she was trying to sort that out and Zoe had her mum staying with her for the weekend.

During the night, Gabe had been texting her. She hadn't wanted to reply because she wanted to enjoy herself but after a few drinks, she had sent several replies. Of course, he had wanted to know where she was and what she was doing. Surely this was because he loved her, she thought as the night wore on.

"Saff, have you had enough drinks?" asked Katy, "the bouncers have just been over to ask if you are ok because of how loud you are being. They said you need to chill or leave."

"Oh, did they now?" shouted Saff, marching over to where the bouncers were stood. She wasn't sure why she suddenly felt invincible while under the influence of alcohol, she became loud and thought she had the strength of ten men, ready to take on the world. She knew she had to tell these bouncers they couldn't tell her what to do.

Before she even had a chance to say a word, they gently but strongly guided her out of the back door and closed it behind her. The cold air whipped around her face, and she shivered, stumbling as she made her way to the main road. It looked like the night was over for her, and she needed to find a taxi.

Around 4am Saff opened her eyes; the room was spinning, and she could hear banging and shouting. *Was someone knocking on the door?* She wasn't sure. She had crashed out, fully clothed on her bed. Swinging her feet off the bed, she put them down on the floor only to feel something wet and slimy on the floor. *Sick, Great!* She had been sick all over the floor! *Gross.* She grabbed a towel from the washing basket near the bed, and quickly wiped her feet.

Groggily she walked down the stairs of her flat and looked through the peephole, steadying herself on the handrail. It was Gabe. Using the key in the lock she unlocked the door to a furious Gabe, who immediately grabbed her by the arm and pulled her outside. Swearing and calling her a few choice names he snarled "Leaving me standing outside at this time in the cold. Let's see how you like it." He carried on pulling her down the garden path and out onto the road. "Do you think I'm some idiot? Do you know how long I've been knocking?" his grip was getting tighter on her slim wrist.

Saff had nothing on her feet and was wearing the little black dress she had worn for her night out. Gabe continued to drag her down the street, disregarding her protests and cries. Saff was twisting and turning her wrist as much as she could and eventually, she managed to escape his grip. In a panic she ran to Zoe's house, she was the nearest friend. She hated having to wake Zoe up at this time, especially when her mum was staying over but she needed to get away from Gabe. She ran as fast as she could, constantly looking back and glad that although Gabe was following her, he wasn't running.

"Saff are you ok?" gasped Zoe as she tied her dressing gown around her and let Saff inside.

"Zoe, I am so sorry to wake you up. It's Gabe. Why does he have to be so horrible?" she sobbed, "I hope he's not following me. I really don't want him to bring trouble to yours. What am I doing? Every time it's getting worse, I have to get away from him."

Zoe bolted the front door behind her and ushered her into the living room, "Whatever you want to do, I'm here for you babe. I know it's not ideal, but have you thought about moving? If you are serious about getting away from him?" Zoe reassured her as she switched a table lamp on.

Saff shivered as she sat down on the sofa and pulled her knees up, wrapping her arms around them "I've thought about it a few times, but I think it's time to do something about it. I need to protect Levi, and myself. He's literally dragged me out of the house like this" she looked down at her bare feet to check them over and was grateful that she hadn't cut them.

Standing up, Zoe walked over to a wicker basket by her fireplace and picked up a couple of blankets. Walking back over to Saff she said "Don't make any big decisions just yet. You look frozen" placing the blankets down next to her.

"I hope I didn't wake your mum up, Zoe. I'm so sorry to have to come here like this" said Saff as she pulled one of the big fluffy blankets over her knees.

"Now, you know my mum would want you to be safe so don't worry about that. Try and get some sleep and we can talk in the morning if you want. Let me grab you some pyjamas."

Saff heard Zoe moving upstairs the next morning, she looked around for a clock wondering what time it was. As she recalled what happened last night, she realised she didn't have her phone. Gabe had been out of order; she knew she didn't deserve what he did to her last night. Her head was banging, and her stomach felt empty. She placed her hand over her face and groaned as she remembered she had been sick on her bedroom floor and retched at the thought of having to clean it up when she got back home. Home. How was she going to get home? Had he gone back to lock her door last night? Was he still there? She had a spare key at her mum's, she would stay away for a bit and then hope for the best. She sat up and groaned as she realised she didn't even have any shoes with her. *Great!* Hopefully, Zoe had something she could fit into, or she wouldn't be going anywhere unless it was barefoot.

Dressed in some clothes and shoes Zoe had kindly lent her, she chanced going home later that day. Saff was relieved that the front door had been locked and Gabe was not around. *At least Gabe had gone back and locked the door, eh?* she thought. She had left Levi at her mum's for one more night, so she could clean up and get her head sorted out. Maybe a hot bath would help, it wasn't going to be easy to relax but she had lit several candles, in the hope they would help to get rid of the smell of her vomit from last night.

After her bath, she sat on the end of her bed drying her hair when the door knocked. She froze and quickly turned the hairdryer off; her heart was pounding, and her mouth felt suddenly dry. She heard the knocking again, and her name being called through the letterbox. It was Gabe.

41

She knew she was not answering the door to him. She had nothing to say to him right now and honestly was scared of what he might do. The knocking continued and Gabe carried on calling through the letterbox for the next 15 minutes, pleading with her to open.

"Saff, please open the door. I'm so sorry. You know it's not me when I behave like that. I will definitely get help this time!" continuing to knock on the door. Her head hurt from all the crying she had been doing; she just wanted him to go away.

"I know you're home; I heard the hair dryer; I can see the lights are on and your key must be in the door because mine won't work. Saff! Saff! Saff!"

"Why don't you leave her alone?" Oh no, that was Jim. He must have come out to defend her, he was so lovely, but Saff didn't want him to get involved. It wasn't fair.

"Do one, old man. It's none of your effin business" snarled Gabe.

"You don't deserve her, she's a lovely young woman and she could do much better than you young man" Jim's voice wobbled, "If I were younger, I would knock your block off for the way you treat her. You're definitely not like your namesake, Angel Gabriel."

"Try it then and see what happens! Get back in your house and shut your mouth."

"If you don't leave, then I will be calling the police" yelled Jim.

"Saff, I'm leaving because of this nugget outside. I can't be arsed with the police, but I will be back. We need to sort this out!"

Saff sighed a sigh of relief that he was leaving but she knew he would be back. Zoe's suggestion of moving had been playing on her mind all day. What did she have to lose? If she moved house, Gabe wouldn't know where she lived, and he would hopefully just leave her alone. She needed to put her and Levi first for once, so she decided to fill in the application, hoping the council would come through quickly with the offer of a new place to live, a safe place. She would miss her little flat and Jim as her neighbour, but she couldn't get away from Fallowfield quick enough.

3

Hopeless

Zoe mixed her cake batter and began portioning it out into the cupcake cases she had lined up on the kitchen side. She was gutted that Saff had moved away, she loved having her live so close, but she knew she needed to get away from Gabe. Surprised the council had offered Saff something after only a few months, another top-floor cottage flat in Didsbury. Saff had snapped it up and moved as quickly as she could. Zoe smiled as she remembered Saff telling her that she felt like she was doing a midnight flit it had happened that quickly.

Checking the temperature of the oven, she slid her cupcake trays into the oven and set a timer. She was humming along to her TLC album *Crazy, Sexy, Cool,* putting the kettle on to make a coffee while her cupcakes were in the oven. She loved her little kitchen; it was her happy place. She had worked hard at her job in the local gym and as a personal trainer which meant she could get her kitchen just right which then helped her pursue her other passion of baking. Just as the kettle whistled on the stove to tell her it was boiled; her phone began to ring. Wiping her hands on her apron she answered, "Hey Saff."

"Zoe, you are NOT going to believe this" Saff exclaimed, "guess who my neighbour is?" pausing to catch her breath, "Lewis flipping Anthony!"

Zoe sat down on one of the kitchen stools, feeling like she had been winded. "Girl, are you joking? Lewis Anthony, as in Gabe's best mate?"

Saff sucked her teeth, "Yep, that's him and no I am not joking. I just can't believe it. I've been unpacking, making it really lovely, and I was putting some curtains up in Levi's room when I saw him walking past."

"Did he see you?"

"I don't think so. I ducked down straight away but how long before he does see me or Levi?"

Zoe felt some of the tension release from her shoulders, "Well that's good that he didn't see you. I can't believe it. You've been there almost two weeks now, haven't you?

"Yeah, two weeks and I haven't seen or spoken to Gabe for a couple of months now. It's not been easy ignoring him because he keeps belling my phone and leaving voicemails literally crying and telling me how sorry he is."

"Well, I should hope he is, but this was meant to be a fresh start for you, and you deserve so much more than him" Zoe checked the timer to see how long she had left for her cupcakes and stood up to make a start on her buttercream.

"I actually thought I was going to get a fresh start, but with Lewis living three doors away how realistic is that going to be?" Saff groaned. "When will I catch a break? When?"

Zoe wished she had an answer for her, but she didn't.

Saff had decided to focus her energies on pursuing her plan to go to university. She was starting at Manchester Metropolitan University to undertake a BA (Hons) in Travel and Tourism. Continuing with her plan to work in the travel industry was important to her. Yes, this plan had been disrupted by having a baby potentially meaning she couldn't travel the world as she had first hoped, but it didn't mean she couldn't still work in the industry, did it? Saff liked to see a plan completed.

Pulling up to the MMU Campus in Fallowfield later that week, she parked her car. It felt good that she was finally driving. It had given her freedom she hadn't realised she needed. Her student loan and a bit of money from her mum had helped her buy a little car. A green Volkswagen Polo, nothing fancy but she loved it. It was her new baby. She looked at the building she was about to enter, it was referred to as the *Toast Rack* as that's what it resembled, a huge concrete toast rack. She shook her head *what were some of these architects thinking? It wasn't the most attractive building.* Collecting her bag, she checked her new notebook and pen were in there and took a deep breath. She was nervous but excited to start this new journey – new house, new car, new course, new start. Her thoughts almost ended with a new me, but she laughed that thought off as she walked into the building.

Two months after moving into the new flat, Saff was in the full swing of studying again, having picked all her books up from the library that she needed for her first assignment, she had them all spread out on the floor for easy access. Levi was at school and as she had only had a few lectures in the morning she was making the most of the time she had in the afternoon when there was a knock at the door. Every time someone knocked on the door, it made Saff jump. She hoped every time that it wasn't Gabe. She had really tried to cut him off by blocking his phone number and she had been proud of herself for not contacting him. Hesitantly she walked down the stairs trying not to make noise on the wooden stairs. Not able to afford new carpets they were still bare floorboards. As she reached the door, she looked through the peephole - Gabe was standing there.

"Saff, is that you?"

Damn, he must have heard me come down the stairs!

"Saff, look I'm really sorry for the way I acted. I don't know why I lose my temper like that. I love you so much and I really want to get help. I've been trying to get hold of you for months and didn't even know you had moved. Saff? Are you gonna open the door?"

She could hear that remorse in his voice. He had to be sorry for what he did, any normal human being would be wouldn't they? *Why did he do this to me?* She found it so much easier to block him out when there was no contact, but now he was here she felt conflicted.

Saff sighed a deep sigh as she unlocked the door. He wasn't going to be easy to avoid, and she couldn't move house again. *Maybe he has changed, maybe he realises that I was serious this time, to even move house.*

She allowed him to come in and talk, which he did, non-stop. Pleading, apologising, and promising that things would change, that he would seek some anger management support. He took up the rest of the afternoon, until she had to collect Levi, so no more studying was done.

Saff wasn't exactly sure why she agreed to get back with him, maybe it was easier than having to avoid him constantly, maybe it was easier than being lonely, maybe she wouldn't do any better than him as he kept reminding her, but whatever her reasons she knew she wouldn't be shouting it from the rooftops.

I know I'm stupid, she told herself, *I feel embarrassed already. I can't tell anyone and if anything, else happens I definitely can't tell anyone! I will look so foolish.*

After a few months of things going well with Gabe, Saff decided to have some friends over. It was probably time to officially let people know they were back together, as she knew her friends had suspected as much. She had begun to relax a little and believed that change was possible. She sent a text to her girls and a few other friends.

Hey, I'm inviting a few people over tonight. I've not really had a housewarming, and Levi is at my mum's for the weekend, hope you can come. Bring a bottle x.

As her friends arrived later that evening, Saff greeted them.

"Throw your jackets in my room on the bed, it's cool" she called from the kitchen as she grabbed some glasses to make everyone a drink.

"Rose or White?" she asked Amy.

"Rose please babe" indicated Amy, "did Zoe get back to you? She said she's got a big cake order this weekend so needs to crack on with that. You know Zo anyway; always choosing work over drinking!"

Gabe came into the kitchen and grabbed her around the waist. He spun her round as if they were dancing, "I'm the DJ tonight" he laughed.

"You're in a good mood," she said as he planted a big kiss on her lips.

This was the Gabe she knew and loved, she felt reassured that tonight had been the night to let everyone know they were back on. Saff left him to control the box of tapes and CDs and felt relieved that he was in a good mood. He had been in a good mood in general recently, and things had been going well. Maybe he had changed. She sat down with Amy and smiled as she heard Gabe put one of the tapes from the Garage Nation tape pack. A bit of DJ EZ would liven people up.

"Everything all ok now then?" Amy said quietly as she nodded her head slightly in the direction of Gabe who was being the life and soul of the party.

Saff felt her shoulders and back tighten slightly, but she smiled back and said "Yeah, it's been really lovely you know. I think that's all in the past now" referring to what Amy had seen and hoping it was true because she had said it out loud.

"I hope so too. No Katy?" noticed Amy.

"No, Jack's out of prison, isn't he? So, she's all loved up with him" smiled Saff.

"Oh yeah, I forgot he was getting out. Did you hear that

Luke got nicked? It was only a matter of time with what he'd been up to but sad. He's got two little kiddies."

Saff was shocked, she hadn't heard but it made her sad, "You'd have thought he would have chilled out a bit after the kids. I just don't get it, you know, what makes some take that path. It really intrigues me."

"Saff you've always been interested in our minds and the psychology of it all." Amy was knocking back her glass of wine and looking like she was going to be needing a refill pretty quickly.

"Doesn't it intrigue you? Look at the people we've grown up around and the people around us now, why do some end up in prison or on drugs, or even dead? Think how many people we've known that have passed already. It's sad Amy, it really is."

Amy leaned forward and tapped Lewis on the shoulder, "Some of that bro please" she said nodding at the spliff he was holding. He handed it to her, and she took a big drag of it.

As she was blowing the smoke out, she spoke through gritted teeth "It is sad Saff; you should study it. You've always got your head in some book anyway. How's uni going?"

"Ah I love it; I absolutely love it. It's not easy but I just love learning and being in that environment. I've met some pretty nice people, but I just see it as a step forward, a way out of this life. Think about those guys we were speaking about, for them, they see their way out as selling drugs to make loads of money or the better path of making it in football, but how many actually make it that way? Uni is that for me, it's GOT to better me, it's GOT to give me a better chance at a job and hopefully get me out of Manchester." Saying it with the confidence that she felt about her plan.

"That still the plan? You've always said that. I'm proud of you girl, sticking to the plan no matter what. You know uni ain't my thing no matter how much me mum and dad shove it down my throat!" said Amy as she put the spliff out to offer it to Saff.

Saff laughed and shook her head, "No thanks, that's not my poison and you know it" and she lifted her glass of wine to take a swig before reaching for the bottle to top up their glasses.

It was around 1am when people started to leave.

"It's been a good night, Saff, thanks for inviting us. Well done for getting on top of your dissertation too! You deserve a good grade, you've worked hard. I don't know how you do it with Levi! I will ring you tomorrow babe," said Amy as she put her coat on, "sure you don't want some help tidying up?"

"Aww, thanks for coming guys. I needed this, I will sort the mess out, you guys get off and I will speak to you tomorrow."

She was already shoving rubbish into a bin bag.

Saff left Gabe sat on the sofa smoking a spliff as she cleared away the glasses and ashtrays humming along to the music that was still playing quietly in the background. She was just getting herself ready for bed when Gabe came into her bedroom.

"Do you think I didn't hear what you said?" he growled; Saff tensed as she didn't know what he was talking about, but she feared what was coming.

"You think you're so much better than people, don't you? Because you're in uni and you want to get away from this place" he said in a mocking voice.

"Gabe, I don't think I'm better than anyone and you know that. I'm only trying to better myself, nothing to do with anyone else and we have spoken about moving away, that's all I meant."

She looked at his face, with his red eyes from smoking weed, and at how angry he was.

"Na, you think you're too good. But who would actually want you? You're lucky that I'm even still with you."

Suddenly, he reached down and picked up a tin of paint that Saff had been decorating with. Before she knew it he had poured it all over her.

Saff stood there in disbelief while pink paint dripped down

her. Gabe marched out of the flat and slammed the front door. Grabbing a towel from the nearby washing basket Saff wiped her face. Slowly she sank to the floor and the tears came.

I can't take this anymore. I HATE MY LIFE, I HATE MYSELF! How have I ended up back here? How am I meant to tell anyone about this?

The shame and embarrassment she felt was overwhelming. Who would believe he had done this to her? It was hard sometimes for her to believe that it was him when he did things like this, and she was the victim of his anger, so she knew it was even harder for their friends to see it. She knew some wouldn't believe her or would think she must have done something to deserve what he did to her. He had gone from being the life and soul of the party to being a monster when no one else was looking. She had to get away from him, again!

Gabe was fuming, he stopped to look down, *Great!* He had splashes of pink paint on his brand-new trainers. He grabbed a tissue from his pocket and tried to wipe it off before making his way over to his car.

There she was again, who did she think she was? He was raging, *she was such a snob, university, moving out of Manchester* he mimicked her as he muttered it under his breath. *What was wrong with Manchester?* Gabe loved it and couldn't imagine being anywhere else, he was proud to be a Manc. And he hated students, dossers, the lot of them. The only benefit of having a university campus so close to Fallowfield was that they all wanted to smoke weed which brought in a bit of money for him. He didn't have any ideas of grandeur for life, he had enough as he was. Saff needed to realise who she was and where she had come from, the sooner she could do that the better.

Being grateful that no one had seen what had happened last week, Saff was still finding spots of pink paint on things. It was like no matter how much she cleaned up, more would appear, it was like a constant reminder. But today Saff had a bigger issue to deal with. She sat in the bathroom on the floor, staring at the pregnancy test she had bought earlier that day. Her head was throbbing with pain, and she knew she was a mess at the moment. Hot tears began falling from her eyes as she berated herself, *how stupid could you be?* She asked herself over and over, repeating the words *stupid, stupid, stupid.* She knew she hadn't been doing a great job at remembering to take the pill every day but being pregnant was the last thing she wanted to be dealing with.

She glanced up at the clock on the wall, again. Three minutes felt like the longest time in her life, she grabbed the stick and scrunched her eyes shut tightly, just wanting this nightmare to be over. *Please God, please God, please God* begging God for a negative result. Opening her eyes to look, she slumped back against the wall. Positive. Disappointment and frustration washed over her. This was not what she had wanted to see. She did not want to bring a baby into this abusive situation, she was struggling to take care of herself and Levi, and her mental health was suffering badly.

The tears continued to come, her whole body felt weak, like it was giving up on her. *Maybe I would be better off dead. I wonder how many tablets you have to take to kill yourself. That would end this whole situation!*

Saff looked in her cupboards and took out all the tablets she had, she started to take them a few at a time. She was sobbing as she did this, *you are so stupid! So, so stupid Saff. You don't deserve to live, you are worthless. All those things Gabe has ever said to you are true. You are weak and pathetic. Who do you think you are? Levi would be better off without you as his mum anyway. I just want this to end, and if this was the only way out, then I'm gonna take it.*

Her phone suddenly started to ring. Honey by Mariah Carey played loudly from her phone, making her jump and snapping her out of her thoughts. *What am I doing?* She didn't want to die, did she?

"Mum" Saff sobbed down the phone, prompting her mum to ask her what was wrong. "How many paracetamols do you have to take for it to be an overdose?" She had no idea how many she had even taken.

Fortunately for Saff, she hadn't taken enough to do any harm. *I couldn't even get taking an overdose right* thought Saff frustratingly, *I can't even get that right.* The hospital had kept her in for a few hours for observation but was happy to let her go home. It had been a cry for help. Saff had also spoken to the hospital about finding out she was pregnant; they had given her some leaflets about her options. Her phone pinged while she was looking through them back at home.

Saff, what's happened? Are you ok babe?

It was a text from Gabe.

Babe? Was he serious? After what he had done to her?
How did he even know? She was fuming and wished people would stay out of her business, but Manchester was a small place, and someone must have seen her in the hospital. She sighed because she knew that she needed to speak to him, he was involved in this pregnancy too and she wouldn't feel right deciding without talking to him no matter how bad he had been to her.

Her jaw tensed when she remembered how bad he had been to her the last time she saw him. The paint, she couldn't shake the cold feeling of it running down her. *Be the bigger person Saff* taking some deep breaths sent a text back.

I'm fine, but we need to talk asap.

He replied.

On way

Five minutes later there was a knock on the door.

Gabe began pacing the living room. He took his hat off and scratched his head, looking like he was trying to process what Saff had just told him "Na Saff, I can't be dealing with that right now you know" he shook his head again, "A baby. Na, na. I can't do it."

Inwardly Saff felt relieved. She didn't want to raise a baby in this volatile situation. She didn't want to be linked to Gabe for the rest of her life, they could barely manage to be in a relationship together, how on earth could they co-parent together? So, the fact that he agreed, meant this decision didn't lie with just her.

"So, we are agreed then? I will make an appointment at the clinic?" Saff tentatively asked him as she nodded her head towards the hospital leaflets, she had showed him.

"Yeah, it's for the best. I'm not ready for all that. Just do what you need to do" Gabe replied. He placed his cap back on his head and turned to leave the flat.

-

Yawning Saff climbed into Amy's car; grateful she had the heating on. It was early morning, that early morning chill was in the air, and she was tired – physically and mentally.

"Babe, sorry about all the mess in the car" Amy jerked her head to the side to indicate all of the stuff littering the car. "I just haven't had the chance to clean it."

Saff smiled slightly, "Amy, your car always looks like this, it's fine. I appreciate you doing this, and the mess in your car is the least of my worries today."

"Not always. I do clean it" Amy said unconvincingly, "Honestly though, it's fine about today. I've been through this myself as you know, so you know I wouldn't judge you. Sometimes you have to do what you've got to do. It's good you've been able to get an appointment so quickly" said Amy as she drove Saff to the clinic. "These things can't wait, can they?"

Saff looked out of the window, trying to tell the tears not to come, closing her eyes to keep them in. She didn't reply to Amy, as she didn't have an answer.

Amy had continued to talk for most of the journey, and although Saff hadn't been listening, she was used to Amy's nonstop talking. Amy pulled up outside the clinic, Saff was surprised to see a queue of people waiting to go inside.

"I'm sorry I can't stay with you Saff; I've got another job interview, mum organised this one for me" rolling her eyes, "but I will be back to pick you up" almost reading Saff's mind as she noticed that most of the ladies in the queue had someone with them.

"It's ok Amy, it's my mess. Thanks for the lift and I will see you later. Good luck with the interview."

She climbed out of the safety of the warm car and walked over to the back of the queue. She didn't have to wait too long before the doors opened and people started to slowly file in, she took a deep intake of breath and pulled her coat tighter around her. It was happening.

The queue was moving slowly, and Saff suddenly noticed a little old lady standing across the road on her own. She was wearing a brown skirt, jacket, and a matching hat. *Was she shouting something?* Saff strained her ears to listen, she was shouting "Don't do it."

Saff felt tears sting her eyes and a lump come to her throat *you have no idea, no idea at all* she thought angrily, as she continued to make her way into the clinic.

That lady wasn't going to be there holding her hand throughout life, she wasn't going to be there in the middle of the night, and she wasn't going to be there when she had to have an abusive, controlling man continue to ruin her life and make her feel even more worthless than she already felt.

Did that woman really think this was just a flippant decision to make? Well, it wasn't! fumed Saff in her mind, recalling those feelings of wanting to end her own life so she didn't have to face this. She closed her eyes and tried to block everything out as she waited for her name to be called.

The next couple of weeks dragged by so she was looking forward to seeing Zoe. Saff had been distracted and finding it hard to focus on her university work. Gabe had rung and texted her several times, but she was trying to avoid him. *How dare he try to run me down now? He had never even responded to me when I told him that I had been to the clinic. It's like he didn't even care, well it wasn't him that had to actually go through with it was it! I really need this relationship to be over and make sure I don't go back. If it's not a place I could bring a baby into then why am I bringing Levi into it or even myself? I just can't face him. I'm not strong enough anymore.*

Zoe handed her a cup of coffee as they sat on the stools at the breakfast bar in her kitchen. Saff loved her kitchen, it felt like a farmhouse kitchen, but not on a farm and Zoe always made amazing cupcakes which Saff was pleased to see were sat on a plate in front of her,

"It's good to see you, Saff. How's Levi?" as she pushed the

plate of cupcakes towards Saff indicating for her to take one.

Saff chose a chocolate one with vanilla buttercream piped beautifully on the top, "He's good thanks…."

Her phone rang as she was speaking, and Saff picked it up and turned it over so she could no longer see the screen. She turned her attention back to her cupcake, peeling back the wrapper so she could take a bite.

"You avoiding someone?" Zoe asked, noticing that Saff had ignored her phone a few times.

"It's Gabe, he won't stop calling and I just want him to leave me alone, for it to be done once and for all. But I just don't want to have that conversation with him" replied Saff wearily, before she took a bite of her cupcake. Seeing Gabe's name on her phone had dampened her enthusiasm for it.

Zoe looked at Saff, she looked tired. Her heart went out to her, "Well, you sound like you've made your mind up so why not just tell him straight?"

Saff sighed, she was so over this whole relationship and how it was making her feel "I guess there will never be the right time, so I might as well, eh?"

She turned her phone over and as he was calling her again, she pressed the answer button,

"Babes, I've been trying to get hold of you for ages. What's going on?" Gabe asked, he sounded like he was speaking through clenched teeth.

"I'm just having a brew with Zoe. Look Gabe we need to talk." Her mouth felt dry, and she rubbed her temple with her free hand as she felt the tension in her head.

"Again?! For God's sake, Saff, it's always something with you!" Gabe snapped. "Why do you always want to talk? I don't even know what I've done this time to upset you."

Saff got up and walked to the next room so she could speak without Zoe hearing. She took a deep breath and said, "I think we both know that this relationship is very toxic and that we shouldn't be together."

There she had said it, she was shaking but she had said it.

"So, what you saying Saff? Go on"

He was really going to make her spell it out, wasn't he?

"It's over Gabe. Me and you, it's over. For good this time"

"You think you can do that yeah? You murdering B***h" He was angry now. "Well, if it's over, then I'm gonna make sure it's worth it yeah" and the call ended.

What did he mean? She wasn't sure but was glad that she had finally been able to say it. Walking back into the kitchen, she realised she was shaking.

"You, ok? Do you want some water?" Zoe asked her, "You look pale."

"My brew will be fine," Saff said picking it up and taking a big gulp to quench her dry mouth.

Saff had managed to eat most of the chocolate cupcake and knew that Zoe was doing her best to talk about anything but Gabe to keep her distracted, but it was still on her mind. There was a feeling of fear searing through her body, her heart was beating fast, and her palms felt sweaty, but she was not sure of what she was fearful.

It had been twenty minutes since she had spoken to Gabe and ended their relationship. They had moved to sit in the living room and Zoe was putting the kettle on to make another brew when there was a knock at the door.

Zoe went to answer and the next minute Saff heard a commotion, the door banged open, and she heard Gabe shout "Where the eff is she?"

Saff stood up but was soon pushed back into the chair by an angry Gabe. He began to pummel her head with punches.

"Over yeah? Well, I hope it was worth it." Raining curse words down on her as quickly as the punches landed.

Saff was trying to protect her head as much as possible as that's where all the punches were landing.

She could hear Zoe screaming "Get off her, Get off her."

Then it seemed as quickly as he had arrived, he was gone.

"Saff, Saff are you ok? I'm calling the police! I can't believe that" Zoe had a few choice words for what she thought about

Gabe at that moment.

Saff was shaking. She sat in shock, tears running down her face, adrenaline rushing through her body and her head was throbbing. *Had that really just happened?*

She had a gut feeling that it wasn't over, he was going to do more. She knew it. He had a key to her flat and she just knew deep down that that was where he had gone.

The police came and took a statement from both Saff and Zoe, but what were they going to do really? The damage was done. He had assaulted her and even taken her mobile phone. The phone could be replaced but he had given her several punches to the head and face, the physical effects would hopefully disappear over time, but the mental and emotional effects would remain for a long time.

"I'm gonna go and stay at my mum's Zoe. I am so sorry that you had to go through that. It's my fault." Saff felt bad that it had happened in Zoe's house. She should never have let him know where she lived.

Zoe grabbed her by her shoulders and said defiantly, "Babe, look at me. That was not your fault. I don't want to hear you saying that. You do what you need to do to feel safe. He's horrible and I hope that's the last we hear of him."

The next day, Saff tentatively returned to the flat with her younger sister Jasmine, dreading what awaited them. Levi was still at her mum's, she needed to check on the damage before he came home.

As she walked into her flat, she was overwhelmed with the damage.

I hadn't expected him to have gone this far.

"Saff this is really bad," her sister Jasmine said in shock as she slowly walked around stepping over broken things, "but come on let's just get it sorted."

Saff was glad she was there with her can-do attitude because she felt exhausted. Every room had been trashed, mirrors smashed, TVs smashed, and even the fridge freezer had been pushed over. They worked for several hours cleaning it all up and making it safe to bring Levi home.

"Jas, I know I have said it before, but this really is it. I am absolutely done with him. I'm getting the locks changed, and getting a new phone and that is it. Please tell me to sort my head out if I ever say I am taking him back. Please!" she meant it, but did she have the strength to walk away this time?

4

Knight in Shining Armour

Kara had been packing up boxes for most of the morning, she looked at her watch wondering where Saff was, she had said she would drive over to help, and it wasn't like her to be late. Looking around the room at all the boxes and mess, she sighed, she needed the help. The kids tried to help after school, but it was quicker to get stuff done while they weren't there.

She saw Saff's green Volkswagen Polo pull up outside through the kitchen window, *finally!* Kara smiled, she was so proud of the way she had picked herself up after what Gabe had done to her, she felt anger rising in her at the thought of him. How Saff had managed to finish university and get her dissertation finished, Kara would never know! And then the police wouldn't stop pestering her to press charges. Kara understood why Saff didn't want to, she was terrified that if he were convicted, he would build up all his anger sat in a cell and this nightmare would not be over for any of them upon his release. She was glad to see the back of him and not hear his name again!

"I'm sorry Mum, I had to drive over and help a friend from uni. Her car wouldn't start so I gave her a jump start. But I'm here now" She grinned, then looked around the room as her smile faded. "Why do you move house so much, mum? You know there's been research done that says moving house is one of the most stressful things you can do!" she said putting her hands on her hips feeling like she had given her mum some insightful advice.

"You know there's been so many bad things happen on the street, shootings, murders, it's just been horrible" Kara grimaced as she remembered those things, "so we are moving back over to Levenshulme, near The Kingsway Pub. It's a nice house."

Saff put her hand on her mum's arm, "You've just reminded me! I forgot to tell you; I got the job!"

"Well done, Sapphire. Is that the one at Blockbuster that you have been wanting for a while now?"

Saff nodded, "Yep. I've only applied about three times. Maybe they got desperate this time?" she laughed.

"No, don't be daft. They should be proud to have you working there. Will the hours fit around Levi?"

"That's the good thing the shifts are perfect. Now your new house will be just around the corner from my work if you can help me with Levi when it's an evening shift, then it will all work out" Saff grinned.

"Whatever I can do to help out with Levi is fine, he's always welcome," Kara said warmly.

"The new place sounds not far from where we used to live when we lived in Levenshulme," said Saff as she pulled a pile of plates out of a cupboard, "Do you remember when we saw the post office getting robbed near there? That was crazy!"

She passed the plates to her mum as she continued to empty the cupboard. Taking the plates and opening some sheets of newspaper, her mum started wrapping each plate up,

"Oh yeah, I remember that. Manchester is a crazy place and we've seen some crazy things" her mum said thoughtfully,

"Yes, Mum I know, and we've moved all around it since I can remember because you've got this weird desire to keep packing your house up and moving around" Saff laughed as she opened another cupboard door. "Do you have any idea how many times you've moved since I was born? I've lost count, to be honest."

"Oh gosh Sapphire, I would have to think back. Do you know that we lived in every one of the four crescents back in Hulme? And remember we even lived in a van at one point."

"We were proper tramps weren't we mum?" Saff joked.

"Eh, we weren't tramps, we were just…...transient! It was a different way of life back then." Kara said wistfully.

They continued to pack up the contents of the kitchen, while they tried to recall all the places they had lived since Saff had been born.

"That's over fifty places. Mum, that's crazy. And you wonder why I've turned out the way I have" She flung her arms in the air in an exaggerated way. "I'm on my second flat since moving out of here and I don't want to move that much. I still want to move out of Manchester, I don't know how you've managed to stay this long after everything we've been through."

Kara was at the sink filling the kettle up, she put it back on its stand and flicked it on, "The kids Sapphire, that's why. It's easier for the kids to see their dad and his family. Once they are older, I will probably be doing the same and moving out of Manchester."

"True. Mum, you really should use these times to have a good sort out of your stuff. Having less stuff means having less mess, and I know you've got better over the years but there's always room for improvement" Saff winked at her mum.

Saff had spent the rest of the afternoon helping her mum and left to pick Levi up from school, she was feeling much lighter these days. When Amy sent a text about a night out at the weekend, Saff jumped at the chance. A night out sounded right up her street. A night to let loose and forget her troubles for a few hours. The problem was that one night out turned into another one, and another one, and another one. If they weren't out clubbing, they were downing a few bottles of wine in her flat, putting the world to rights. Saff was enjoying the company of her girlfriends and getting to know herself again, she was trying to forget her pain and keep herself as numb as she could.

She was also enjoying her new job, and so was Levi.

"Mum I can't believe we get to take all these films and games home for free every week." He loved coming to her work and choosing his videos and games.

Saff laughed as they walked in the doors of the Blockbuster store, "You go and look at the games, while I just go and speak to my boss."

She walked over to the managers station, "Hi Simon, how's it been going? Are the shifts done for next week?"

Simon walked over with a sheet of paper, "I have just finished them. Are they going to be ok for you?" as he handed her the rota.

Saff glanced it over, she was a shift supervisor, and she was pleased as she looked at the rota, at the staff she had with her on her shifts. "Yep, that looks good" as she handed him the rota back.

He placed it back down by the manager's station and said

"I'm just nipping out for a cig. Be back in a sec."

Levi was running back to her, "Mum can I get two games and a video? Pleeeeeaaase?" he whined in his best pleading voice.

Saff pretended to think about it and said yes, taking them to the counter to be checked out.

"Hey Lola, can I check these out please?" placing Levi's choices on the countertop, "And I see that you're on my shifts next week."

"Yeaaaaahhh I get to work with the one and only Sapphire. That's so good!" Lola said with genuine enthusiasm, Saff loved working with her, she was so much fun and not to mention beautiful. She had the longest blond hair Saff had seen.

Simon was coming back in from smoking his cigarette. He was a prolific smoker and could finish a cigarette quicker than Saff had ever seen. The maddest thing was, he told everyone his wife didn't know he smoked. That had always baffled Saff as she could smell it on him as soon as she was near him, but he was adamant his wife didn't know.

"Oh Saff, don't forget about the interviews for the Assistant Manager post next week. I really think you've got a good chance of getting it." Simon called across the shop floor as he rushed to the back of the store, "Just nipping to wash my hands."

Saff felt good that he had that faith in her, she hadn't worked there for that long, but he felt she had what it took, so that filled her with confidence. And now she had finished university she would need the money.

-

The girls had been out in Baby Grand in Manchester since just after 9pm. It was Saturday night, and the nightclub was packed. R&B music thumped out of the huge speakers around the venue.

"Is that the third bottle of wine Amy?" asked Zoe, holding her bottle of J20.

"It's actually the fourth" giggled Amy as she shakily waved her glass in front of Zoe's face, spilling wine on the floor.

"Whoops" Amy laughed, "Anyway, girls come here, come here." She bent her head and gestured with her hands for them to come closer, "Shall we get some sniff?" she thought she was whispering but had said it much louder than she realised.

"Sshhhh Amy," Saff said as she looked around hoping no one had heard her or had realised she was referring to getting some cocaine.

"You are so extra, Amy. Where you gonna get some of that?" Saff asked much quieter than Amy.

Amy put her finger on her cheek and looked up like she was thinking deeply. "Dante" she replied triumphantly, "I've got his number I think" as she fumbled in her bag for her phone.

Dante Knight was well known for being able to supply all sorts of drugs, including cocaine. Amy drunkenly made her way to the toilets and made a drunken call to him. He had gladly agreed to meet them in Baby Grand as he was already out in Manchester with his boys.

He and his boy Reggie turned up about 30 minutes later. That fourth bottle of wine had been drunk and the fifth was almost half empty. Dante and Reggie swaggered over to them. The one thing Saff knew about him, was that he had an assurance about himself, a confidence but not overly cocky, it was an attractive confidence. Saff watched him as he made his way through the crowds to where they were stood, his gold tooth glinting every now and then in the disco lights which also made his caramel skin glow. His short dreads moved rhythmically as he bopped his head in time to the music.

As the night went on, Saff noticed Dante looking at her a few times and smiled back at him. His smile drew her in, his gold tooth flashing at her. She was on a high from the coke they had sniffed from Amy's house key in the toilets, she wasn't going to let the other girls have all the fun and she was feeling good about herself.

"Go and dance with him girl," said Zoe, as she pushed Saff toward him.

Feeling confident because of the alcohol and drugs in her system, she walked over to where he was standing dancing. He quickly turned to stand in front of her and dance with her.

"You're looking nice you know Sapphire" he shouted into her ear over the bass, "You deserve a man who will treat you nice."

After Gabe, she hadn't been looking for another relationship but those feelings and desires of being loved, of wanting to settle down with a man who loved her hadn't gone away. No one could treat her worse than Gabe had she reasoned in her drunken mind, so she laughed and danced closer to Dante putting her arms around his neck as he pulled her closer.

Zoe turned up the fire in the living room and looked around the room, making sure that everyone's glasses were full and that there were plenty of snacks on offer.

"Zoe, you really are the hostess with the mostess," laughed Saff as she put a cupcake and some crisps on one of the paper plates Zoe had laid out for them.

Amy grabbed a bottle of wine, and put it down by her feet, "Just keeping it within reach girls. I need it tonight, my parents are driving me mad, always going on and on and on. It's soooooo boring."

Zoe frowned and sat down on the floor crossed-legged.

"Amy, they are only trying to help you. I don't know why you rebel so much, isn't it time to grow up?" she nibbled on a few cashews.

"Zoe, you sound just like them. Do you not ever want to just have fun?"

Saff raised her eyebrows, looking at Amy.

Amy continued, "You really need to loosen up. Have you found a fella yet? I think you need to get laid. It helps me relax, and I'm sure Saff would agree" She took a big swig of her glass of wine.

"Erm, leave me out of this" spluttered Saff as she had just taken a drink of her wine, "it's Zoe's choice to not have a fella and she definitely has less troubles in her life than me and you. Doesn't she?"

"Uh oh, here comes the mum tone" Amy responded, "doesn't she?" mimicking the way Saff had said it.

"Anyway, moving on" Zoe turned her face to Saff, "while we are speaking of fella's. How's it going with Dante?"

"Aww Zo, it's mad, it feels like I've known him forever. He makes me feel so comfortable around him. Not like with Gabe where I always felt on edge. He never lets me pay for anything and he's really funny! It just feels relaxed, no matter what we do, we seem to have fun. It could be going for a walk, watching TV, or a night out," Saff's eyes glazed over as she thought dreamily about these things, "I know my cheeks will hurt from laughing and I go to bed feeling content. I feel like he really listens when I talk and takes an interest in what I'm saying."

Zoe smiled "You look happy, that's good! After what you've been through with Gabe, you deserve to be treated nicely."

"Mmmm he's a good catch Saff" said Amy as she winked at Saff, "verrrrrry nice."

Saff half smiled at Amy's odd comment, not sure how to take it "Yeah thanks. I do feel a bit on edge after all that, but honestly I don't think I have ever heard Dante say a cross word about anyone or even lose his temper. Well actually, the only time I did see even a flicker was when talking about Gabe and what he had done. He said he doesn't have time for waste men like him, and if there was one thing he didn't like, it was women beaters. He said he witnessed that stuff growing up, which is sad, isn't it? But he has reassured me that our relationship won't be like that, and I can just relax. Let's hope it lasts, eh?" laughed Saff, lifting her glass to chink it against the girl's drinks.

"Top up girls?" enquired Amy as she peered into the bottom of her empty glass.

The smell of the freshly baked chocolate cupcakes wafted in the air as Zoe placed them on a plate ready for when Saff arrived, she knew she enjoyed them.

"It was good to hang out the other night," said Zoe as Saff pulled a stool up to the breakfast bar in the kitchen, "I actually can't believe how much Amy managed to drink. She didn't wake up the next morning until 1pm" pushing the plate of cupcakes towards Saff and placing a cup of coffee in front of her.

"It was a lot of fun, but I worry about Amy. Not even just her drinking, just her attitude to life at the moment but she won't hear what we've got to say to her will she?" said Saff in between nibbles of the chocolate cupcake.

Zoe slumped down on one of the stools, "Ugh, I have no idea how to get through to her. That morning, I had already done a couple of PT sessions, picked up a few bits from the shop, AND baked a few cakes before she woke up." She sat up straighter on the stool, "Actually Saff, I thought I saw Dante when I nipped into Tesco, but I couldn't be sure because he was with a blonde girl," said Zoe, not making eye contact with Saff and picking up the packet of cigarettes that were on the counter.

Saff looked thoughtfully as her appetite for the cupcake rapidly faded, "Oh really? Mmmm, I don't know, I can't remember if he mentioned anything. You smoking again?"

"Ah it might have been nothing, I was just sure it was him.

You don't think he's messing about do you?" Zoe gave her a hooded look and stuffed the packet of cigarettes in a kitchen drawer. "And yeah, I always pick up the ciggies again when mum's health starts flaring up, it stresses me out."

Saff was caught off guard by Zoe's accusations of Dante messing about with another girl, flustered, and hoped the flush in her face wasn't noticeable to Zoe, "It probably wasn't him you know." Shrugging her shoulders, she changed the subject "How's your mum doing this time? Is it the arthritis again?"

Saff's mind was reeling when she left Zoe's. She got into her car and started the engine. It wasn't the first or the last time, one of her friends had said they had seen Dante with another girl, and it wasn't always a blonde girl! The car CD playing kicked in and Mariah Carey's voice began to sing from the speakers, *'Shake it Off'*. Zoe wasn't the type to lie or make something like that up and to be honest, Saff didn't want to believe it was true, but it was beginning to bother her more every day. She decided she would ring him once she got back home and ask him directly. Turning up the volume of the music she sang along with Mariah to the songs on her favourite album *The Emancipation of Mimi*.

Dante laughed a deep belly laugh down the phone, "Saff don't listen to people chatting makka. Haters. You're my girl and that's it."

Could she believe him? She wanted to believe him, but something still felt off and she was going to get to the bottom of it. She thought about trying to get hold of his phone, he had more than one due to the nature of what he did, so that was going to be tricky as he didn't let them out of his sight. She would have to think of a better plan to see what she could find out.

It turned out that Saff didn't have to plan anything, because a few days later she got a call from an unknown number.

"Hello," Saff answered curtly thinking it might be one of those telemarketing calls.

"Hi, is that Saff?" a girl's voice asked.

"Who's speaking please?" Saff was ready to hang up thinking she had been right; it was going to be a telemarketer.

"My name's Freya, I got your number from a friend of yours and I just wanted to let you know that I've been with Dante on and off for the last few years, but we just got back together three weeks ago."

Saff's stomach was churning, she felt herself shaking with anger as Freya continued to talk, "A mutual friend of ours told me he's been seeing you and another girl, Hazel."

Saff's mouth was dry, she took a big gulp from her bottle of water so she could speak "Right, ok. This is the first I'm hearing about this, and you do realise I have been with him for a few months now?"

"Well, I realise that now, but he told me you and him weren't even a thing Saff" she replied with a hint of attitude. "This is what he does, he's done it to me for years," She sounded bored.

Saff wondered why she continued to get back with him then if this is what he does she said mockingly in her head. But she was disappointed in herself getting into another relationship where a guy treated her badly. She was fuming that someone had given her number to Freya, she mustn't forget to pull her girls about that. Dante treated her like a Queen in every other way, what was she going to do? She didn't want him to reject her like so many others had, but she was going to have to confront him, again!

"Baby girl, she's lying. She wants me back but Freya and me are over – O V E R, overrrrrrr" Dante reassured her. "And Hazel, I don't even know who that is. Freya's just trying to get under your skin and wind you up. Forget her! I love you and only you."

Saff wanted to believe him so badly, this was the first relationship where she had a guy who made her feel so good about herself and she wasn't ready to give that up just yet.

He treats you good and he does not treat you like Gabe did

Saff told herself, persuading herself that this kind of treatment was ok in comparison to the abuse she had experienced previously. *I just want to be loved, and he loves me, I know that* she continued thinking as Dante continued to rain kisses and cuddles on her. Dante was so attentive to Saff. In between his work, they spent so much time together, it was hard to imagine how he could ever find time to cheat on her.

Dante did love her; she wasn't like the other girls. They all wanted him for his money or for clout, to be seen with him and his boys. Saff wasn't like that, she had a brain and had goals and ambition. He liked that. He had the same aspirations for his life, all this was just temporary, a way to bring in money to get to where he wanted. *I didn't choose this life, it chose me,* he would often think. Selling drugs was just a stepping stone, he would clean the money up eventually, get out of Manchester, and then maybe he would settle down and stop messing about. For now, he enjoyed the fun he was having but he didn't want to hurt Saff, he did want to see her achieve everything she was planning and dreaming about, and he would help her in any way he could. She deserved it.

5

Restless

Saff had been feeling restless, not that anything was going bad for her, the last two years had been pretty ok. She just had a feeling that she wanted more. She felt unsatisfied. She was at work and sat behind the managers station in Blockbuster on a Wednesday night shift. It had been a quiet one so far and she was watching the clock for closing time. 9.20pm, she yawned *only another 40 minutes to go.*

Most of the staff that worked there were students studying at one of the local universities so there was a high turnover of staff. The staff moved on as this was just a job to most of them, not part of their career path. Having been there for a couple of years, Saff had got to meet some characters, it was one of the parts of the job she enjoyed the most.

"The course I did had been part of my plan to travel the world," she told Lola who was emptying the bins, "and that's just not realistic anymore with Levi."

"Aww Levi, he is just the cutest Saff," Lola grinned as she

tied the full bin bag "But yeah travelling the world with him –
that would be hard."

"I love my job here," said Saff.

"Yeaaahh now you're an Ass Man" laughed Lola.

"Course, I love being Assistant Manager. It pays the bills,
and it honestly doesn't feel like work when I'm on with people
like you. But it's not forever you know. I see so many people
coming and then going on to do what they love" Saff stood
up and stretched, she should make a start on closing down the
tills. "I want to do more; I want to do something more with
my life. I want to do something I love. Probably a job where
I'm helping people because I always seem to be helping and
advising friends and family, why not find a job that pays me to
do that?"

Lola stopped and turned to face Saff, "Saff you could totally
do that. You give the best advice, and you could do anything
you want. You can't be stuck here in Blockbuster for the rest of
your life, even if you are the best Ass Man!" putting a fist up in
the air as she said it.

Later that night, she ran an idea by Dante as they lay in bed.

"That's sick Saff, you would make a good social worker" he
encouraged her.

"You don't think it's too much?" she asked, wrinkling her

nose as she spoke.

"Naaaa, babes you need to believe in yourself a bit more. Do it!" Dante responded. He really did champion her and help her to believe in herself.

"It means going back to uni though and makes me feel like I wasted my time with my first degree. All that hard work for nothing" she said sadly.

"Yeah, you can do that. You've always got your head in a book. Smarter than me for sure! Nothing is wasted. I'm sure it will help you the next time round" Dante laughed.

"Is it mad that I love learning?" looking at Dante to gauge his reaction.

"I mean it's not my thing, learning like that but if you do, then do your thing," he leaned over to look at his phone as it vibrated, he clicked the button to silence it and put it back down. He glanced at Saff to see if she had seen who was calling, but she was still in her thoughts, staring off into the distance.

"It is my thing, I just see it as my way out you know, a way to give me and Levi a better life. Gabe hated that about me" Saff grimaced.

Dante lay back down next to her, he took hold of her hand "Cha, forget him! If anyone is going to get it done, then it's you Saff. You will make it happen."

"That means a lot, thank you. I'm going to drive to the library tomorrow morning and start having a look on one of the computers there." Squeezing his hand back, she was so glad he had her back. "I'm tired, so I'm gonna go to sleep," Saff said as she snuggled under the covers.

Dante kissed her forehead, "Good night baby girl. I'm gonna go watch some TV to chill out for a bit" as he quietly left the room with his phones.

Saff tossed and turned to get comfy, but she knew what she had seen out of the corner of her eye. She wasn't stupid; she had noticed Dante silence his phone and it was his personal phone, not the work one. Saff had bitten her tongue, not wanting to ruin the vibe because if she started, she knew she would get angry, and he would probably leave. She felt excited about the future, but she wondered if Dante would ever be able to commit to her. She told herself that she was his main girl, and these others wouldn't last, he loved her.

Dante sat down in the living room and put a movie on, turning the volume down so he could let Saff sleep. He did have her back. It would be good if she was all legit and carried out her plan to leave Manchester. Things had started to get a bit on top for him with his work, he needed to think harder about his future. He hadn't planned on selling drugs for this long, but the money was too good. Where else was he going to make this much money? But he had to think smarter, he needed to start cleaning some of this money and then maybe he would think about letting some of those girls go and trying to make it work with Saff. He believed in her and knew that she would see her plan through to the end. If she had decided she wanted to be a social worker, he knew that's exactly what she was going to do. Dante picked up one of his phones to return the call he had silenced, settling back in his seat he felt pleased that Saff hadn't noticed who was ringing him.

Amy was sitting at the breakfast bar in her parent's kitchen. It was a large open-plan kitchen diner with big glass doors looking out onto the beautifully landscaped garden. Her head was pounding from her hangover but also because her mum would not stop talking. She wasn't happy that she had had to decide to move back home after enjoying her own space.

"Amy are you even listening?" her mum asked, "we are worried about you. You really need to think about your future. What are you doing with your life? We are happy that you are back here with us, where we know you are safe, but we just want to be assured that you are thinking seriously."

Her mum was cleaning up like she always did, and Amy was sure she was banging the pots and pans extra hard to get on her nerves. She closed her eyes and took a deep breath, praying that her mum would shut her mouth.

"Why can't you both leave me alone? I don't want to do what you want me to do and right now, I don't want to do anything" Amy stared up at the small TV on the kitchen wall at the 10 o'clock news, her parents seemed obsessed with the news, and what was going on in the world. "You may be happy that I'm back here but I'm not. It wasn't a choice I wanted to make. I want to live and enjoy my life, so why can't you and Dad get that through your thick heads?"

Her mum slammed the pan in her hand down onto the marble counter, "Excuse me?"

"Mum!" Amy shouted, "Just leave it. I am fine. Just leave me alone!" As she stormed out of the room, grabbing her bag and coat she slammed the front door behind her.

She stomped over to where her car was parked and got in. She was angry, her mum always made her feel like this. Why couldn't she just let her live her own life? Just because they had a perfect life and were childhood sweethearts, didn't mean it would be the same for her. She opened her bag looking for her cigarettes and lighter and pulled out her phone.

She needed to go somewhere, somewhere she could blow off steam and forget. Scrolling through the contacts, crossing people's names off mentally as she got to them - Cameron.

Didn't he say his missus was working away for a month in Dubai? She was sure he did, and he always had a good stash of coke. Clicking call on her phone she waited for him to answer while she started the car ready to drive straight over to his.

6

Fatherless

Caroline sat perched on her chair with her legs crossed, twirling her foot in the air with her notepad balanced on her knee. She was sat with Saff in her office. She had enjoyed having Saff as a student, she enjoyed having student's full stop. It was encouraging to her that people wanted to become social workers. Caroline had been a social worker on the Looked After Children's Team in Salford for almost 12 years now and enjoyed having students, particularly ones like Saff.

"This is going to be one of our last supervision sessions now. It's been really great having you on the team here, you've done some fabulous pieces of work. Did you know there was a job coming up on the Leaving Care team?" She asked Saff, "You are coming to the end of your second 100-day placement, and I know you've got a couple of assignments to finish off, but it might be good for you to apply."

"Really? Do you think I would be ready for it?" Saff asked hesitantly, she still didn't believe in herself.

"Of course! You have been great on placement, believe in yourself a little more" Caroline smiled warmly, "the applications will be closing in the next two weeks so I would encourage you to make a start."

Saff couldn't believe it when she was offered the job! It was due to start a few weeks after her placement was finished.

"Me, a qualified social worker! Can you believe it? And going straight from my placement into a job!" she laughed down the phone to Dante.

"Of course I can. I knew you could do it from the first time you told me your plan. I believed in you. Let's celebrate. Let me spoil you."

Saff felt so warm and happy and couldn't stop smiling. "Yes, let's celebrate! I have a job as a Social Worker, wow! I know I need the money; these last two years as a student, money has been super tight! I was gutted I had to leave Blockbusters, but it was too much. Aaaaaand I have some other good news" she said excitedly, "You know I've been offered one of the properties I bid on?"

"No way, that's sick! Things are finally going your way babes. Finally making that move, getting that money. You deserve it all" Dante was behind her move as he felt the same about Manchester and wanted to get away.

"Aww thank you. I have so many bad memories in that flat I need to get away. A fresh start you know, and this feels like this is it." There was a desperation in her voice as she spoke, she had to get away.

Within a few weeks, she was moving into her new property almost twenty miles away from where she had been living.

"I actually can't believe it's happening. A little house, with a front AND back garden!" Saff excitedly exclaimed to Zoe as they drove across to Leigh.

"I can't believe you didn't tell anyone until now" replied Zoe, still baffled as to why she had only found out this week.

"Zoe, it felt so unreal that I didn't want to jinx it by telling anyone. I mean, what if it fell through and then I looked like a right idiot? I only told my mum and Dante, and of course Levi. I felt like it was going to be snatched away from me at any point" stopping at the lights as she waited to turn right off the East Lancashire Road. "The drive over makes me feel all warm inside. I love the trees, the hills, the views" Saff said dreamily.

"I know what you mean Saff. It's not felt that far driving over but look at all these fields and trees" pointing out of the window at what she could see around her, "how does Levi feel about changing schools?" she hoped the move wasn't too much for him.

"Levi seems excited. I didn't want him to move schools like I did, so one change is better than having two changes. But I had to get out of Manchester, you know I have wanted to get out for ages. So many of the lads we've grown up with end up in prison or selling drugs and even dead. Look at Dante's cousin, getting stabbed to death at a party a few years ago. Just horrible! I can't bear another funeral, or another prison visit you know. And I absolutely DO NOT want that life for Levi, the only way I feel I can change that for him is to just get out, getaway. He can't become another statistic; I refuse to let it happen!" Saff banged the steering wheel as she spoke.

"I agree Hun!" cheered Zoe.

"It actually makes my head spin. I've got a new job, a new house in a totally new area and a man who I love. This has got to be the start of things turning round for me and leaving all my crap behind in Manchester."

Zoe smiled and hoped it was. She had heard a rumour last week that Dante had been seen with Freya again, she didn't have the heart to tell Saff right now and burst her bubble, but she would need to tell her at some point.

Saff pulled up outside her house, reversing onto the driveway. "We are here," she said excitedly.

Zoe opened the car door and looked at the little house, it was lovely, and she could see how happy and relaxed Saff looked, "Aww it's lovely. Let's get some of these bits inside, and I hope there's a kettle in one of these boxes as I could do with a brew."

Saff brought the last box inside and shut the door. Finding the box with the kettle and brew-making things, she put it on the kitchen side and began unpacking it. "Good job, we stopped for some milk on the way, and I forgot I even put a packet of biscuits in this box. Chocolate digestives too. So how's things with you Zoe? How's your mum doing?"

"She's not too bad you know, thanks for asking. She's always asking about you and Levi. But I've had a letter from The Salvation Army, saying someone is trying to trace me. The only person I can think of who would even do that would be my dad."

"Oh really? Wow" exclaimed Saff, unwrapping two cups from a box while the kettle boiled. "Do you really think it could be him? What will you do?"

Zoe pulled herself up to sit on the kitchen ledge, "Well I had to chat to my mum first because I didn't want to upset her, you know. She's raised me and has already been through her fair share of drama and pain. She was cool you know, she said it's my choice and she would be behind me no matter what I chose to do, and to be honest I kind of knew that would be her response but felt it was only right to run it by her first."

"Aww, she's really lovely and understanding. She only wants the best for you. I can't even imagine what I would do if my dad got in touch like that" replied Saff as she unscrewed the jar of coffee and put a scoop in each cup. "Can you pass me that milk please?"

Zoe picked up the small carton of milk they had bought on the way and passed it over to Saff, "But honestly, I don't know what to do. I'm 28 years old, life is going ok at the moment, but then maybe that means that now is the right time. It's always been there in the back of my mind, but my mum made sure that me and my brother were taken care of, and I've never really had a desire to go searching for him. And my brother's not bothered, because we don't have the same dad, and he's got a good relationship with his. So much so that I can't even remember the last time me or mum even spoke to him."

"Really?" Saff responded, the shock visible in her response, "I remember you saying that he was doing well after moving away to America but yous haven't even spoken? Sounds like my brother to be honest. Maybe it's a guy thing or a leaving the country thing?"

Zoe took hold of the handle of the hot cup of coffee Saff handed to her and placed it on the ledge next to her, closed her eyes and tried to recall how long it had been since she and her brother had spoken, "I would say it's been about 18 months now, and that's since I stopped reaching out. It was all one-sided Saff, and I haven't got time for relationships where there is no effort being put in from the other person. He's clearly living his best life and has no room in it for me, and I've come to terms with it now. But then this with my dad, sheesh. I know that I don't feel comfortable speaking with him straight away, but email contact feels enough for now, so I did let The Salvation Army know that they could pass my email address over to him."

"And?" said Saff wide-eyed.

Zoe jumped down off the ledge, and picked up her coffee to take a sip, "And, he's emailed already. Basically, he got ill last year, and it made him think about me more and the need to be in touch and he's over the moon that he has found me. He lives in Scotland, is married, has three children, and wants to meet me."

Saff's eyes were wide, "Bonny Scotland eh?" she said in a fake Scottish accent, "married, kids, your head must be going crazy. That's a lot, Zoe."

"It's a bit scary and sudden. I can't get my head around it, and it's gonna feel super weird meeting him after all these years, so I really need to decide if that's what I want to do."

"You don't have to meet him, but you might always think what if, if you don't babes. But at the same time, I guess there's no rush from your side. Just take your time in making a decision."

They spent the rest of the day unpacking boxes, and discussing the plans Zoe might make in taking a trip to Scotland to meet a man that she hadn't known for the majority of her life.

A couple of weeks later, Zoe sat on the train heading up to Scotland, she settled herself into her seat, taking out the books and magazines she had brought to read along the way. The train from Manchester Piccadilly was filling up, and she was glad she had reserved a seat at a table. She had never been to Edinburgh before and was surprised it was only a little over three hours on the train.

Her dad was picking her up from Edinburgh train station and she wasn't sure how she felt. Part of her just wanted to get it over with. The only time Zoe saw these types of reunions was on TV shows like Jeremy Kyle. Those people always hugged each other so tightly and cried their eyes out. Is that how it would be for her? Zoe didn't want to cry. She was preparing herself. To her, she was going to meet a stranger and she didn't even like hugs with people she knew, let alone strangers.

Pulling into the train station, Zoe gathered all her belongings and steeled herself for the upcoming reunion. Stepping off the train, she pulled her coat tighter around her as she felt the chill in the air and began walking up the platform.

There he was, she could see him. There weren't many Black people in the train station, and her mum had shown her a few photos of him when he was younger, so she knew it was him. He was stood with two boys by his side. *Did he look nervous?* She wondered as she slowed her pace.

As she got closer, she thought it looked like he was crying, oh he was. As she reached him, with a half-smile on her face, he pulled her into an embrace, and she could feel his body shaking with the tears. Zoe felt her body stiffen, she wasn't a hugger in general, but she needed time to open up, so she held back, feeling uncomfortable and waiting for the embrace to be over.

The next three days passed in a blur, getting to know her dad, his new wife and their three children. It had been a nice couple of days but weird at the same time. While she had been there, there had been a few comments made that had made Zoe feel uncomfortable and she needed to address them. There were comments made about her mum, her darling mum who had sacrificed everything to care for Zoe and help her be who she had become. There was no way she was going to let this man, pass any judgement on her mum, and she made that very clear to him which hadn't gone down well. She realised that she wasn't the daughter her dad had thought he was finding, and she couldn't match up to his expectations. It felt like he was disappointed in her. They had invited her to visit again in a few months, but Zoe wondered if it was going to work out, this father-daughter relationship. Was this what she wanted?

The weights were stacked neatly, and the mats had all been put away in the studio room after the morning gym classes had finished. Zoe headed to the staff room to take a short break before her personal training session Saff had booked with her. She was looking forward to seeing Saff and glad she had found time to come back to the gym, the place where they had first become friends. Saff had booked a PT session with her and explained that she had a baby at home and needed something for herself. They had become friends after that session. Outside of the kitchen, the gym was one of Zoe's favourite places to be, it brought her focus and calm that she didn't take for granted.

She unpacked her mid-morning snack of an apple and a tub of peanut butter and sipped on her water. The last few months had been a challenge, all this stuff with her dad whirring through her brain. She looked forward to chatting things through with Saff a bit more, she knew she understood as she had grown up without her dad.

Zoe dipped a piece of apple into her peanut butter and grimaced as she recalled Amy's reaction to it all. She really didn't know what she had in her parents, they did everything for her and most of the time she was ungrateful. Zoe shook her head as she remembered what Amy had said *"Oh how I wish my dad would disappear sometimes, he does my head in!"* *Amy, Amy, Amy,* thought Zoe, I really hope you grow up one day. It was Zoe who had introduced Amy and Saff to each other, some days she regretted that decision because of how stupid Amy acted sometimes, but Saff was a grown woman and could make her own decisions about who she was friends with. Zoe on the other hand felt more burdened with Amy than anything, their mums had been close friends growing up, so she was almost like family to her.

There was a gentle knock on the open staff door, Zoe looked up to see Saff standing there ready in her gym gear and a bottle of water.

"I'm not early am I?" asked Saff looking at her watch.

Zoe stood up and grabbed a paper towel to wipe her hands, "No, not at all. I was just taking a minute. Are you ready to get started?"

Saff grimaced, "Depends on what you've got planned for me?"

"Come on, girl" laughed Zoe, as she headed towards the area she had set up in the gym to do some circuit training, "you've got it and we can go at your pace to begin with."

Walking over to the section Zoe had set up, Saff placed her water bottle and mobile phone on a window ledge. "I feel like it's been ages since I've actually seen you. I'm glad I was able to squeeze this last session in with you before I have to cancel my membership."

"That's because it has been a few months, and I'm sure there will be good trainers at your new gym. We will start with some stretches, to get warmed up, so just copy me" said Zoe as she stretched her right arm across her chest. "I've just ended up with loads of cake orders, obviously my hours here at the gym, and then I've been to see my dad twice."

Saff stretched her right arm across her chest to copy Zoe, "I know you've told me a bit through text and that, but you will have to fill me in."

"Well you know I've always felt different, growing up" taking her left arm to cross over her body, "My brother knows his dad and his dad's family. I've just always felt left out and a bit of a loner, and don't get me wrong, his dad's families have done things to include me but it's not the same. I had hoped meeting my dad and spending time with him would have made me feel different and answered some questions about my identity. Or filled in that gap I had, like something was missing. But it didn't. Is that weird?"

Saff had looked thoughtfully before replying, as they moved into a leg stretch "It's not weird, no. You know I didn't grow up with my dad so I can relate to wanting those questions answered. I don't even know how I would feel if I got the chance to meet my dad. I don't even know if I would want to" Saff grimaced and you could see a physical shiver go through her body, "And we've got the cultural difference to deal with too. My dad's Pakistani, and your dad's Black, while we've both been brought up by White mums."

"Yes! Exactly Saff, you get it. Being mixed race most of my life wasn't a massive issue and it's not something that has really been in my face you know, well until someone else noticed and wants to come with some racist nonsense!" Zoe and Saff recalled the times they had experienced racism growing up, and the impact that had had on them over the years as they finished their warmup stretches. "We are going to start with twelve squat jumps and then you can have a 45-second rest which I will time. So let me demonstrate it first and then you can go."

Once Zoe had demonstrated a couple, she gave Saff the nod to begin "That's good – two, three" as she counted Saff through the reps, "and rest for 45 seconds, and then we will move on to push-ups, twelve of them" Zoe started her timer for the 45 seconds of rest. "The first visit to my dad's was ok. I've told you most of that stuff but this second time around" Zoe shrugged her shoulders and twisted her mouth in a grimace, "there was just too much that didn't sit right with me.

"What happened?" asked Saff as she got down into a push-up position, waiting for Zoe to give her the go-ahead.

"We had a big argument! I had to address some of the comments he had made last time I was there, especially those about my mum!" Zoe started her timer, "ok let's go. One, try to get as close to the floor as possible and up. Great. Two, that's it."

"How many is that now?" Saff said struggling for breath, "I don't know if I can do anymore" she wailed.

Zoe knelt by the mat, "You've done nine now which is really good. Let's try for one more and then you can rest."

Saff pushed her way through one more press-up and collapsed onto the mat, red faced. "I am so unfit. This is only exercise two and I feel like crying."

Zoe laughed and passed her a sheet of blue paper from the machine, "Well use this to wipe your tears and be ready for the next exercise which will be 15 calf raises."

"Those I can manage!" asserted Saff pulling herself up to standing, I can't believe your dad was calling your mum like that, he was out of order. Who does he think he is? Your mum's done her best to bring you up on her own. And to have the cheek to ask you if you've ever eaten curried goat when you make the nicest goat I've ever had."

"Honestly Saff, I don't know. He must think Mum's had me living under a flipping rock or summat. I've survived all these years of my life without a dad, so to be honest I can carry on in the same way. And it wasn't just hearing him bad mouth her, but denying parts of our lives that I believe my mum has been truthful about."

"I hope you told him that" Saff encouraged her, as she began the 15 calf raises.

Zoe looked at her, "This is me we are talking about" she laughed, "Of course I did babe. I don't like being confrontational, but it needed to be said" she laughed. "I don't know, maybe I'm just too set in my ways or I'm being too defensive, but I've done well for myself managing without him, I've got two successful businesses which I've built on my own, I've got my mum, and my little house. I just don't need the stress you know. And rest. We will move onto Bench Dips over here on this bench" moving towards it.

Saff followed her, sitting on the floor in front of the bench ready to get in position. "Zoe you are a boss, since I've known you, you are a go-getter and you've never needed a man to help you in that sense."

Zoe was in position next to Saff, "Aww thanks Hun, Right, you are going to do twelve of these, just like this" as she demonstrated the bench dips. "For me, it's time to focus again, men are a distraction from my goals, and I don't need any more of those in my life especially not from a guy who doesn't know me, hasn't been there for me, and doesn't seem to respect the person I've become" standing back up, "ok let's go. One – two."

"We are almost at the end of the circuit now" assured Zoe, "some abdominal crunches and then 60 seconds of the skipping rope will be the end of the circuit and then we go again but next time round we are gonna focus and push through."

Saff groaned, "Sit-ups. Ugh, not my fav, but ok. I think it's a good thing that your dads got in touch, as it takes away the what if aspect but I'm sorry it's not worked out for you, in terms of having a dad/daughter relationship."

"I know, and thanks. It's happened, and it is what it is, to be honest" said Zoe as she lay on her back on the mat, patting the side next to her to indicate for Saff to join her, "I've felt confused about my identity at times and then combine that with just not knowing your dad, not knowing how to have a relationship with a man - it can *really* mess you up but I think that's why I just stay away from guys full stop. To protect myself."

Saff laughed, "But with me, it's gone the other way, unfortunately. Like I'm seeking some kind of validation from guys but looking in ALL the wrong places."

"That is true babe. It affects us all in different ways" said Zoe. "Right let's get on with this circuit and focus."

7

Alone Again

Amy was waving through the living room window with a big cheesy grin on her face. Saff opened the door as Amy was singing.

"We're all going on a summer holiday" laughing and dancing around, "Tenerife, here we come!"

"So, it's all booked then? Two weeks in the sun. I can't wait" Saff sighed. "Work is super intense so it will be amazing to just chill out and it's so nice that I can actually afford to do stuff like this now!"

Amy was still dancing around the living room "I know, I can't wait. Oh sunshine, beaches, cocktails!" She sang, "And at least my parents are good for something eh?"

"It's really nice of them to have paid for you Amy, they are good parents" Saff responded, "But it's been years since I've been anywhere, it still feels like a dream. Levi is going to be buzzing! I can't wait to tell him when he gets back from school."

Amy finally sat down, "Aw he will be, won't he? Is he settling at his new school?"

Saff nodded "Yeah, he has. I was worried about moving him. You know I went to three primary schools and it's not easy changing but at least this is only one change, and it was to give him a better life" Saff sat down on the sofa and pulled her knees up to her chest, hugging them into her, feeling like she needed to give herself that reassurance.

"That's good, he's a good kid. And Dante? Will he be cool about you going away without him?" asked Amy.

"Yeah, I already told him that we were planning it, he's cool about it and said he will do the airport runs. Ah, I can't wait!"

The holiday was amazing, just what she and Levi needed. It was so much fun having Amy there too, even on the days she drank a little more than everyone else, but she was looking forward to getting back to see Dante. As the plane landed Saff turned her phone on to let him know they were arriving.

"Has he texted back yet?" Amy asked while they waited for their luggage,

"No, and I have tried a few more times. The messages aren't being delivered and it's going to answerphone when I ring. I will literally kill him!" fumed Saff. How could he do this to her? Her relaxed holiday feeling was rapidly fading. They decided to call a taxi as Saff continued to try and get hold of Dante. The thing that made her the angriest was that he was meant to be picking her up in her car as she had let him use it while she was away to keep it ticking over. She was fuming but also had a sinking feeling that something bad had happened.

That feeling was confirmed the next day when Saff opened her front door to two members of the Greater Manchester police. Dante had been arrested and her car had been impounded! *He had been doing that in MY car?!!* Saff wanted to laugh and cry at the same time. He had been arrested on a drug-related charge and was looking at a custodial sentence. Well at least she knew why he hadn't picked her up but now she had to get two buses to Longsight police station to collect her car which had been subject to *"a thorough search"* the officer had said.

It was a few weeks before she was able to go and see him in person on a visit to prison. Prison was a place she occasionally needed to visit for work as a social worker, but she hadn't thought she would be visiting for personal reasons anymore. It made her feel very uncomfortable being there under these circumstances.

HMP Manchester, or Strangeways as it was formerly known, was a high-security prison. The visiting process was very intrusive, being searched and sniffed by sniffer dogs, and having your fingerprint taken. Saff felt criminalised by the time she got through all the security checks into the visiting room, and there had been a lot of waiting around!

She entered the visiting room, her eyes looked round the room until she saw Dante and sat down in the seat opposite him. He was sitting there with his arms folded and a serious face.

"Dante, what the heck happened?" Saff asked, relieved to see him.

Dante rolled his eyes and started looking around the room letting out a yawn like she was boring him.

"Erm, hello," said Saff, trying to catch Dante's eye. "Can you see me sat here? I've just been through all those security checks to sit here and see you. You can at least look at me."

"No one told you to come Saff" still not making eye contact.

"Are you joking Dante? You sent me the visiting order to come!" Saff was searching his face, "What is going on with you?"

Dante shrugged and let out a stretch before folding his arms again. Tears were stinging Saff's eyes, why was he being like this? She sat there for a few minutes longer, waiting, willing him to say something but he didn't. She got up and walked out of the room ending the visit, hot tears streaming down her face and her heart hammering in her chest. She needed to get out of this building before she passed out.

That night Saff was going out with her friends, the night now became a night to let loose. Dante had been a rock to her, but she knew it was over. Why had he treated her like that? She knew she didn't deserve it, but she also knew she couldn't be with someone who was in prison for committing a crime. She had to think about her new job, the new life she was trying to create.

"Slow down Saff" Zoe had laughed, "We can't keep up!"

"Zo, I'm so annoyed. He's really upset me you know. I plan to get smashed. Absolutely smashed so I can't remember what a crap day it's been today. And I plan to move on as fast as I can" she was fuming, but she had a twinkle in her eye. She knew how to get over Dante and hurt him in the process, and that's what she planned to do.

The drinks were flowing, and the music was thumping.

"Saff, you remember Christos from the gym?" Zoe shouted in her ear. Saff looked at where she was pointing, her vision was blurry by now as the number of drinks she had drank was taking effect, she nodded and took a swig of her drink splashing most of it all over the floor.

"Whoops, sorry" she slurred. "Yeah, tell him to come say hi" Saff giggled.

Zoe called Christos over, and he chinked his glass against Saff's making more of it splash out onto the floor.

"Let me get you another drink" he slurred into her ear, sounding as drunk as she was.

Saff lifted her glass and shouted, "Lead the way."

Saff woke up the next day and covered her eyes, *ouch!* Why was it so light? It was hurting her eyes. She slowly opened them again, *oh no, where am I?* She did not recognise this room, had she been that drunk? She sat up and looked at who was sleeping next to her in the bed. It was Christos. *Eeeek, had they spent the night together?* Saff's mouth was dry, and she had no idea what time it was.

Christos stirred, he was cute with his tanned olive skin and mop of black curls, and what she could remember of the night, she had had fun. But she couldn't remember leaving the club or anything after. She reached for her phone, 9.20am. Well, she was awake now, so she might as well ring a taxi and get back home.

"You ok Saff?" Christos said sleepily, he still had his eyes closed.

"Yeah, I'm gonna get off though if that's ok. I have to get back to Levi. Can you tell me the address so I can call a taxi please?"

Christos gave the address, and she ordered the taxi. Five minutes later, she heard the taxi beep outside.

"Text me when you get home, ok?" said Christos from his bed, "and just post the key back through, please. I think my Gran has gone out."

Saff winced forgetting that he lived with his gran. She closed the front door and turning the key in the lock, dropped it gently through the letterbox and walked to the taxi.

Amy woke up and stretched her brown legs out on the crisp white sheets of the hotel room. She turned over disappointed to see that her lover for the night hadn't stuck around, she sighed *oh well. I had a great night and I'm sure I can get him to do it again.* She checked her phone, 10.05am. She still had time for a shower and to grab some breakfast before she made her way to her shift at her new job.

She walked into the hotel bathroom and turned on the shower, while she brushed her teeth. Her new job hadn't been too bad so far, it was in a tattoo shop in Manchester, and she was the new receptionist. She laughed as she remembered her mum's response when she had told her where her new job was, the smile had dropped from her face pretty quickly, and then came a flurry of questions about the dangers of tattoos and the people that go into those types of establishments. Her mum needed to relax, and she might even see if she could get a few freebies while she was there so she could do her mum's head in. Putting her toothbrush back in the glass by the sink, she stepped into the hot shower.

Her shift had flown by, and she had secured herself an appointment with one of the tattoo artists that she had spent the day flirting with. She had been begging Saff to come out to a party all week and couldn't understand why Saff was hesitant when she kept telling her that she hadn't had a great week, she was struggling to get through each day, waking up with a hangover most days because she was trying to drink her problems away, craving that numbing feeling, wanting to forget. Amy couldn't see the problem as she felt the same most of the time and did the same, the only difference was she didn't have any kids to deal with. Saff kept going on about Dante too, didn't she realise that there were plenty more fish in the sea, and she just needed to get back out there, which was what Amy was trying to help her do.

"We just need to pick up a bottle or two on the way. Is that ok boss?" Amy asked the taxi driver who indicated it was. "We will stop at one of the shops on Wilmslow Road. I'm so pleased you finally agreed to come to this party Saff."

Once they reached Wilmslow Road in Rusholme, Amy

indicated the shop to the taxi driver and she jumped out, pulling Saff with her.

"Shall we get two bottles of Rose? Or one white and one rose?" Amy was asking as they walked down the alcohol aisle in the shop.

Saff was following behind her but wasn't answering.

"Saff, which one?" said Amy turning to see Saff frozen in the middle of aisle, looking like she'd seen a ghost. "Saff, what you doing?" she turned to look at where Saff was looking, Gabe was coming down the aisle from the other direction and he did not look happy.

"I thought it was you! A little grass aren't ya?" he snarled, "what are you doing round here? No one wants you round here. Trying to get man sent to jail and that."

Before Saff could even respond or react, Gabe spat in her face and pushing past her stormed out of the shop. Saff was visibly shaking. Amy searched in her handbag and shoved a tissue in her hand. "Oh my God Saff, are you ok? He is an absolute nutter! Do you want to go home or still go to the party? I don't even know what to do or say."

Saff closed her eyes and took a deep breath. Scrunching the tissue up that she had just used to wipe her face, she looked at the shelves where the bottles of wine were and said, "Amy, get two bottles just for me!"

"You sure?" said Amy, "shall we just make the most of the night and move on from that absolute tool?!"

Saff nodded. Inside she was shaking and feeling scared. "Amy, this was exactly why I hadn't wanted to pursue things with the police, the best thing for my safety is to put it all behind me and try to forget him as much as I can."

The evening had ended up being a blur, Saff was sure she had drunk more than those two bottles of rose, but she couldn't remember, and doubted Amy could either. She was grateful that her mum was helping with Levi, but she also knew that she couldn't carry on like this. Losing Dante, seeing Gabe, being humiliated, and drinking it was all leading her down the path of depression. She was grateful that her GP was understanding and had agreed to give her a sick note. This gave her the time she needed to figure stuff out.

It had been nice to spend time with Christos, she wasn't in the right place to be in a relationship, she knew that, but he was different from the guys she usually went for. He had a normal job for a start, working in an office 9-5 type of job. He wasn't her usual type in looks with his olive skin, mop of black hair, and twinkling light brown eyes, but she felt attracted to him. Christos also knew Dante, and Saff knew they didn't get on. If she was honest with herself, this had been part of the attraction.

They had gone to school together and had always had this dislike of each other.

Saff's heart was still firmly attached to Dante, and she missed him, but she tried to put on a strong front and push those thoughts away. She finally had a chance to have a normal relationship where she thought the chance of family and stability was possible, with a man who was not Gabe or Dante. Christos had spoken to her about just wanting to be a family man and settle down. Maybe this was her chance to do that too.

Going back to work was daunting, but the time off had helped clear her head and she was back to taking anti-depressants. Anytime things were going well, it was important to Saff to try to function without them, but she found that she kept needing to go back to them.

"It's good to have you back Saff," said her manager Alice, "It's a phased return so please keep in communication and let me know what we can do to support you. These are the cases that you will start picking back up again" placing a printout in front of Saff.

Saff glanced it over and was pleased to see some of the names on the list, "I've missed working with these kids you know. It's good to be back. I want to make a difference in their lives, it's why I qualified."

Alice snorted in a kind of laugh as she turned her chair back towards her desk, "Well remember we are only doing damage limitation at this point. For most of these kids, the damage is already done, unfortunately".

Saff's heart fell, she hadn't gone into this wanting to "just do damage limitation", she had wanted to use her own experiences to help these kids, to give them a better start in life which she felt she had been doing. And no matter what Alice had said to her, she was going to do her best to continue making a difference.

She made her way back to her desk, it felt strange to be back, but she sat down and turned her computer on, waiting for it to load up.

"Hi Saff, it's so nice to see you back. Can I get you a drink? I'm going to the kitchen to make one anyway" asked Thea. Thea Obrien was on her social work placement, she had deep red hair, green eyes, and a soft Irish accent.

"I will have tea, please. No sugar, just milk. Thanks, Thea, that's really kind." Saff already felt more relaxed. She tapped her login details into the computer, pleased she could remember them.

Thea brought a hot cup of tea back to her desk a few minutes later, sitting at one of the other desks in the room. Saff picked up her drink and took a sip, she suddenly felt herself retching.

"Is that milk ok Thea?"

Thea looked up, "Yeah I'm sure it is" sniffing her drink and taking a sip of it, "It tastes fine. Are you ok?"

Saff didn't feel great, but the nausea seemed to have passed for the moment. "Yeah, I just felt funny for a moment. Thanks for the drink" Saff didn't risk taking another sip, and she didn't want Thea to think she had made a bad cup of tea. She was such a lovely girl, Saff was sure she had told her she went to church, so she didn't want to upset her for no reason.

Fortunately, Thea was going out to see a young person, so didn't see that Saff poured the rest of the cup down the sink. *What's wrong with me? I hope I'm not coming down with anything.*

Back at home, the pregnancy test sat on the side of the bath, while Saff sat on the floor. She was leaning against the bath with her eyes closed. *Why was time going so slow?* She looked at the timer on her phone with 1 minute remaining. *Come on, come on.* She mentally wished the time to go faster.

Beep, Beep. Beep, Beep. She picked up the stick, horrified to see the two lines that had appeared, indicating she was pregnant. One thing it seemed she didn't have a problem with, was getting pregnant. *God, there are people out there who try so hard to get pregnant, and they don't. And then there are other people who are not trying and are on bloody contraception and just get pregnant. Just like that! Why?*

Even at the age of 28 years old, she was still failing at remembering to take contraception daily, no matter how hard she tried, it didn't work for her.

Fortunately, Christos was happy about the pregnancy; it would finally get his family off his back about starting his own family and getting married. The pressure was becoming more and more, he knew this wasn't what they had wanted ideally but it was enough to shut them up for a while. Which was why it was him that suggested moving in with Saff and Levi so he could help out more and show his family he was committed to this.

As the pregnancy developed he suggested he should put in some extra hours at work, the overtime would help them financially.

"Overtime?" Saff asked, "You have already been doing loads of overtime, I think you actually spend more time in the office than you do anywhere else." She laughed, but it was like it had just dawned on her, he was in the office a lot. Those suspicious feelings crept up on her, and she hoped he wasn't at the office doing anything else. She shook her head; no these were just old fears rising to the top because of what she had been through, Christos wasn't like the others.

8

Caught Out

Pregnancy wasn't something Saff enjoyed. She could never understand why the medical term was morning sickness when she felt sick all day long! She wasn't physically sick, there was just a constant feeling of nausea. Food didn't taste the same, there was a metallic taste in her mouth and the only time she felt ok was when she was asleep or in the bath.

She wasn't sleeping too well and that wasn't being helped by her neighbours. When she had first moved in, her neighbours had all seemed fine, and Saff was hoping to keep herself to herself anyway. But houses on council estates were usually built quite close to each other. Saff was in an end terrace, but she felt like she could hear every word of the neighbours next door, especially during their arguments, which seemed to be every day. The screaming matches were horrible, their language colourful, and it broke Saff's heart when she could hear the kids crying.

The lady on the other side, who was the first house in

the next block of terraces, was lovely. An elderly lady who reminded her of her old neighbour Bill. She took great care of her garden, even though it was only little, it was her pride and joy. It was just a shame about the neighbours on the other side.

"I forgot to tell you what happened this morning Christos," Saff said one evening as they watched TV. Christos hadn't been in long from work, he didn't even join them for dinner anymore with all the overtime.

"Go on" Christos looked over at her, waiting to hear what happened this morning.

"The police were all over here, the front and the back at about 8am. I was in the bathroom brushing my teeth and looking out of the window and could see a few at the back, even in our garden!"

"What on earth?!" he asked, Christos left for work before 7.30am to get to the office on time. "Looking for the guy next door?"

"Yep" nodded Saff, "they ended up booting the front door in and dragging him out in cuffs. So frustrating that we've ended up living next to what appears to be the worst neighbours on the street."

"If he's been arrested, hopefully, it means there won't be any noise or arguing for a while and you can get some sleep. "How are you finding work?" asked Christos.

Saff squirmed in her seat trying to change position as she couldn't get comfortable, and her feet were aching. "It's hard you know Christos, I'm tired and obviously want to protect the baby so I am trying to make fewer visits to the young people. Just to keep safe really."

"It won't be long now, and you will be able to go on maternity leave. I'm still happy to be doing the extra hours at work" said Christos.

Saff looked at him as he was watching the TV, they hadn't been spending much time together and she felt like they were behaving more like friends than boyfriend and girlfriend. There certainly hadn't been any intimacy for a while which had suited Saff as she felt hot and bothered most of the time as her bump grew each day.

"Is everything ok Christos?" Saff tentatively asked, not sure if she really wanted to know the answer.

"Yeah, course" Christos replied quickly, glancing at her and then quickly pulling his gaze back to the TV.

"Erm are you sure?" she asked again.

Christos sighed and shook his head. "Can I be honest with you Saff?"

Saff felt a lump in her throat and her heart beat faster, "I think you should Christos, yeah."

Christos cleared his throat, "I'm not sure if things are really working out with us. I know it's the worst possible time as we are expecting a baby and I am really happy about that, but I just feel like we aren't moving forward as a couple in the way I thought we would."

Saff was silent for a minute and was thinking before she responded. "Wow, erm I don't think I was expecting this but I kind of agree. I don't really know what else to say."

"Let me go and run you a bath, I'm not trying to stress you out. We can talk about it another time" he spoke as he jumped up and began his way up the stairs to the bathroom.

Saff sat there stunned. She was not expecting it but there was a part of her that understood. Her mind was racing. She was going to be a single parent, again!

Suddenly there was a buzzing. A phone was vibrating as messages were coming through. Saff looked over to where Christos was sitting, he had left his phone. An overwhelming urge came over her to take a look. Pushing herself up from the sofa with her bump, she snatched the phone and punched in the pin. She had seen Christos put it in enough times.

The messages that had buzzed through were from Amelia. Saff could feel her heart rate speeding up and she felt a little faint. She lowered herself onto the chair Christos had been sitting on and listened for him upstairs, she realised she still had a few minutes before he came back down.

The messages were very intimate and flirtatious. Scrolling through them, many of them were trying to make plans to be on the same shifts together. Then there were messages of plans to meet up outside of work. She felt the anger rise within her, the sound of her blood pumping becoming loud in her ears.

Saff racked her brains to check the dates of a few of those times and realised that he had told her he was working at those times. How could she not have picked up the signs earlier? She had had enough experience of being cheated on by Dante. She felt anger rising inside her How dare he? Another guy taking her for a fool again?!

"Saff are you coming upstairs for this bath?" he called as he bounced down the stairs and into the living room. He halted in his steps as he saw Saff with his phone.

Reaching towards her for it, he asked "Did it ring or something?"

"Messages" Saff replied flatly, "from Amelia."

Christos cleared his throat, "Did you read them?"

Saff nodded, holding his gaze, determined to keep eye contact.

"Look she's a girl at work, who I get on with. Nothing has happened" he exclaimed.

Saff's eyes suddenly widened, "So this is why you've been doing all that overtime?! Not to earn money for us and our baby."

"I mean it didn't start like that, I was doing it for us, for the money. But I guess the last few weeks, it's been nice to work with her more. I'm sorry you know, and I will support you and the baby, and Levi but I think it's probably best I go back to my grans. You don't deserve to be treated like this and I am so sorry."

Hot tears rolled from her eyes. How many times had Saff heard that line? Had she been taken for a fool again?

Christos started packing his things up to move out by the weekend. His Gran or his Yaya as family called her would be happy to welcome him back into her home. He hadn't been totally honest with Saff when he had mentioned Amelia. He had told Saff nothing had happened, but he knew he had crossed a line and regretted treating Saff like that. He did like her but knew she was rebounding from Dante Knight. Dante, even the thought of his name made his skin crawl. He didn't like him or how he had treated Saff, and a few other girls he knew. He was glad Saff was no longer with him, but the guilt that he carried knowing him and Amelia had begun a level of intimacy, not exactly physical, but it may as well have been. And he had rushed into this relationship with Saff due to his family's pressure.

A sudden dark thought crossed his mind, maybe he and Dante were not that dissimilar? NO! He shook his head. No, he was *nothing* like him, what he had done with Amelia didn't compare. He shook his head, pulled his shoulders back, and smugly pushed that thought far away.

It was nice to have Zoe pop over bringing gifts for all three of them. "I've just turned 29 so it's the big 3-0 next year," Saff told Zoe, "I feel like my priorities are changing. My maternity leave is coming to an end and it feels like it's flown by because I took it about two months before she was due, and I just don't feel like I can cope with going back. It's such an emotionally demanding job" bouncing baby Sienna on her knee as she squealed. "While I was pregnant, I was so tired, and I don't know how many times the midwives told me I needed to relax and reduce my stress, reduce my blood pressure. Like I wasn't trying to do that, but all while being sick and not sleeping, and processing what happened with Christos. I've loved going to baby classes and meeting other mums. I want to focus on being a mum for a while."

Zoe cooed at Sienna, shaking one of the new toys she had bought at her, "If I were you, I would want to stay at home with this little cutie too. She's gorgeous, look at all her curly hair. I'm an April baby too but I don't hit the big 3- 0 until the year after you, how are you feeling in yourself?" looking sympathetically at Saff.

Saff sighed, "I'm ok but just not 100% you know. Most days I feel like I'm going through the motions. I just keep going on to mess things up. Repeating horrible cycles, and I don't know how to change things. But I love being a mum and as long as my kids are ok, then I will be ok" She sounded like she was trying to make herself believe this as much as she wanted Zoe to believe it.

"And how have you been since things with Christos, you know since he left? I feel so bad for the way he has treated you Saff, after I introduced you to each other too" she said sympathetically.

Saff smiled, "I've been ok you know. I wasn't ready for a relationship and my feelings were all still wrapped up in Dante. I can't blame Christos for meeting someone else. Amelia is lovely and it makes sense why he was spending so much time at work. Don't get me wrong I was so angry with him, but I just want to get on with my life and start making better choices."

Zoe had enjoyed her time with Saff and the kids, she did feel broody at times but had no desire to be in a relationship with a man, or a woman, as some people often dared to ask her if she was gay because they never saw her with a guy. The drive back home wasn't too long from Saff's, and she made a mental note to make more of an effort to visit and spend time with the kids.

Her phone began to ring on the seat beside her, an unknown caller. She didn't like to answer while driving, so once she checked it was safe she pulled into a lay-by on the A580. It was the hospital to say her mum had had a fall and had been taken to St. Mary's Hospital. She immediately drove to the hospital, rushing to the ward she was in.

"Mum, what... how... are you ok?" her words came out in gasps as she approached the hospital bed the nurse had pointed her to.

Her mum, Elizabeth took hold of her hand, "Zoe, baby I'm fine, I'm fine" tapping her hand on top of hers to comfort her.

"Well, you are clearly not fine because here you are" Zoe spread her hands out in front of her, exasperated.

Elizabeth tutted and smoothed the blanket over her lap, "I fell. I don't know what all the fuss is about. Tony from next door found me when he brought the paper around as he does every afternoon. It was he that insisted I come here."

Zoe sat on the chair next to the bed and took her coat off, "Well thank you, Tony. I will make sure I pass on my gratitude to him. I might even send him a batch of cupcakes but Mum, it's got to be time now."

Elizabeth flicked her hand in the air as if brushing Zoe's words away, "You know I like my independence and I don't want to become a burden to you and get in the way" knowing what Zoe was referring to but not wanting to accept it. "And what if you meet someone, I don't want you to have to worry about your mum making things awkward."

"I have space for you at my house mum, I have time to look after you and you will never become a burden to me or get in my way. It's an offer I have put to you for years and it will stay on the table until you accept it." Zoe knew how hard her mum had worked to take care of her and her brother, and she would do anything to repay that and look after her when the time came, or when her mum stopped being so stubborn. "And mum, you don't have to worry about me meeting someone, I have no desire for that kind of distraction right now. You are more important than my love life, please stop worrying about that."

Elizabeth tutted, "Zoe you are a beautiful young woman, who works hard, and you have every right to meet a beautiful man who values you. Not every relationship ends like mine did, don't use that as a measure for yours."

Zoe sighed and rubbed her eyes, "I know Mum and I appreciate you saying that. Honestly, I'm just not interested right now. Will you think about my offer please?"

Smiling, Elizabeth nodded, as the nurse on the ward approached the bed. "Ms. Ross, are you ready for us to do some checks to see if we can look at getting you home?"

9

Repeating Cycles

Walking into the church grounds, Saff looked around. She wanted to be alone but deep down she hoped someone would see her and ask her if she was ok. The last six months had been hard, and she had found herself stuck in the same cycles. Finding a little set of stone steps, leading to the vestry door at the back of the church, she sat down. The stone felt hard and cold. The church grounds looked vibrant with all the leaves falling from the trees. Reds, yellows, oranges. It was Autumn. She was reflecting, and contemplating the decision she was about to make. She cried at the very thought of it all.

The church was one of those "proper" churches, with a spire and stained-glass windows. Saff lived within walking distance. She had found herself drawn to the church because of her situation, she felt like she was stuck in a difficult situation, and she needed help, she needed saving. She needed someone to tell her what the right thing to do was even though she knew the answer. This was a situation she had never wanted to be

in again. She had been here before, many years ago. A shiver
went down her spine as she thought about that relationship.
That abusive relationship with Gabe, she didn't even like
hearing his name all these years later. She had told herself that
she would never, ever find herself back in this situation. Yet
here she was.

Almost 30 years old, a single parent of two children, and
feeling completely alone. She knew no one else could make
this decision for her. Saff was struggling to care for the two
children she already had, being in an area on her own with no
family or friends out here. Levi was now eleven and Sienna
had turned one earlier in the year. Depression was something
she had suffered with on and off throughout most of her adult
life and it was a dark pit she was falling back into. She looked
around, still deep-down longing for someone to find her.

Feeling the cold from the concrete steps on her legs, she
searched her mind and heart for the answer, but she couldn't
find it. She was the one who would struggle, and her children
would suffer. She knew it was her actions that had got her to
this place but that didn't make things easier it just made her
hate herself even more than she already did.

She had never thought of herself as a bad person, but she
knew that the decision she was going to make was not fair. It
wasn't the decision she wanted to make, but she could see no

way out. She wasn't thinking straight, no she COULD NOT think straight! She could not see how this would work out for her and her two children without fighting a battle she did not have the strength for.

Hadn't she already been through enough? She was tired of being strong. Tired of being alone. Tired of trying to better her life only to keep returning to these self-destructing cycles. On one hand, she had achieved so much, even as a single parent. She had completed a degree, completed a master's, and qualified as a social worker; she had moved away from Manchester where so much of her pain took place. But what did any of that really mean when here she was, in a cycle, in a predicament that she knew she could only blame herself for. Oh yes, she was fine with taking responsibility and could do a great job berating herself. Saff could honestly be her own worst enemy.

No matter what happened she knew it would be something she would have to deal with on her own. She would not be telling many people. It was not something she wanted to shout from the rooftops. It was something that she was utterly and absolutely ashamed of.

Saff had chosen the grounds of a church to sit and reflect because she felt that she was at a point in her life where there had to be more than this. There had to be something bigger than her. There was something oddly peaceful about the grounds of a church. The gardens usually looked so well looked after. The grass was well maintained, there were so many different types of bushes and flowers, and trees. It was beautiful.

She had been in the church a few times as it was linked to Levi's primary school. It had those hard wooden benches to sit on, but it was pretty, with its stained-glass windows. The windows had pictures of people in the designs, people she had no idea who they were. Her visits to the church had only been for little things the school had put on, and Levi went to the youth club there. Saff did know a lady who went here, she had met her at a baby class.

As she thought of her children, she thought about her bad decision making which had led to them having different dads. It was never planned and something she didn't want to happen as that is how she had grown up. Saff and her siblings had different dads. But as she sat reflecting, she realised she was repeating generational cycles that she silently prayed would break. That she could break them. This is why she had come to the church grounds. Prayer was all she had right now, but she didn't even know God like that.

She believed he was real, but she had been living her life and God didn't fit into that lifestyle. She enjoyed a good night out on a Saturday and the hangover from all the drink and drugs was too much to consider attending a Sunday morning service. Can you even imagine?! She looked up at the church, at the stained-glass windows and it made her smile to even think about trying to rock up here on a Sunday morning!

If God were real, he wouldn't be interested in her, she was sure of that. Especially not right now. Not the way she was living. Drinking, partying, sexual relationships, her language was foul! She was sure God didn't like swearing. Saff thought of herself as a fairly good person but was that enough? She had trained as a social worker because she wanted to help people, to give back. She had fought so many battles and often fought them alone. Trauma can cause us to be very independent and try to fight these things with our own strength. But she was flipping tired of fighting. Why wasn't God helping her? That's what he was supposed to do, wasn't he? Help people? Or maybe he just helped people like those that went to this church, who already had their lives sorted and on the straight and narrow.

Something had to change. She had made so many physical changes to her life. Got new jobs, found a new boyfriend, finished a new college or university course, moved house, redecorated, gained weight, lost weight - you know how it goes! But still here she was, still her, still plodding on, still trying to keep it together even if just for the kids' sake.

She felt like she wanted to run away. Run away from a situation, a person, a place or even herself. That's how she felt. No matter what she did, where she went, what she achieved or didn't, she was still her. So, running away wasn't going to change anything, was it? She had to stand and face this.

With a heavy heart, she knew the decision she was going to make. A decision that she felt she had no choice to make. Little did she know how life-changing this would be.

She got up to start the short walk home. Her mum was coming to visit. She didn't see her as much these days as she had moved away to Yorkshire adding more house moves to the many she had racked up over the years. As she rounded the corner to her street, she could see her mum stood outside her house waiting. She hugged her as they greeted each other and went inside.

Saff put the kettle on to make a brew.

"Do you want a drink, mum?" she asked, knowing the answer would be yes.

"Oh yeah, that will be nice. Where have you just come from?" her mum asked her.

"I just went for a walk, needed to clear my head" Saff replied as she grabbed two cups to make the coffee. "Sorry Sienna isn't here, Christos picked her up last night as they have a family thing today, and she won't be back until bedtime."

"Aww, no worries. How you feeling love? Do you feel any clearer about the situation?" asked her mum. She had always been open with her mum.

"Well, I ended up sitting in the church grounds for a bit. You know that church on the main road?"

"Church?" her mum's eyes went wide with her question.

"Yes church" Saff laughed.

"I know it's hard, but you need to do what you need to do Sapphire, you know we will support you no matter what."

Saff knew she would get some support from a few family members and a couple of friends, but this would be support from afar and ultimately, she had to go through this alone.

Waking up the next morning, Saff felt a familiar feeling. Nausea.

"Mum, I can't find my new tie," shouted Levi.

Saff sighed "How could you have lost that already Levi? It was on top of your uniform pile."

Levi had started high school this week and she didn't want to be feeling like this. She didn't even want to get out of bed but that's impossible when you are a single parent with children! And this was part of her struggle and why she knew she couldn't manage any other way. She needed to get her head back in the game to be able to take care of her kids. They needed her.

"Found it mum, it had fell down the back of the drawers."

By the time she had made it downstairs, Levi had made himself some cereal and was getting ready to leave for his bus. He had several friends from primary school at his new high school, so he was with some familiar faces on the journey to school. Sienna wanted some breakfast, Saff struggled in the kitchen with the nausea, so she threw some toast and banana together and ran out of the room before she was sick.

While Sienna ate her breakfast, Saff prepared herself to make a phone call to her GP to make an appointment. Surprisingly, she got one for later that day albeit a telephone appointment but at least it was today. She needed to get things sorted quickly before she got in her head or before it was too late. Her mum had told her yesterday she could look after the kids and her friend Amy would pick her up and drop her off.

Saff could not explain the turmoil she felt inside her head, her heart. She remembered that first time she had been through this all those years ago. She could still hear that little old lady in her head, shouting across the road *"You don't have to do this,"* she thought of it often. Saff knew she was stupid to be in this situation again, she didn't need anyone to remind her of that. Some things didn't change. It seemed she didn't change.

But she had to.

The GP rang later that afternoon. It was Dr Devi. Saff explained her situation to her and why she had called. She needed an appointment as soon as possible.

Dr Devi asked some questions about her situation and then she said "Referring you for this, is not something I personally want to do. It's not something I believe in, but if that's what you need then I will."

Saff was taken aback. She suddenly remembered that the doctor she had gone to the first time had said something similar to her, were they even allowed to say things like that? She wasn't sure and she really didn't need to hear it because she personally didn't want to do it either.

Dr Devi said she would refer her to the clinic at St. Mary's Hospital. With it being a hospital, hopefully, no one would know why she was there if they saw her. And hopefully, no one would be outside telling her not to do it because they were not the ones who had to go through this. She knew that some people had a flippant attitude to situations like this and just did what they could to make it go away but she didn't feel like that. She felt backed into a corner. She felt out of control. She didn't take any of this lightly.

10

I Hate Myself

Two weeks later, Amy pulled up outside to pick her up. Her mum was there and told her she didn't need to worry about the kids.

"Sorry let me move this stuff out of the way, just ignore the mess," said Amy as she began shoving all the papers and empty crisps wrappers into the back, "How you doing?"

"Pretty crap to be honest. My heads all over the place" responded Saff as she clicked her seatbelt into place, "so sick of being in this place and going through the same crap over and over. Why do they not teach you this stuff in school? All we got taught was science stuff. I don't remember ever being taught about the emotional side of all this, that relationships and sex can end up in pain and hurt. You see heartbreak in films but not stuff like this. And, come on, real-life relationships never look like what they do in films."

"True," said Amy "but no one's relationship looks like that

really. I feel ya pain babe. Have you spoken to Christos?"

"Yeah, he knows where I'm going. He just doesn't want Amelia to find out, and to be honest I don't either." Saff put her head back and closed her eyes. "We shouldn't have slept together again, it was a mistake, and I don't want to hurt her, neither does he."

Amy snorted, "Well he should have thought about that shouldn't he and kept it in his pants!"

"Yeah, but it's not just his fault, is it? It was just sex, but it shouldn't have happened. Isn't sex meant to be fun?" Saff looked out of the window as she felt tears roll down her cheeks. "Well, I don't see how STDs, babies, abortions, pain, grief – I don't see how any of that is fun, because it definitely doesn't feel like it is right now."

Amy reached across and squeezed her hand before passing her a tissue.

"You know that I absolutely adore babies, I'm always broody, and my babies are absolutely gorgeous. I love them so much and just want the best for them." More tears streamed from her eyes, doing her best to use the tissue to catch them all, "We can all agree that I do not like being pregnant with all that sickness, but here I am, driving to the hospital to get rid of my baby. Who even am I? How has my life got to this point?"

"Saff, this is a horrible situation, I know, I've been here

before, a few times but I hate that it's always us women left to deal with it. I'm here for you, you know that. You are not a bad person; you are just being forced to make a horrible decision and you have to do what's right for you, what makes you happy. We are here now, so I will wait for their call, and be straight back, ok?" said Amy.

Saff smiled and said "thank you" before getting out of the car and walking to the reception to check-in.

As the general anaesthetic began to wear off, Saff slowly came around. There was a nurse nearby who smiled and said "Hello, how are you feeling?"

Saff felt groggy and uncomfortable but overall, not too bad, physically.

"Everything went well. Let me just grab you a drink and a bite to eat" said the nurse warmly as she walked out of the cubicle.

Saff tried to sit up slightly and make herself comfortable. There was a glass of water on the table next to her which she reached for and took a much-needed gulp of water.

The nurse came back with a hot cup of tea and a slice of toast.

"Here you go lovey. If it's ok, I wanted to talk to you about what's next. Have you thought about future contraception?"

This was something Saff had felt she had never figured out properly. She explained to the nurse her previous experiences and she needed to try something different now. This could not and would not happen again. Firstly, she did not plan to have sex ever again, but that might not be the most realistic plan.

The nurse smiled and said "I agree, it is a hopeful plan but not realistic. You are a young lady, and you have a lot of life left to live. How about the implant?" and the nurse went on to explain how it would work.

Saff was very squeamish and thinking about having something inserted in her arm made her shiver, but after what she had just been through it was pretty minor. So, she agreed to have an implant fitted in her arm. The fact that it could last up to three years before needing to be changed was a big plus.

Back at home, Saff wanted to get back into the swing of things and be there for her kids. She no longer felt nauseas which she was relieved about, but wow did she feel low and emotional. Her mum greeted her when she got to the front door and packed her off to bed which was a relief because she could not stop crying. She didn't want to let her kids see her like that. She didn't want them to worry anymore, Levi had already started to worry when she was feeling sick. She had to find a way to pull herself together.

"Sapphire," her mum said as she knocked on the bedroom door. She came in with a cup of tea and some toast. "The kids are eating some food; do you want anything?"

Saff shook her head and took the tea and toast saying that this was enough. "I'm so peed off Mum. Just don't want to start going down that spiral of depression again you know but I can feel it creeping up. Just feels dark."

Her mum nodded, she knew from her own experience what depression was like and Saff knew she understood.

Saff was beating herself up. Berating herself for what she had done. She had always struggled with how she felt about herself, but right now she really hated herself. She couldn't even look at herself in the mirror.

"Did the hospital offer you anything like counselling?" asked her mum.

Saff nodded as she drank her cup of tea. "Yeah, which is good. So, we'll see how that goes. I need to ring them and get an appointment" It was a relief to be offered it because she needed to talk to someone, talk to someone who could professionally help her.

Saff had dropped Sienna off with her sister and made her way back to the hospital that she had only been at a couple of weeks before. She had been so emotional and was hoping today's session would help. Saff hurried to the entrance after parking her car. She really did not want to see anyone and absolutely didn't want anyone to know why she was there because this was not something Saff wanted to share right now. She didn't want to hear anyone's views or judgements on what she had done. She already knew and honestly, she felt the same.

The counsellor, Moira, greeted her. She was an older lady with short brown hair that Saff could see was beginning to grey above her ears. Moira went through how the sessions would work and explained the confidentiality of the sessions. Already Saff was thinking *I wonder what she really thinks of me and why I'm here?*

Moira smiled and asked Saff where she wanted to start.

Saff explained how she was feeling "I feel a lot of emotions right now all mixed up together. I feel guilty, ashamed but I also feel loss."

Moira looked at her sympathetically and nodded "I understand."

Saff replied "I just don't think many others will understand. I feel like I'm not allowed to feel loss, but I do. It breaks my heart" she sobbed.

Moira passed her a box of tissues "There is no right or wrong way to be feeling right now. What you feel are very real feelings and hopefully we can work together through that together."

Saff felt like her words were spilling out of her mouth as she explained "I didn't want to be in this place right now. I lost my baby. I felt like I made a decision, but it wasn't the decision I really wanted to make. I just don't know if I can forgive myself for that. How do I move forward? I really don't know. I actually really hate men right now. It seems so much easier for them. They get to just walk away but it's our bodies that have to go through this stuff!" she was angry "I never want to be with anyone again! Men just want sex but for me, sex ends in pain and heartbreak. I actually feel disgusted with myself." She took a moment to blow her nose before she continued "The thought of being with a man now makes me feel sick. I don't even want to make any effort with my appearance in case it made a man look at me. I actually can't bear it!"

Moira paused thoughtfully before she spoke "People can have psychological problems that do affect their sex life, it is very normal. These can be problems around lack of desire and especially after what you've been through its understandable. There are specific therapists that work in that area, but it is not an area I am qualified in. So, if it is something you want to explore more, I can look at making a referral, but I do feel we can unpack some of the other feelings you are feeling if you like?"

Saff shook her head. She wasn't planning to have any relations with anyone for a while "Not right now, I think I would just want to carry on with these sessions and see how I get on."

Moira nodded and smiled warmly as they continued the session.

11

Do Something Different

It felt like torture in her mind every day. Saff had made a decision in the hope that she could get back to herself and be there for her kids but now she was a mess in a different way. It was a lonely place to be. It was not something she was going to bring up when someone said, "Oh hey, how are you?"

That typical British question we ask but we don't really want the answer to, or we want the answer to come back "I'm good, thanks" because anything else might inconvenience our day or make us feel uncomfortable. So, it was easier to hide away, and avoid that question altogether. Saff knew if someone asked her, she was sure she would tell them the truth because she was not good!

Saff was grateful she hadn't returned to work once her maternity leave had ended. She couldn't imagine working as a social worker while having a baby at home, not only was it stressful but it was emotionally and mentally hard at times.

She was now a stay-at-home single mum. That running

away feeling was still there but how could she run away from this? How could she run away from herself? How was that even possible? No new job, new house or new man was going to fix this. *Lesson learnt* she thought grimly.

Amy had come round to see how she was doing. They sat in the living room with a brew while Sienna napped upstairs.

"Them riots in London are awful, aren't they?" Amy said as Saff pulled her dressing gown tighter around her, she hadn't even bothered to get dressed the last few days. Amy nodded towards the news on the TV screen. "It's to do with a lad getting shot, Mark Duggan."

"I don't even know what's been going on, my heads been all over the place. But it doesn't sound good." Said Saff glancing at the TV.

Amy sat back with her brew in one hand and a biscuit in the other, "You know my parents always have the news on, so it's been all they've been talking about at mine. How you doing?"

"My heads mashed up. I just don't know if I'm gonna be able to forgive myself this time round you know? It just feels so much bigger than me if that makes sense."

"Girl, I hear you but you're gonna have to forgive yourself or you're gonna be in a real mess" Amy stated, always straight to the point.

Saff laughed "I'm gonna be in a real mess? I already am!

Look at me" she said exasperated, and took a sip of her coffee, her mouth feeling dry. "This is gonna sound mad so don't laugh, but there's this niggling feeling that I need God to forgive me for what I've done."

Amy's eyes widened slightly, and she nodded, saying "Okayyyy...."

"I know, it sounds mad when we aren't like that, but I believe there's something out there and the thought just won't leave me alone."

"So, what you gonna do about that then?" Amy asked sipping her coffee.

Saff sighed; she didn't know.

"How do I know what God is saying OR if He would forgive me? What did God think about me? That's IF He thinks about me at all. Trying to process this stuff in my brain makes my head hurt. I just don't know how I'm going to move forward this time round. Like...." Saff paused trying to gather her thoughts, "EVERYTHING has changed. Things feel like they will never be the same, but I know I need to do something different than I've been doing" She looked at Amy who was sitting there staring at her, she looked almost scared. Saff realised she had been rambling and spilling out the thoughts in her head which didn't even make sense to her so how would they make sense to anyone else?

Saff was thinking a lot about God and what he thought about her. This need for him to forgive her got stronger and stronger to the point where she could no longer ignore it. She picked up her phone and sent a text to Lucy. Lucy was the lady she had met at a baby class, and she knew she went to the church round the corner.

Hi Lucy, I hope you are well. I wondered if you could let me know what time your church starts on a Sunday please x

A text pinged back pretty much straight away.

Hi Saff, so lovely to hear from you. It starts at 10am and it would be lovely to see you there x

Saff decided she would attend the service and see what happened.

She hadn't been going out partying recently, she hadn't been doing much socialising at all. Apart from her mum, Amy, the kids, and the mums at the few baby classes she had managed to drag herself and Sienna to, she hadn't seen many other people. *Things have to change and what do I have to lose when I have lost so much already?* If she wanted to find God and find out what he thought about all of this, surely the best place to start was in a church.

Sunday morning came around and Saff had spent the morning worrying about what to wear, should you wear your

Sunday best, or had things changed and it was a bit more relaxed now? She had no idea so settled on some jeans with a blazer jacket.

She plucked up the courage to walk through the doors for the 10am service, arriving five minutes before so she could find a seat.

As she walked into the foyer, a very kind lady approached her and welcomed her, "Good morning, how lovely to see you. My name is Joy. Is this your first time with us?" She instantly made Saff feel more relaxed.

Joy showed Saff into the main church and helped her find a seat on the hard wooden pews. Saff wondered how long the service was on for and wished she had asked Lucy that question too. She was still feeling slightly uncomfortable as she had no idea of what to expect. She looked around but couldn't see Lucy's face yet.

The service was nice enough. They had a band and sang some songs, some of which Saff remembered from all those years ago when she had been to church as a child.

There was Great Is the Lord:

And Lord we want to lift Your name on high.

And Lord we want to thank You.

For the works You've done in our lives

And Lord we trust in Your unfailing love.

For You alone are God eternal

Throughout earth and heaven above

And Lord I Lift Your Name on High:

You came from heaven to earth.

To show the way

From the earth to the cross

My debt to pay.

From the cross to the grave

From the grave to the sky

Lord, I lift Your name on high.

Saff couldn't believe how easily the lyrics and melodies came back to her mind, and that they were still singing them all these years later. It was a fairly big church, and the seats were mostly full which felt strange as she lived so close but didn't know these people.

The vicar spoke and gave a message about loving our enemies. It was hard to concentrate, knowing why she had come to church. She was trying to block her thoughts out, but they were intrusive, reminding her of what she had done. *You shouldn't be sat in this place! What if people knew what you had done?!* She wanted to run away right there and then, to silence the voice in her head but she did not want to draw attention to herself.

Finally, the service was over, which was a relief as her bottom was beginning to feel numb.

"Saff, how nice to see you" beamed Lucy as she came over to where Saff was sitting. "They are serving tea and coffee in the foyer if you want a cup. They have biscuits too."

Saff could do with a brew, so she walked with Lucy to the foyer who introduced her to one or two people along the way.

"No Sienna today? Is she with her dad?" asked Lucy as she asked the lady serving the drinks for a coffee.

"Yes, she will be back later this afternoon and I left Levi in bed sleeping, early mornings aren't his thing." The serving lady asked her if she wanted coffee or tea. The coffee cups already had a scoop of coffee in the bottom, and the tea was poured from huge metal teapots. "Coffee please" Saff responded as the serving lady poured boiling water into one of the cups from the urn behind her.

Lucy guided them to a couple of free chairs lined up along the foyer walls, "So how did you find this morning?"

"It was actually really nice. I used to go to church when I was younger, Ivy Cottage in Manchester" Saff explained to Lucy, "And it's funny because I recognised some of the songs today."

"Oh wow, how long ago was that?" asked Lucy.

Saff mentally tried to figure out how long ago it was, "Mmmm, I must have been about ten years old. We went for a few years but then my mum came away from the church and that was that. But it's been nice today, and really nice to meet some other local people. It's not been easy to meet new people since I moved from Manchester. The main way has been through baby classes."

"Well I'm glad we met at one of those classes, do you think you will bring Sienna and Levi with you one day? Well that's if you are hoping to come back again!" said Lucy, offering Saff another biscuit from the plate on the table nearby.

Choosing a chocolate digestive biscuit, Saff replied "Thank you. With Sienna being with her dad at weekends, she might not come with me as often unless there is a random Sunday I have her. And with Levi, it might be a struggle to get him out of bed this early on a Sunday morning, but I will ask him."

"I can't imagine what I would do with a free night from little Eve," said Lucy, looking dreamily, referring to her baby "Oooo maybe an early night. That would be nice."

"Ah Lucy, I agree. It was hard not having Sienna home at weekends but now I know that I get something many other parents get and I try to make the most of that time and be kind to myself. Which does mean having an early night at times," laughed Saff. She finished her coffee, chatted for a little while longer, and then made her exit. It had all been very overwhelming but overall, she had enjoyed herself and knew she would be back again.

Saff had been back to the church a few Sundays running now and was beginning to understand things more, learning more of the songs and about the Bible.

"So you recognise some of the songs then? asked her mum during a phone call.

"I actually do! But the music is something I'm finding hard. They are definitely not what I'm used to listening to!"

"What did you expect Sapphire, a bit of R&B or Bassline?" laughed her mum.

"No, of course not mum. I guess I didn't think much about the music, but music is an important part of life. You've brought me up on some classics, and then I've gone on to like my own stuff but it's nothing like the church songs. I just don't know if I will ever get into them. Did you when you went to church?" asked Saff.

"I was into the rave scene before I went to church, so I get it. I think once you get more familiar with them it will get easier. Can't believe they are still singing some of the same songs all these years later" replied her mum.

Saff still found it amusing picturing her mum transitioning from the rave scene to church life, "Mum, you really have been through some transitions in life. You've been a Muslim, a hippie, a raver, a Christian and I guess you are back to being a bit of a hippie again."

"What can I say? I've lived life!" her mum said, "Have you made any friends?"

Saff pulled her feet up on the sofa, and curled them under her, "Mmmm, it's early days I think. I know Lucy obviously and everyone has been so nice. It does feel strange sitting there, not really knowing anyone, AND not wanting to tell anyone why I wanted to come either. That's hard but I do want to make friends. People are definitely different to any of the friends I already have" she laughed, "but you know me, I'm capable of sitting in a room with different types of people and getting on ok."

"I know you will be fine Sapphire. Speaking of your friends; do they know you've been going to church?" asked her mum.

Saff sighed, "They know but I think it's just weird to them. Amy has been kind and polite, but I don't think she really understands why I need to do this."

"You know why you are doing this, and I believe you will be fine. You can't control what other people think about you and what you do" reassured her mum.

Saff was making her way home on the short walk from church one Sunday afternoon when her phone started vibrating, indicating an incoming call. She kept her phone set to vibrate these days, long gone the days of choosing a ringtone.

She looked at the screen and frowned, it was a number she didn't have stored, so she answered tentatively.

"Hello"

"Sapphire!! What you saying baby girl?" rang the voice down the phone. Dante Knight. He must be out of prison. Saff really couldn't deal with any drama right now but there was a pang of familiarity about hearing his voice and she was curious how he was out already.

"Hello Dante," she said through gritted teeth, remembering the last time she saw him, "when did you get out?"

"Yesterday! Thought I best shout you first you know after seeing my ma and all that. So, what's going on?"

Saff doubted she was the first girl he had called since getting out yesterday if that was when he got out. She couldn't believe anything he said to her anymore which made Saff feel sad because he had been her best friend at one time. She felt so comfortable with him and could have spoken to him about anything, but he had taken advantage of that relationship many times, was a prolific cheater, and let's not forget his behaviour during her one and only visit to him in prison. He was not someone Saff needed in her life right now but even the sound of his voice brought about a familiarity that she longed for.

"I've actually just been to church," Saff told him confidently.

"Church?!" Dante burst out laughing "Rah, what you doing there? Had to be for a wedding or suttin?"

No Dante, not a wedding or anything else, just a normal Sunday morning service. I've been going for a while now." She replied, not even trying to hide the annoyance in her voice.

"Rah, just never saw you as a church girl init." He replied casually.

"Well, I've changed, a lot!" declared Saff.

"Mmmm changed, eh? That's cool Saff, and so have I! Soooooo when can I see you baby girl?" he drawled.

Saff knew Dante hadn't changed "To be honest, you can't see me. I've got stuff going on and I'm trying to sort myself out." She meant it, she was not about to let him start messing things up.

"Let me help you, Saff. I need to fly by and pick those bits up that I've got at yours anyway. Come on……." Saff sighed; he did have stuff at hers that she had kept safe for him while he had been in prison, some clothes and trainers.

"You're lucky that stuff is still at mine, and I didn't sell it!"

she said in frustration remembering how he had had the cheek to get another girl to ring her to try to pick the stuff up! A girl who claimed she was his girlfriend, well join the flipping queue love because there are a few of us here.

"Yeah, well I appreciate that, but I still need to get it aaaaand I still wanna see you." He was trying to use that pleading but sexy tone he had to get his own way.

She had to stay strong, "Look you can come pick it up, but there's nothing between us anymore. I meant it when I said I have changed, things have changed, life has changed. So come this afternoon and then just draw a line yeah."

"Cool, I will fly over bout 3ish. Not sure about drawing that line though" he laughed, and she ended the call.

She really couldn't be bothered with Dante coming round but she did want his stuff out of the house. She didn't want to be around him and his flirtatious ways. She got changed and chose a pair of tracksuit bottoms and a big baggy jumper, her hair scraped up into a scruffy bun. *Gosh, you look tired Saff,* she said to herself while looking in the mirror. She felt tired too and hoped her general appearance would put Dante off her for good.

The bass of his music could be heard before she even saw his car. He was always so extra and wanted people to look at him. She stood up as a shiny brand-new black Volkswagen

Golf pulled up outside her house, sighing as she saw him jump out of the car. He looked like he had been making use of the gym while he had been locked up, his dreads had grown so they were almost touching his shoulders, and she could tell he was dressed in brand-new expensive clothes, everything looked clean and crisp.

Did her heart just do a little leap seeing him again after all these years? No, she had to be strong she told herself.

She opened the front door before he got the chance to knock, "Saff, Saffy, Sapphire, shining bright like a jewel!" he sang to her and brought her into a big bear hug before she could even protest.

She managed to wriggle her way free from his hug and she knew she was definitely not shining bright like a jewel; he really was a charmer. "Save it, Dante. Your stuff is in the cupboard in the kitchen."

"What? No offer of a brew? You really gonna do man like that? Come on babes" Saff sighed and turned to walk back into the house to the kitchen to put the kettle on. She could do with a drink herself, but she really wanted him to leave as quickly as possible. She heard him close the door behind him.

"Got it looking nice in here now init girl," he said as he looked around, "So, you good yeah? Do you need anything?" for his faults, he had always been generous, but I guess you could be when you were making money the way he did and from the looks of it, things were not going to change even after a stint in prison.

"I'm good Dante, it's cool. Are you gonna sort your life out now?" raising her eyebrows as she poured the boiling water into two cups of tea.

Dante laughed, "Always straight to the point you!" reaching out to touch her arm in a playful way, Saff winced and quickly stepped back. His touch had been electric, sparking memories that she quickly tried to subdue.

"Erm, my life is good. But it would be better with you" he flashed her a smile.

Even after everything he had done to her, she still loved him, but she couldn't be with him anymore, she had to move on no matter how much it hurt.

"Nope, not gonna happen. I'm sure you will move on quickly, I have, and I am double sure you've got many, many options." She said confidently.

Dante stayed a little while longer, reminiscing about their good times. That was his thing, always bringing the good times up to stir up emotions in her but she couldn't forget how he made her feel in the bad times, how betrayed she felt when he cheated, and how devastated she was when he had given her the cold shoulder on that prison visit. That was the deepest cut for her.

She was glad when he finally loaded his stuff in his car. His parting words were a promise that he would come see her again. She had joked that she hoped it wasn't too soon, but she meant it, she didn't want him coming back around. Life was different for her now and she questioned what love even was. The relationships she had been in had been bad ones, even the ones she had thought were good at the time! Surely that wasn't love, but would she ever find out what real love was?

12

Breaking the Mould

Saff walked into The Royal Sovereign pub in Salford to meet for Sunday lunch and Thea O'Brien stood up and hugged her. "It's so nice to catch up with you Saff" she beamed with her warm smile.

"Aww Thea, thanks for agreeing to meet up. It's been about four years, hasn't it?" she was just as Saff remembered her.

"I think it has and look at these wee ones" bending down to say hi to Sienna in her pram.

Thea already had a table, and Saff unclipped the pram straps to sit Sienna in a highchair.

"Saff it looks like there have been some big changes since I last saw you. Levi, you've got much bigger" she said smiling at Levi.

"Definitely some big changes, we've got this little one now" Saff laughed as Sienna blew a raspberry at her brother. "And I wanted to let you know that we have been going to church. I remember that you went to church." Saff said it hesitantly so she could be sure she had been right.

"Yes, I go to church, and Saff, that's amazing. Let's order some food and then tell me all about it." Saff remembered she had been a great listener so after they had put their orders in Saff told her all about the church and a number of the people she had met, how it was making her feel. She didn't explain why she had gone to church in the first place, that was a conversation for another time if it happened at all. Right now, Saff wanted to focus on the good.

"I know that church! I have some friends that go there" exclaimed Thea.

"Really? How crazy is that? It's such a small world" Saff couldn't believe it, but it made her feel like she had made the right choice with the church. Thea shared that she had been a Christian all her life, growing up in the faith. Saff listened, soaking it all up. It was really exciting, and she was looking forward to reconnecting with her friend.

Thea began inviting Saff to events, Christian events. It was like this whole new world opened up before her. There were music events, film events, meals, and Christmas events. Thea was very involved in youth work in her local area and there were often opportunities for Saff to help.

One thing Saff had was time! She wasn't working as she was still a stay-at-home mum, and Sienna was with her dad at weekends, so she was able to attend most things she was invited to. The more time she spent at church and around Christians, the more she began to realise this was more than she had ever imagined. Thea was great, patient and graceful, answering any questions Saff had, and she had a lot!

"I feel like I haven't seen you in forever" moaned Amy as they walked into Costa Coffee in Manchester, "Saturday night was so good. I even saw Dante; they sent a bottle of champagne over to our table," she looked very pleased about that.

Saff looked over at Amy while they joined the queue for coffee, "Well I am very glad that I was not there! Going out to those places just aren't where I need to be right now."

"Mmmm because you're too busy with your church things, eh?" laughed Amy, but Saff could hear it again, that polite judgement. "You are different though you know, there's just something about you. I've not figured it out properly but there's something" Amy said.

Saff knew she was right, she felt different, and she was glad people around her were beginning to notice too. "I just feel like there is hope now, I've been through so much Amy, and I've tried so much to better myself, better my life, and none of it has worked. I'm sure even you could agree to that. But this just feels like this is it, this is what I have been looking for."

Amy shuddered "Not for me all that, it freaks me out. No drinking and no sex equals no fun. Why would you even want to follow all them rules or read that boring book? If you want rules you should move into mine with me Mum and Dad"

"It hasn't been like that though, that's the thing. Right now, I am still trying to understand it all, so I definitely don't have all the answers. But where has drinking and sex got us so far?" Saff asked raising her eyebrows.

"A good time, that's where!" laughed Amy as she danced to the till to order her drink.

Amy had enjoyed catching up with Saff and headed straight to the sunbed shop afterward. She had a couple of nights out coming up and that required a few beauty treatments, so she looked her best. She picked up the cleaning spray and some paper towels to clean the sunbed before it came on.

She missed her partner in crime, her party buddy, Saff. Zoe was cool to hang out with, but she was more like an annoying big sister. They had grown up together with their mums being friends from before they were pregnant with Amy and Zoe, but Zoe didn't drink, she didn't date guys, she didn't seem to do anything but work and chill with her mum, which Amy couldn't think of anything worse.

The sunbed was clean, she stripped down to just her knickers and lay down, sticking the goggles to her eyes to protect her from the UV rays. The sun bed clicked on, and the lights sprang into action. She let out a satisfying sigh and thought about how she didn't understand why Saff was making all these changes and going to Church. Amy had thought it was just going to be a phase from the guilt she had felt after having an abortion.

The sunbed began to heat up and she relished in the warmth on her skin. Life was about doing what made you happy and she loved doing just that. Screw what everyone else thought or wanted her to do, she did whatever she wanted to do, and no one could stop her. She began tapping her toes along to the house music she could hear playing over the speakers in the room, the music was getting her in the mood. She might even grab a sneaky glass of wine at one of the wine bars before she went on to her hair appointment. The thought made her feel warm inside and she felt the flutters of excitement in her tummy.

Yes, she told herself that's what she would do because it made her happy and she deserved to be happy.

It was a Saturday morning and Saff sat in the kitchen with a cup of tea reflecting on the last six months. Levi was still in bed and Sienna was at her dad's. She couldn't believe it was six months since she had started going to church. Levi had been with her a few times, and Saff smiled as she remembered what he had said.

"Why is everyone so nice Mum?" he had asked her during their walk home one Sunday, he was very serious, and it had made her laugh.

"They are really nice aren't they son? It's because they know Jesus." It was nice to be in an environment where people weren't hating on you or trying to stab you in the back. It was also nice to know that even Levi could see the difference in people. Seeing that difference in people and realising it was because they knew Jesus, had made her realise that going to church and being a Christian wasn't what she had once thought it was.

This God thing is more than that. It means something to the people I've met. But can I be like them? She sipped her cup of tea as she thought; *Can I be like them? I just don't know.* She had been worrying about this recently, what would people think if they knew the real her? The life she had led. *Thea seemed ok about things when I shared with her,* she thought, *but that was Thea.*

All these people she had met were nice, seeming to be from nice normal families, nice stable backgrounds and she just didn't fit that mould. Saff was different, she listened to different music, had different life experiences, had different language, and enjoyed different things. How could she become a Christian when she was so different from all those she had met? *I am changing,* she told herself, *but do I really want to change completely? Who will I become? How can someone like me, having done the things I have done, become like those people in church?* She couldn't see how it was possible nor work out if that's what she wanted.

Saff had a lot to think about, she put her cup in the sink and made her way into the living room which was covered in boxes. *Where to start today?* She thought. She was moving house again, not too far from her current home, but to a bigger house so Sienna could have her room and they could move away from the next-door neighbours. Unfortunately, the guy seemed to be in and out of prison, and when he was out the screaming arguments went on late into the night and so did the early morning police visits. Saff's heart went out to the kids, she had hoped to have moved away from this stuff when she left Manchester.

She began putting books into a sturdy cardboard box when she heard Levi making his way downstairs.

"Morning Mum," he said as he plonked himself onto the sofa.

"Good morning, did you sleep well Levi?"

Levi yawned and shrugged before he asked, "What are we doing today?"

"Well, I'm packing, so if you could carry on putting your things in boxes in your room, that would be helpful."

Levi screwed his face up and moaned, "Why do we have to move *again?*"

"You know Sienna needs her own room, and that's why. We've been in this house for four years now, that's a long time for me! You know Nana used to move around a lot when I was younger. We haven't moved around as much as that and hopefully, this next house is the house we will stay in for many many years. Ok?" she knew he had made friends on this street, and she knew how hard it was to move but it wasn't far, and he could still come back and play.

"Will I get the biggest room like you said?"

"Yes, you will get the biggest room, like I said" she smiled, thinking of the new place.

It was a great size with a huge back garden, but it needed some work doing, decorating and carpets and she needed help. Family had offered to help with the decorating, but it was mainly her church friends offering to help in different ways. Saff had only known them for a few months, and they wanted to help her, not only practically but financially. They were offering more help than people she had known for years. She was blown away by their generosity and gratefully accepted any help offered.

Easter was approaching, and Thea had invited Saff to an event in Manchester City Centre being hosted by Make Jesus Known. They had a big stage outside Manchester Town Hall with a sound system. Saff and Thea had helped with handing out flyers to encourage people to attend and were now listening to some of the bands on the stage. It felt a bit awkward being here in her hometown. Was it all going to be cringy? What if she saw someone she knew?

"Hi Craig, this is Saff. Saff this is Craig, he will be performing."

"Nice to meet you," said Craig.

Saff heard a familiar accent "Are you from Manny?"

"Yeah, are you?" replied Craig.

"Well, I moved out a few years ago but yeah South Manchester."

Craig chatted with them for a while, then had to get ready to perform on stage. He had told Saff he used to be a drug dealer in Manchester but was now a Christian and shared his faith through his music. Saff waited for his performance because she wasn't sure what Christian rap was going to sound like, but it was really good!

After his performance, she told Craig that she had really liked his music, "Music is something I have been struggling with since going to church. I'm not really into the songs we sing you know. They are fine in church but at home, I'm not so sure. But what am I meant to listen to? Everything I listen to has swearing in it or talking about sex!" she explained. Craig listened and said he completely understood. He said he would be happy to send her some music artists he would recommend.

On the walk back to the car, Saff gushed "This has really blown me away you know Thea; I think Craig is the first person I've met who I feel is like me or WAS like me."

"That's really good then! You can relate to where he has come from but look at what God has done in his life."

"I know, it's mad. I feel like it's answered a lot of my worries, like I can still be me, but I can also be a Christian, if that make sense?"

"Totally!" said Thea, she always had a way of making Saff's feelings feel validated, she had been a real blessing in her life.

13

Redeeming Love

Saff was lying on her single mattress on the bare floorboards surrounded by boxes and bags. Her bedroom was the last room to finish upstairs in their new place, the kids' rooms had taken priority. She wasn't bothered because she knew these things take time.

Picking up the book she was reading she went to pick Sienna up from her cot and take her downstairs. Settling her on the floor with some toys, she sat down and opened the book. A lady at church had lent it to her and Saff hadn't been able to put it down, she loved reading, and this was a great book.

It was a book Saff could relate to. It was inspired by the story of Hosea in the Bible, not that Saff had read that story in the Bible yet, but she understood it was a story about Gods' unconditional love. A love that Saff didn't have much experience of. She had her mum's love, and she loved her children but not a father's unconditional love and not the unconditional love of a husband.

The woman in the book had ended up a prostitute, being used by men and although Saff had never been a prostitute, she could relate to being used by men, being promiscuous, thinking that's what men wanted from her. But in this book, the man Hosea, loved her and wanted her despite the things she had done.

Was that even possible? That a man could love her despite her past and the things she had done? It was something Saff hoped for herself, to be loved unconditionally and not to be judged because she knew that wasn't who she was anymore.

Over the last few months of chatting with Thea and being at church, she had begun to realise that God loved her, and it was unconditional. He loved her as a father should love his child, something she had never experienced.

She put the book down, checked that Sienna was safe, and closed her eyes. It was time.

"God, I've come to know enough to know you are real. I've met so many amazing people these last six months and I want what they have. I want to know you like they do. I want to be changed like they have been. I realise that I have been trying too hard to change my life myself, but I need you to change my heart. I have made such a mess of things and I need Jesus to help me. I believe that you are the son of God. I believe you died on the cross for my sins and that you rose again. Please forgive me for what I've done and help me to become who you have called me to be" Saff continued to pray and ask God into her life, to take the steering wheel of her life.

Opening her eyes, she looked around. Was she meant to feel different straight away? Because she didn't feel any different just yet, nothing "magical" seemed to have happened so she wondered if anything would change after that prayer.

Later that day she was listening to music as she was pottering in the kitchen making her and Sienna lunch. As promised Craig, the rapper she had met in Manchester, had sent her an email with some music recommendations, she had already checked them out on Spotify and had got a couple of albums – Lecrae, Kirk Franklin, Andy Mineo. It was surprising for her how good they were. Music that did not glorify violence, sex, drugs, or swearing but yet still sounded good, who knew?

A text pinged through on her phone, she sat down on one of the kitchen chairs and sighed as she read it. Dante, again! He hadn't stopped texting her these last few days.

Remember that mad night out in Leeds we had? Orrrr it was sick! You were so drunk, we had jokes that night xxxxxxx

He kept doing this, bringing up good memories they had together, trying to take her to that emotional place but it wasn't working. She didn't even reply, she had already told him straight that it wasn't going to happen. But it seemed he wasn't going to give up just yet!

It was a real challenge for Saff, she didn't like being on her own and the desire to be with a man, to spend the rest of their lives together, to get married was very strong. But now she was different, she was unsure how that was going to happen. The guys she went for seemed to be a certain type; she would openly admit that she had liked a bad boy! And would also admit that this hadn't served her well.

Another text pinged through from Amy.

Baby Grand, this Saturday? You coming?? The girls are out out! xx

It seemed that all the temptations were coming at her today. But the thought of a night out in Manchester sent shivers down her spine. It sounded like a nightmare right now. The girls would be expecting "Drunk Saff" to show up, but she wasn't available anymore.

Thanks for the invite, Amy, but it's just not my scene right now. I'm trying not to drink, and I know that you all will be, so it's easier if I don't come. Sorry x

She could have guessed what Amy's response would be.

Buzz kill you Saff lol proper boring since you been going to church. Still love ya babes but you're missing out x

What was she missing? Having a hangover the next day? Spending loads of money that she didn't have? Doing something embarrassing while drunk? Nope, Saff was pretty sure she would not miss any of those things.

Saff put Sienna in her highchair and strapped her in, placing the dish of pasta she had made for her in front of her. She sat down with her bowl of pasta and realised that her desires had begun to slowly change, the things she was choosing to do with her social time were changing, and the music she wanted to listen to was changing. She was also reading her Bible. Thea had bought her one as she didn't have one and had advised her to start in the New Testament with the book of Matthew. She had read Matthew, and Mark and was currently reading Luke reading all about the life of Jesus.

It was hard to talk to friends about this, friends like Amy anyway because as much as she said she was happy for Saff, she knew it made her feel uncomfortable and that Amy didn't like some of the changes Saff was making. She knew her friends didn't understand why she wanted to stop drinking and taking drugs. She assumed they would all be laughing about her on their night out on Saturday, but this was something that Saff was determined to do. She was committed to knowing more about Jesus and what that meant for her life. So far, she had made quite a mess of her life, bad choices everywhere which had affected her children too. She had to make things better, for herself and them. They deserved it and so did she.

She used to wake up feeling like she was living in the film Groundhog Day, dreading another day of trials and battles, and feeling hopeless with no future. But now she found she was waking up excited. Excited for what God may do, what the day might bring, what she would learn, who she would meet. She knew each day she was becoming more like God as he led her and shaped her, and the exciting thing was that was an ongoing process, so it was only going to get better!

There was a Bible verse that Saff had written on a post-it note and stuck to her wall by her bed to remind her that she was now a new creation. *"Therefore if anyone is in Christ, he is a new creature; the old things passed away; behold, new things have come." 2 Corinthians 5:17.* It was a strange feeling to wake up each day excited, but it was a great feeling too. This was the type of buzz she only felt when she had been high on drugs, but now she was buzzing while stone-cold sober!!

Another text pinged through from Dante.

Will I see your pretty face at Baby Grand on Sat? xxxx

Saff sighed but decided she would reply, hoping he would give it a rest.

Nope, sorry Dante. I'm not going but the girls will be out. Just not for me anymore!

*Not for you babes? I will treat you to a bottle of wine and
we can have some fun xxx*

*I'm trying not to drink at the moment Dante but thank you
for the offer. Have a good night.*

*It won't be the same without you babes. Come on, we've
not been out for ages, all the drinks are on me because I
know you like a glass or two. Or I could come check you
instead? Xxxxx*

He wasn't making this easy! She did miss hanging out with
him, he made her laugh so much. Saff thought about it, maybe
they could hang out instead but shook her head, what was she
thinking?

Maybe another time

She hoped that that would be the end of it.

She felt like she was starting a new life, it hadn't even felt
like this when she had moved out of Manchester as exciting
as that was, she was still her and still had the same problems.
But now, she felt lighter, she could think clearer, and she was
beginning to see that she had much more hope and purpose
in her life than she ever realised before. Saff had also been
praying, this was usually during her Bible reading time, but it
was becoming something she wanted to do more, simply to talk
to God. She wondered if it was ok to pray and ask God for help
in her friend situation.

Saff loved her friends; they were great friends. But she was finding it harder and harder to be around them, particularly on nights out or nights in. Nearly every social gathering for as far as she could remember involved drink and more often than not, drugs. It was just the norm. And there was often a pressure or an encouragement to join in, not from Zoe, she avoided drinking anyway. Saff knew she wasn't addicted, and for a while, it would be fun, until she was too drunk or too high, then it became stupid and sometimes dangerous. Waking up and not remembering all of the night, what had she said, what had she done? Sometimes it would take the next week to piece it together, hearing bits from different people. It was mortifying at times, but yet she did it again, and again.

She was drawing a line now. Yes, she could still be there and say no. But she didn't feel strong enough to maintain these new standards herself, she knew that they would be relentless in trying to get her to have a drink, telling her there was no harm in it and there was no fun without it, especially Amy. Saff was worried they would wear her down until she gave in. It was too early for her to be strong enough to not give in to the peer pressure.

Finding some new friends would help, she had nothing to lose. "God, I am really enjoying this new life that you have given me. I am struggling socially, with my friends. I don't want to do the things I used to do but this means I need some new friends and some new invites, please. I hope that's ok. Amen"

Hoping that prayer was ok, Saff took herself and Sienna into the living room and got settled on the sofa ready to read some more of her book, hoping that Sienna would be ok playing with her toys and let her read.

A little while later she put her bookmark in to mark her page, she put her book down. Standing up to stretch her legs she walked to the kitchen to put the kettle on for a brew. Sienna had been playing fine by herself, although the living room looked like there had been about five kids playing with the amount of mess she had made with her toys. She picked her phone up from the kitchen table where she had left at and looked at the three messages that had come through.

She had three invitations to social events from Thea and people from church. Had that been an answer to her prayer earlier? Checking her diary, she was pleased that she was able to accept all three invitations. A ladies' breakfast at a local tearoom this Saturday morning, a music/quiz night in Salford with Thea next Friday, and a birthday party in a few weeks.

The rest of the week seemed to fly by and before Saff knew it, it was Saturday morning, and she was on her way to the ladies' breakfast. She enjoyed a good coffee and pastry and was looking forward to getting to know some of the church ladies. Recognising many faces from a Sunday morning made her feel at ease. The one question that seemed to pop up time and time again was what had brought her to the church? How was she going to answer? Was this the right place to be honest? Did she want to let people know?

"I live just round the corner, and had met Lucy when I worked with her, so I thought I would come and check it out. And I'm still here" Saff smiled, hoping that response was sufficient because it was true, it just left out the finer details.

The ladies' breakfast was on every other month and Saff was looking forward to the next one. It was so refreshing to be in an environment where there was no alcohol, she noticed no one was swearing, and the topics of conversation felt different but comfortable. That's how Saff felt, comfortable.

Comfortable was the opposite of how she felt later that night when she heard Dante's car pull up outside her house. She looked at her phone, 10.30pm, *was he for real?!*

Opening the door when he knocked, she glared at him "What are you doing?"

He grinned sheepishly "Missed you on the night out so I swerved it and flew up here."

"I'm about to get into bed Dante, I'm tired, it's late and I hope you haven't woken Levi up!" Saff said not even trying to hide her frustration.

"I could join you" he suggested with a glint in his eye.

"Good night, Dante" and she closed the door, as quietly as she could hoping the conversation hadn't woken Levi up. She felt bad because he had driven all this way, but it was uninvited, and with him being so persistent, she wasn't sure she had the willpower to keep him away. It was like temptation was literally knocking on her front door.

The next few months flew by. Saff had begun helping out at church where she could, she was accepting all the social invites she received from church friends and was now taking Sienna to a toddler group run by the church. It was here she was able to get to know other mums and make friends, and Sienna loved it!

"Betty, what groups are there at church for my son? He's 13 now" Saff asked one of the toddler group organisers one morning.

Levi had started going to a Tuesday night youth group at the church for the local kids, but she hadn't noticed anything at the church that would help the kids explore faith as she was.

"Oooo there hasn't been anything for a while for that age. We just can't get the workers."

Saff thanked Betty and smiled; her thinking cap was on.

Later that day she ran her idea by Thea on the phone.

"Do you think I could do it? I know I'm not that far into my faith journey yet, but I wish I had had something when I was younger. Life might have been different. I might have valued myself more. I just want to be able to use my experiences to help others not have to go through the same."

"Definitely Saff. Speak to the vicar at the church and ask Josh and Lisa Moore. They would be a good couple to do it with" encouraged Thea.

Once Saff set her mind on something, she always saw it through.

Within a few weeks, Saff, Josh, and Lisa had set up a youth Bible study for the youth at church. There was a small number of kids similar age to Levi whose parents all went to the church, and Saff really wanted something for Levi. This is what she did, she saw a need, tried to find a solution, and took some action.

Working with the young people was great, it meant giving up her Friday nights every week, but Saff felt it was more than worth it. Her Friday nights were no longer for going out so why not use her time to try to make a difference?

They had been able to have a meeting with the vicar at church and discuss plans and resources they would be able to use, and the planning of where and when they would hold the group. It was also great getting to know Josh and Lisa, they were turning into really good friends.

"Drugs eh Saff? I can't even imagine you doing that" laughed Josh one Friday while they were setting up for the group.

She had heard that a few times since sharing some of her background with more people at church.

"I've never fancied them myself, just not been my thing" he shrugged "but it's good to hear your story, especially for the young people."

Saff was also hearing that more, that she should share her story.

"Do you fancy sharing some of your story at one of the ladies' days?" smiled Lisa, "because I agree, but us older people need to hear it too!"

"It's been good to be able to share bits with the youth group, if my experiences can help them to not go through the same, then that's a win for me! Yeah, I guess I could also share with the ladies" Saff said nervously.

She desperately wanted people to experience what she was experiencing. There was a hunger inside her for more, to know more about God and to see where this was taking her. She felt complete, she felt loved – finally! But she also wanted to tell everyone, which she did on her Facebook, every status update was sharing how amazing she felt, how different life was, how hopeful she felt, and how good God was!

One person who was noticing changes in Saff was Christos. She had mentioned she had been going to church, but he had really started to see changes in her.

"She's like one of those God botherers now, isn't she?!" scoffed Amelia, when it had come up in conversation.

Christos suddenly felt protective of Saff, as he could see this change was positive for her and Sienna, "Amelia, chill and don't say stuff like that" he responded.

"Ok, ok, it's just weird. Going to church for a christening or a wedding is cool but to go EVERY Sunday and want to talk about God ALL the time. Ugh," Amelia didn't hide her distaste for this new activity.

"Look, Amelia, it's Saff's choice. And she seems happier, she seems more chilled and easier going. Let's just see what happens eh?" He didn't fully understand all the God stuff either, but he wanted to end the conversation and noted not to bring this up again with Amelia.

-

The next ladies' day was a few weeks away, so Saff had time to prepare. She sat at the kitchen table with a pad of lined paper and a pen. The day was about identity, which was something Saff had struggled with for most of her life so surely she had a lot to share about it. Who was she? Battling with her ethnicity after experiencing racism, growing up without a dad, having siblings with different dads, moving around so much, changing schools, being a teen mum, depression, hating who she was, the list went on! She tapped the pen on the paper as her mind swirled with all the thoughts. Where would she start?

During a recent message at church, the vicar had spoken about praying and asking God for guidance. She decided this was the best thing to do as she didn't want to share everything, and she didn't want to waffle on with herself. Putting her pen down and closing her eyes she said out loud "Dear God, it's me, Saff. Erm, would you mind helping me figure out what to speak about for this ladies' day, please? Amen."

Hoping that prayer was ok, she picked up her pen and set about writing her experiences related to identity. As she wrote, she felt amazed, sometimes you need to see it written in black and white to take it all in. So much had happened in her life, but so much more had happened in the time she had been coming to church for which she was grateful. It was like a miracle. Life wasn't perfect by any means, but she knew the work was starting on the inside.

"Thanks for the help God" she whispered as she continued to shape her short talk.

-

The ladies day was in Church House which was the old vicarage building in the grounds of the church. It was a big old building with huge rooms and incredibly high ceilings. It was one of those buildings that was either cold or made you sweat and made lots of creaking sounds.

The women who had planned the day had decorated the room with lovely different coloured buntings. The tables were all covered with tablecloths and covered with plates of biscuits, cakes, bowls of crisps, and bowls of fruit. Saff looked around the room as she sat down with a cup of coffee and a couple of chocolate biscuits She was pleased that she recognised most of the ladies there, that made her feel more comfortable about sharing. There were the odd few faces that she didn't recognise, but she knew they would have been invited by one of the ladies she knew. She had wanted to invite her friends, but Amy had declined, and Zoe was genuinely busy with work. Thea was there and joined her where she was sitting, "How are you feeling?"

"Nervous. It's one thing writing your experiences down in a way that you can share them, but it's going to be a totally other thing to actually stand up and share them with everyone" gulped Saff, grateful that Thea was there with her.

"Aww, you will be great," said Thea, gently patting Saff's

knee, "I am excited to hear you and will sit at the front so if you get nervous just look at me."

"Thank you so much for coming today. I'm nervous but excited too. I've got ten minutes in the first session, before the break so I will sit with you until then."

After she had shared, there was a break time for refreshments. She had felt herself getting emotional as she had shared, which she hadn't expected, and she was glad it was over. Saff was so surprised at how many of the ladies came up to her to thank her for sharing, some said that what she had shared had spoken to them or they had been through something similar at one time in their life. Some were emotional themselves. Saff was overwhelmed and in awe that God would use her in this way.

Over the next few months, Saff was asked to share on different occasions, and she said yes, every time, wanting to share this hope she had found. It was so exciting, she wanted to shout it from the rooftops. But no matter how many times she shared her experiences, for some reason, there was something inside of her that felt she was not yet able to share about her initial reason of coming to church. Why she needed God to forgive her.

She had concluded that this was because she was still

unable to forgive herself for the abortions. The Bible was full of stories about forgiveness, she had learned that God didn't keep a record of our sins and that if we repent then we were forgiven. But this part of her still felt ugly and hidden. It was one thing to read it in her Bible but to really feel it and know that God had forgiven her, seemed much harder. The few select Christian friends she had shared with had all told her that God had forgiven her. She kind of believed that he had but there was still a sense of shame and guilt.

"I feel like God has wiped my slate clean Thea. Like he has really given me a chance for a fresh start but for some reason that issue just feels like I can't face it just yet. I do believe in my heart that God has forgiven me because I am truly so sorry for what I did and it will never happen again, but that feeling isn't matching up to my thoughts and how I still feel about it" she explained one day to Thea as they met for a coffee.

"Forgiveness can be a process. You will hopefully get to a place where you no longer dwell on what you did, where it no longer has the same hold over you. It's important that you believe that God has forgiven you, that was why he sent his son Jesus to die on the cross for our sins, to take that punishment for us. It's important that you are able to forgive yourself, but there is no pressure for that right now. It's so great that overall, you feel like you've been given a fresh start because you are a new creation! Focus on that and let God do the healing work"

smiled Thea.

14

Metamorphosis

Over the next few years, Saff threw herself into her faith, it encompassed all she did and who she was. She got involved in what she could - youth events, joined the PCC (Parochial Church Council), volunteered in the church coffee shop as a supervisor, helped the church go about looking for a youth worker, set up regular prayer meetings, helped with singles nights, volunteered in a local high school to support the chaplaincy work, took their youth Bible study group to a Christian camp for young people. Whatever she could do to serve she did, she wanted to make a difference, especially in young people's lives because she was so thankful to God for changing her life.

"I really wish someone like me had spoken into my life when I was a teen or even younger. To tell me their experiences or to even show me that being a Christian wasn't as cheesy and embarrassing as it had been made out to be. Who knows how different my life could have been?" Saff explained to

Lisa and Josh while they were debriefing about the trip to a youth camping holiday camp in Stafford. "Taking our group away and being able to take Levi into that environment was just amazing. Honestly. I didn't even know this kind of stuff existed! I think I've enjoyed it just as much as the kids did. We are going again next year, aren't we?" she laughed.

"Even better. Do you fancy coming to another festival? Same setup but different venue and more for adults" said Lisa.

"Erm, yes. Sign me up! If I can get the kids sorted, then I am definitely up for that!" said Saff excitedly.

Josh and Lisa were becoming real friends, and Saff had noticed that the invitations and contact from Amy and her other friends had dwindled. She hadn't expected anything else, why should they keep inviting her if she kept saying no? She missed Amy, but she knew she thought Saff was a bit crazy and that she had turned into the "God squad." To be honest she had, and she didn't regret any of it. The only real regret was not doing it sooner. Being able to finally look at herself in a mirror and say she liked herself was a big thing.

Kara was moving again; her lease was up on the room she was renting, and she had found a new place in a shared house. She looked around her room after all the packing, she had never been precious about belongings and found it easy to part with things. *Easy come, easy go* she thought. She began to take her bags and boxes to the front door ready for when Saff arrived to take her to the new place. Saff was on time, as she always was, a trait she picked up from Kara. Once the car was loaded up, they set off to the new place which was only a 7-minute drive from where they were.

"Can you let me know the dates you are wanting me to come and watch the kids please?"

Saff kept her eyes on the road, "Oh yeah I will give them to you when we get to your new place. These roads are awful to drive on mum, so steep and winding! I hope the new place is much more accessible".

Kara tutted, "They aren't that bad Sapphire."

Saff laughed, "I was joking Mum, and you would say that because you don't have to drive on them."

They unpacked the car at the new place, and Saff helped her mum take her bags and boxes to her new room before she put the kettle on. Saff was talking about the changes she felt she was experiencing.

"I've noticed the change, Sapphire; it's been lovely to see. I knew that time at church when you were younger would plant some seeds."

"Well yeah mum, it must have done. I appreciate you planting those seeds" she joked with her mum.

Her mum had left the church many years ago, and although she had been supportive and encouraging of Saff finding God herself, she didn't seem to want to open that door again for herself.

"So much has changed. Have you noticed that I haven't been swearing? It's like those words are just gone, it's weird. I also got rid of loads of CD's. Just didn't feel right having them anymore, I mean I wasn't going to listen to them again. A lot of them remind me of my old life and as the Bible says my old life has passed away and the new has come!"

"I have noticed, and it's really good. If you are happy then so am I. Change is good as long as it's positive."

"You know that stage a caterpillar goes through when they change to a butterfly? Metamorphosis. It can look like nothing is going on, but actually, big changes are happening inside the cocoon. I looked it up and this stage can last a few weeks, a month, or even longer. The caterpillar actually turns into a big pile of messy goo before coming out as a beautiful butterfly. This is how I feel about my changes. It feels messy at times, a lot of the time. Some things feel like they've fallen away easily, like the desire to drink alcohol or take drugs, or the swearing, but others have been more challenging" Saff paused. "The musical change has definitely been hard, music has been a big part of our lives but now I've found sooooo many good

Christian artists that play genres of music that I really enjoy, I can't complain about that anymore".

Kara nodded in agreement, "It can feel like that in life, that messy metamorphosis process. I know I've been through a few of them in my life."

Saff looked around the kitchen of her mum's new place, "Who was it that you said lives here Mum?"

"There are two women, one of whom owns the house and then me and the other woman are the lodgers. I know them both already so it should be easy to settle in. They are both out until the evening today." She picked up the cafetiere, "Do you want a refill?"

Saff shook her head, "No I'm ok thanks. I need to get off soon anyway. Erm mum, you've been single for quite a long time now haven't you?"

Kara laughed, "Yes, I guess I have. It's not something I think about much at the moment. Why?"

Shrugging, Saff said "It's just been a new season for me, a season of being single which I haven't had for a very very long time, but I feel it's another one of my changes. I am really enjoying being single." A picture of Dante's flirtatious smile flashed into her mind; she shook her head. "But it's hard too, Dante keeps popping up, texting, ringing but I feel deep down that I just need a good run of being on my own. To figure out who I am, who God says I am. Plus there is a freedom that comes with being single, I actually have time to volunteer at church and all that."

"You're at a different stage of life to me," Kara said as she picked up her freshly topped-up cup of coffee to take a sip. "We've both had crap relationships and it's good to have that time to be on your own, it's important and especially as you are going through these changes. I know when I was at church, it was hard navigating that with my before life, my non-church friends, there was always this tug of war between the two lives. And eventually, one way pulls harder."

Saff sat forward to lean her elbows on the table, "Yes that is what it's like" she affirmed. "I don't want to go back to my before life, but it is getting harder to accept invitations." Saff grimaced, "I've seen Gabe a few times at things like birthdays or weddings, and that's been hard. I don't feel comfortable being around him, it actually scares me."

Kara's brows furrowed, "He hasn't said or done anything to you again has he? They are definitely places you don't need to be. Please be careful."

"Don't worry mum, I really am and to be honest it's not just seeing him, it's all the stuff. The drinking, the drugs, the music, Gabe, oh, and the questions *"Why don't I want a drink?"* People just taking the mick asking, *"You really believe all them stories in the Bible?"* *"Well, what do you think about gay*

people?" *"Na God ain't real because why does he let all them*

kids starve in Africa?" *"Where was Party Saff/Drunk Saff? She*

used to be fun" the list goes on. I'm sure you must have had

similar all those years back, and it's not that I don't want to talk

about it, because I actually do but I don't have all the answers

right now. I even feel anxious before going to family events

where I know I will be the only Christian. I feel like I become

a target." Saff grimaced but was grateful that she had been able

to let her mum know how she had been feeling.

The plans for the trip away with Josh and Lisa were moving

forward.

"Thea, I am so excited that you are coming with us. I'm

happy to drive and my mum is coming to stay with the kids.

We need to set off early as it's a long drive to Bristol, so will

you be ready if I pick you up on the way?" Saff asked as she

was mentally preparing and organising herself for the trip.

They were sharing a tent, and she was looking forward to

spending this time with Thea, Josh, Lisa, and the others that

were camping with her. Five thousand people were descending

on The Bath and West Showground in Bristol, for six days of

worship, teaching, and fellowship. Six full days, without the

children, to spend time getting to know God more, learning

more about the Bible, and meeting new friends, Saff was overwhelmed with joy.

Once they had arrived and set up their camp, it was time for the first evening meeting of the event. They had a huge, big top tent, the kind you see at a circus with a massive stage at the front. The floor was covered with carpeted boards and the tent was filled with people. The band at the front started playing music, worship songs but this was not like it was at Saff's church. This was loud and modern. The atmosphere was just electric, it was like she could feel God, she could feel his spirit moving in this tent. No drug could top this.

Over the six days, Saff attended seminars to hear talks by different speakers, there was always a morning and an evening meeting in the big tent. Just gathering each day with everyone was beautiful. There was also a lot of time to socialise. They had several other people in their camping group, friends of Josh and Lisa's and they had a shared space under a large gazebo.

"You're a professional camper aren't you, Josh?" Saff teased as Josh hooked up some lights to an electric point we were camping nearby, "This is definitely not what I expected when you said camping, but this is more my style. I can't believe we've even got carpet!."

"Come on now, we always do things this way! Can't be slumming it now can we Saff?" he laughed.

Saff had not felt this relaxed for as long as she could remember. She thought maybe this was a taste of heaven.

She sat in her camping chair as the sun shone one afternoon reading the programme for the line-up of seminars and talks today; a seminar called Soul Sista: The Keys to True Peace caught her attention. The description said the speaker would be looking at who God says we really are.

"Thea, do you fancy this one this afternoon?" she asked as she circled that one in her programme. Fortunately, she did, so they went along that afternoon.

The speaker was an American lady with short blond hair and tanned skin. She shared some of her background with them, which turned out to be one Saff didn't expect. She had been involved in drugs but was now married, with children and a Christian ministry. Her talk was encouraging and inspiring but one thing she said stuck out to Saff, she was talking about finding a partner and what she was looking for.

"Run as fast as you can towards God, and when you turn to the side, see who has been able to keep up. That's your guy."

Saff suddenly realised that was what she wanted, a man who wanted God as much as she did, a man who was serving like she was, a man who had the same fire and passion or even more. She wanted him to be able to lead and protect her as the Bible spoke about, didn't she? Did that even exist? Saff was not sure.

After dinner later that night, people were sat around chatting on camping chairs or on blankets on the floor. Being August, it was still warm. Saff was sat with a few of the girls.

"A lot of people meet their future partners at events like this. It's where I met Josh" grinned Lisa.

Saff could see how that made sense. She hadn't met many single men, there were a few in her church but none that she had been attracted to or interested in.

"Statistics say there are fewer single men in church than single women" grimaced Thea, "these events are great to meet people that you wouldn't necessarily meet in your church."

Saff was unsure how men would react to her already having two children, it wasn't something she was ever going to hide she had had both of their names tattooed on her wrists years ago. Would she meet someone here at this event? Was she even looking right now? She was thinking about what that speaker had said and that was going to be the main thing she looked for, a man running as fast as she was after God.

"Anyone want a cold beer or cider?" one of the lads asked the group. A few said yes and were handed a bottle. "Saff?" asked one of the girls, holding out a bottle of cider.

Saff hadn't had any desire to drink since this change had happened in her life, and she knew she didn't want to drink in her old life environments as that kind of drinking ended up with being drunk. But this was the first time with her Christian friends she had been offered one. She looked around the group, almost everyone had a bottle of something in their hand, *Will they think I'm weird if I said no? Do I want to drink it? What was the right thing to do?* All these questions quickly flew through her mind, but she didn't want to make a fuss, "Well if everyone else is, then yeah why not?" Saff tentatively said and she took the cold bottle of cider.

The group hung out for another couple of hours, and Saff had a laugh and made some new friends. They had already spoken about coming again next year and she was down for that, as long as her mum was ok with looking after the kids again! She glanced down at her bottle of cider, she had only taken a few swigs of it and felt bad wasting it, but she didn't feel right drinking it. She had thought that Christians didn't drink, and she felt confused about it. Her mind was in turmoil about how to handle this situation as alcohol had played such a part in her life and been at the forefront of a lot of the bad things that she had been through.

Saff felt so refreshed and excited upon her return from her trip. This time of really focussing on God in so many different ways had been amazing, and to think she had never even known things like this existed. If people had thought she was on fire and enthusiastic about her faith before this trip, they wouldn't know what had hit them now! Saff was eager to go. But returning to church felt slightly weird on the Sunday after their trip away. She sat down on a pew in her usual place in the church, the band started the music and Saff honestly felt a little deflated. She had just come from worshipping with five thousand people with a huge live band in a big top tent to church with their small band and around one hundred people, it felt very different and would take a bit of time to adjust back to the norm.

There was a guest speaker that morning, Chris Rowling, Young Adults Missioner for Manchester and surrounding areas, including Leigh. He shared his heart for reaching young adults, for training them up in evangelism and mission. It had been very interesting, and Saff suddenly felt her spirits rise again, and was interested in finding out more. She made her way over to Chris after the service and shared some of the things she had been up to with the church.

"Listen, I'm about to launch a discipleship course over in Bolton. I think it would be great for you if you were able to get there & the vicar here was ok about it. It's every week on a Monday for a year. What do you think?" he asked her.

"That sounds amazing and something I would love to do.

Can you send me the details so I can show the vicar and work it out please?" Maybe things weren't going to be so bad after coming back from her trip.

The following weekend, Saff drove over to Yorkshire to see her mum and go for a coffee.

"So, how's things going Sapphire?" her mum asked as they sat down at a table near the window in the coffee shop. Her mum had introduced Sapphire as her daughter as she said hello to a few people on their way to their table.

"Good, really good. Thanks so much for coming and looking after the kids while I went away" said Saff and she let her know about her conversation with Chris Rowling.

"Things sound like they are going really well for you Sapphire. It's about time, eh?"

"I know mum, it's just so nice to be in this place now. I really feel like I'm becoming who I was meant to be. I can't wait for this course to start, the vicar said he was okay with giving me the rubber stamp to attend. It's like a Bible course and you know how much I love learning" Saff laughed.

One of the ladies on the next table suddenly turned round, "Sorry to eavesdrop sweeties, but I do recall your mother telling me you had started going to church."

Kara had already introduced Sapphire to her, Sadie,

and Saff was pretty sure that she wasn't sorry she was eavesdropping.

"Erm, yes I do," said Saff, looking at her mum for some help with the potential conversation that was about to start. Her mum just smiled and took a drink from her coffee cup.

"Oh you look like such a beautiful young woman, why do you need to let the church interfere with your life?" Sadie said, quite loudly. She wasn't really making eye contact and Saff couldn't be sure she was really wanting to have a conversation or just talk to put on a show for everyone in the coffee shop.

"I am not sure what you mean. Interfere with my life? My life has actually changed for the better since being at church" Saff hoped that speaking quieter would encourage Sadie to do the same. It didn't work.

"Oh Darrrrling, the church is there to ruin your fun. I bet they have told you not to have sex before marriage?" she did make eye contact at this point like she was searching Saffs face for the answer.

"They haven't *told* me not to have sex before marriage, but I am aware of what the Bible says about it," Saff said wishing this conversation would end, she didn't mind discussing her faith with people, but she was trying to catch up with her mum and Sadie was gathering quite an audience.

"You can choose what to do with your body. Sex is freeing.

Have it. Do it. Have loads of it, whenever you want and with whomever you want! And don't let anyone tell you otherwise."

"Look Sadie, I'm just trying to catch up with my mum and I didn't really want to have a conversation about my sex life with a stranger but ok. Since becoming a Christian I have felt a freedom I have never experienced before. All my life has been shaped by bad decisions I have made, and many have involved sex. This has been a part of a lot of pain for me. I absolutely and completely can see why God, who loves me, would want to protect me from that and wait until I was married. Because if I did then I would have saved myself, and my children from a lot of pain." Saff's heart was beating fast as she turned back to face her mum.

Saff heard a few faint claps, and she was sure she heard a "whoop whoop."

"Sorry Mum, I don't want to be rude to your friends but I'm sick of people judging me for finally making a good decision in my life. I don't understand why I have to feel like I have to justify myself to people."

Kara smiled, "Love, I don't have a problem with you sticking up for yourself and what you believe. It makes me proud to see. Now let's get back to catching up."

-

Lucy approached Saff during one of the Wednesday toddler

sessions at church to invite her for a walk and some lunch afterward with a few other mums. Once all the toddlers were strapped into their prams and wrapped up from the autumnal chill in the air, the group set off on the short walk to the local park. Lucy had asked Saff all about the trips away and Saff was enjoying filling her in.

"So what's next for you then?" she asked Saff after they had stopped at the sandwich shop on the way to pick up a few things for lunch. Saff filled her in about the new discipleship course she had started at the beginning of September. It was held at Bolton Parish Church, and despite Saff being the only female student, it hasn't turned out as bad as she had originally thought it would. Chris Rowling delivered some of the teachings, with the rest coming from guest speakers and video teaching provided by the organisation, New Wine.

Saff gushed, "It's a whole day each week just to study the Bible and learn, and I love it. I look forward to my Mondays and it's been good getting to know the other students. Chris and his wife Sarah have become real friends. I've been over to their house for dinner and met their kids. It feels like a proper safe space to grow."

The group made their way over to the playground area in the park and those toddlers that were still awake were unstrapped to run around in the fenced in area. Janet, one of the mums turned to Saff, "Did I hear you say you are doing a Bible study course?" Saff nodded as she took a bite of her cheese and onion pastie. "I went to Bible college and absolutely loved it. It's actually where me and Mark met."

The conversation turned to where the women had met their partners, Saff was fascinated and was taking it all in, asking Lucy where she had met her husband.

"We met at university, down in Cambridge, and got married pretty soon after we had graduated. Then a job opportunity for Simon moved us to sunny Leigh and we've been here ever since." Smiled Lucy as she kept one eye on the children playing.

"I don't think I've seen him at church yet Lucy, does he work on Sundays?" Saff enquired.

Lucy laughed, "No, Sunday is not a workday, but he's not really interested in faith and church I'm afraid."

"Oh I'm sorry, I didn't know." Said Saff, regretting asking the question and reminding herself to not be so nosy.

"It's fine Saff, honestly. I've tried, I've prayed, I've fasted." Lucy sighed.

Janet picked her son Lucas up, "We've tried too. Mark has taken him out a few times and invited him to men's events."

"He's sympathetic to our faith and is happy for me to take Eve to church and be as involved as I like but he's made it clear that he's just not interested. It hasn't been easy and to be honest, although I grew up in church, during my college and university years it wasn't my main focus and I lost myself for a while. It wasn't until a few years into the marriage that I had an interest again as I had suddenly remembered my first love, Jesus." Lucy's face seemed to glow when she spoke of Jesus.

"God's not done with him yet though Lucy, we keep praying and we keep believing alongside you," Janet said determinedly.

"Sienna, no that's not nice" shouted Saff, as she walked quickly to where Sienna stood, apologising to the ladies for needing to step away. Sienne had just pushed a little boy out of the way so she could get to the steps to the slide and was about to make her way up them!

Saff felt she had established some strong friendships with people in her church and was feeling safe and secure in her world. And Thea remained a strong presence in her life, continuing to invite and include her in things.

"It's a group of girls I went to uni with, we are meeting on Friday if you want to come?" Thea mentioned to her one day.

"Yeah, sounds good. Where and what time?" Saff rarely said no to an invitation from Thea unless she genuinely couldn't make it due to other plans or childcare.

"7pm at Slug and Lettuce in Didsbury." Hearing Thea's

response, Saff suddenly felt sick. Her mouth felt dry, and she felt her tummy doing somersaults.

"Are you ok, Saff?" Thea asked, looking concerned, "You look a little pale."

"I, um, just didn't realise it was back in Manchester, in Didsbury. I'm just not ready to go back there, to the pubs where I used to go. Especially on a Friday night" Saff felt panicky. It was an unexpected feeling, realising that she wasn't ready to put herself back in places that reminded her of her old life.

Saff was trying to focus all of her time and energy on the new things in her life, her new friends, the new places she was enjoying, the discipleship course, and the youth group, all of it brought so much joy to Saff's life. When the discipleship year ended, she felt a loss for the group, for the structure, for the learning, and for the fellowship. She was grateful that Chris and Sarah continued to be friends.

"Last year's course went so well; we are running it again this year with a new group of students," Chris told her while they were all eating dinner one evening.

"Aww, I miss it so much. You guys are such great leaders and I know the students will love it" Saff replied as she cut into the lasagne Sarah had made.

"Why don't you come and help out? She could do that

couldn't she Chris?" Sarah asked.

"We would love you to do that! You really have matured in your faith since we first met you. You would be a great addition to the team" responded Chris.

"Really? Because I don't need to be asked twice you know!" laughed Saff. She had gone from being a student on the course to now being able to help facilitate the course! This was amazing news. Things were going so well, and Saff was in a much better place than she had been for a long time.

15

Computer Love

Dating and the idea of meeting someone often popped into Saff's head. She would look around her church and her social circles and couldn't see anyone who she thought could be a match. Would she be able to meet someone who would understand and accept her background? Would she be able to meet someone she was attracted to? Or would God ask her to settle for something completely different? She had had a few Christian men approach her and she had tried to be as gracious as she could without being rude. One guy had approached her at the end of a church service and told her that he owned his own house, had his own business, and had a car before he asked her out. She knew it must have taken a lot of courage to approach her, but she wasn't attracted to him or felt they had anything in common.

An old school friend had recently contacted her on Facebook, and had told her he had always been interested in her, would she be up for a date? She had told him, as nicely

as she could, she was now on a new path and she was looking
for someone who shared her faith, even though he wasn't her
type despite this, she was trying to be nice. The conversation
that ensued left Saff feeling awful. He told her they could still
be together even if she had her beliefs and he had his own, she
could go to church and pray but he wouldn't have any part of
it. The thought of a relationship like that made Saff's head hurt,
and she thought back to Lucy and how open she had been with
them that day in the park about the struggles of being married
to someone who didn't share her faith, it was just a challenge
she didn't want to face if she had the choice.

The Facebook conversation with Anti-God Man carried on
with him asking her if she thought she was better than him,
along with some mocking that she believed in this fairytale
man in the sky. Saff tried to point out this was exactly why she
wouldn't want to be with someone who didn't believe the same
and who actually disbelieved. For Saff, it wasn't just about
sharing a faith, it was more than that, she wanted someone who
had the same passion as her, who would understand why she
went so hard after God. The Bible verse *'Do not be unequally
yoked with unbelievers' (2 Corinthians 6:14)* to Saff's
understanding, was more than just not being with someone
who didn't believe, but being with someone who identifies as a
Christian but wasn't living for Jesus. There was an unequalness

in people's faith, and it was not a healthy foundation for a marriage, it could create real problems and while she was at the stage where she had a choice to pursue someone with the same faith or not, then she could and would.

Anti-God Man's messages got progressively rude and disrespectful and realising there was no resolution with him, and he would never understand, Saff blocked him.

Thea had mentioned that someone she knew had met their husband on a Christian dating site. Saff hadn't even realised they existed, she was aware of dating sites and had been on them before, but it seemed that most guys were looking for casual hookups! She decided she would give one of the Christian sites a go, what did she have to lose?

Saff had winced when creating her profile on the site she had chosen and there had been an option to click if you wanted to meet someone with children or not. Of course, it was an individual's choice, but it did make her feel like she was less worthy than those women who were yet to have children. But we all have our criteria, she told herself.

Within a few days of Saff signing up and creating her profile, she was pleasantly surprised to see she had several messages. Feeling slightly obliged to respond to each one, she took some time to look at each profile individually before responding. She had ensured she was specific in her profile about certain things such as the fact that she had children and didn't want to connect with guys who lived too far away or even in another country. So when responding to some of the messages, it was fairly easy to respond when she could see on their profile that they either didn't want to meet someone with children, or they lived hundreds of miles away.

After she had responded carefully to all the messages she had received, she took some to look through the profiles and see if there was anyone she may want to connect with. Could you really get a feel for someone from some photographs and what they had written? It was all she had to work with for now, and at least she knew they would share a faith. She sent a couple of messages, not wanting to overdo it, and would check it again the next day.

Sitting in front of her laptop a few days later, she checked her messages again. Trainee Pilot Man had responded to her message, he seemed nice. He was training to be a pilot and had initiated contact with her, so Saff was open to chatting, which they had been doing for the past couple of days. She replied to his message as she was reading through the rest, and a reply came back shortly after as he was online. There had been a steady flow of messages going back and forth between them when Saff mentioned one of her kids. He responded shocked and asked if she had children. To which she had said yes and that she had made it pretty clear in her profile. He responded that he hadn't really read her profile and had only looked at her photos, but he wasn't interested in meeting anyone with kids as he didn't want them for a long time. He was suddenly no longer showing as being online.

Saff sat back in her seat feeling flabbergasted. Had he just ended communication and blocked her? She felt frustrated as she had really tried to be very clear right from the off and had believed that those messaging would have read her profile. She didn't want to waste her or their time. It was early days, so she resolved to not let the interaction with Trainee Pilot Man get her down and discourage her, so she kept on looking.

There were a few messages that just said "hello" or "hi there" which Saff mulled over. It wasn't the most interesting way to start a conversation, and it was definitely not how she was doing it as she was trying to put some effort into her opening message. There were also several accounts without photos, some had written in their profile that they wanted someone of substance, that wasn't just attracted to them for how they looked. Saff sighed; she understood what they were trying to say but it was very hard to start communicating with someone who you wouldn't even be able to recognise in the street. Or was she being shallow? What was the etiquette for all this online dating? There was obviously so much to learn!

The vicar was giving the church notices during a Sunday morning service, these were a standard part of the service and where you could find out all of the upcoming events and news.

"We will be putting together a baptism service in a couple of weeks, so if you are interested in getting baptised, then please come and speak to Joy after the service," he began searching the congregation "Joy, can you give us a wave?"

Joy stood up in her pew and waved to everyone. Saff felt her stomach do a few excited somersaults, she hadn't been baptised yet and knew she had to find Joy after the service to sign up! The vicar went on to read the rest of the notices. A local singles night. Did Saff hear that correctly? What were the chances of that? She would definitely be picking up a flyer about that.

After grabbing a flyer for the singles night at the end of the service, Saff went to find Joy. She explained that they would be holding an evening in the vicarage a week before the baptisms to check that we all understood what we were doing and why. Saff couldn't wait and put her details down on the sign-up sheet. She knew baptism was an important part of her journey and an outward show of the commitment she had made to God.

Saff picked up the phone later that afternoon to invite Thea to her baptism.

"Of course, I will be there!" she responded enthusiastically, "and I wanted to let you know that I've met someone. Well, it's still very early days but it's a friend of my brother and we have spent some time together at a few dinner parties at my brother's. I think we are going to go on a date."

Saff felt the physical warmth fill her body, "I'm so happy for you, you are so lovely and deserve to meet a great guy. Oh, I'm so excited for you!" and she genuinely was.

Thea laughed, "Well we will see how it goes, as I said it's early days. How is the online dating going?"

"Erm, it's interesting! But honestly, it isn't going as well as I would have hoped! You know I want to meet a guy who is on fire for Jesus and so far, I don't think I have. One guy was telling me the other day all about how he doesn't need to be part of a church but for me, that's really important."

"Oh no Saff, of course, it's important. Have there been any guys that seem like they might be ok?"

"Mmmm maybe, I've started a few conversations, but it seems that having children is not a big selling point! I really believe that the right guy will be much more understanding that at our age, well my age, you may meet someone who has lived a bit of life before, but so far the ones I have spoken to don't seem to get it."

"That's awful Saff, you are right. The right guy will be and the ones that are being funny about it, forget them. How horrible."

"I need to update my profile to make it clearer that I've got kids. I think some guys just look at your photos and don't read much, so if I can put it at the very start it might save me, and them, some time. And in the meantime one of the local churches are holding a singles night, so I guess I will give that a try too."

The singles night was being put together by Ruth who attended the Parish church. It was an effort for the churches to gather together and give the singles more opportunities to meet together. The meeting was in the room they served tea and coffee after the service. As expected the room was cold, old churches were not easy to heat despite the number of heaters Saff could see around the room. The room had extremely high ceilings and wood-clad walls where various flyers and notices were blue-tacked to the wall. Saff had arrived promptly at 7.30pm, the advertised start time and was stood by the coffee bar as Ruth was pouring boiling water from the urn into her coffee cup.

"I've been single myself for a number of years now. I went through a terrible divorce and couldn't face going through all the rigmarole of meeting someone, so just put it off" Ruth was explaining, "but since I have been looking I have realised it isn't an easy task. I mean look around this room" she nodded her head towards the room as she poured some milk into Saffs cup before handing it over to her, "where are all the men?."

She wasn't wrong. So far, only a few women had arrived.

"It's only 7.35pm" Saff said looking at the time on her phone screen. "There's still time for people to turn up."

Saff guessed that Ruth was probably in her late 50's, possibly early 60's but looked good for her age. She looked like she looked after herself and was quite glam in a lovely red dress with heels. Saff thought she was probably quite intimidating to some men with how glamourous she was and having only met her, Saff could tell she was very confident and able to lead people, as she was now calling across to the other women in the room to come and get a drink while she was making them. It sounded a little like a command.

Saff sat down near one of the heaters, hoping it would warm her up but glad she had worn a scarf and gloves, which she had kept on. Over the next 15 minutes or so, a number of other people arrived including two men. Nine women and two men. The two men who had arrived were much older than Saff, she would probably guess they were both in their 60's. Richard was tall, not bad looking for an older chap and smelled lovely. He was wearing a flat cap, scarf, and jeans. Graham was much shorter and seemed shy. He was wearing a green woollen jumper with beige trousers and kept looking at the door, nervously.

Saff knew this wasn't going to be a night she was going to meet anyone or even meet anyone her age. She was definitely the youngest in the room, but she was here so she may as well get to know some of the ladies at least.

"Thanks for coming, so sorry it wasn't well attended" Ruth was calling after people as they left. Saff helped to clear the tables and wash the cups.

"Oh Sapphire, thank you so much for staying to help," Ruth said as she closed the door behind the last person to leave.

Saff had told them her full name, and Ruth had insisted on calling her by it for the rest of the night. "How boring this night must have been for you with only two old men turning up!" she tutted.

"Ruth, it's been nice and I'm really grateful for you putting the event on. I think Richard may have had his eye on you."

"Pfft," Ruth said waving her well-manicured hand in the air as if brushing away the whole night. "Not my type."

"I thought he was quite good-looking, and he seemed well travelled, confident and the way he shared about how he came to know Jesus" Saff blew air out of her mouth, "that was powerful."

"Well, we will see if he contacts me after the event. Saff, a bit of advice, we let the men do the chasing and we never make the first move" wagging her finger at Saff. "I will organise another event in a couple of months and try to widen the invitations and get more along, hopefully, some younger men for you to consider."

Saff laughed as she zipped her coat up and readied herself for the cold walk back to her car. "I look forward to it Ruth."

This was not turning out how she expected. What was going on God?

16

Betrayed

The music could be heard loud, and the bass was thumping, and she knew who was pulling up. She couldn't believe that he was still trying to pursue her.

"Hi, Dante. What's going on?" called Saff as she came out of the front door and walked over to the gate. She hoped this would stop him from coming into the house and staying too long. She dismissed the feeling she was feeling in her stomach, she hated that he still stirred things inside of her.

"Nothing just thought I would fly over and see how my baby girl was doing, and I can see that you are looking good" flashing his gold tooth at her as he smiled and leaning on the gate in between them.

He looked good, he always did, and he smelt fresh, she gave her head a shake and replied "Erm I'm not your baby girl anymore, remember? Think it's time to knock that on the head! Have you been keeping out of trouble?" trying to change the subject.

"You know me, always keeping out of trouble" he laughed. "You seen Amy recently?"

Why did he suddenly look so sheepish when he asked her that? "Nooooo, why?" she asked hesitantly.

"Cool, cool. No reason, no reason. Anyway, how's the kiddies? Bet Levi is big now."

He had always made time for Levi, which was nice, he wasn't bothered that she had kids, he still wanted her, and to be honest it had never seemed to be a problem. So why now was it an issue for Christian men? She was perplexed but needed to keep her focus while Dante was around, so she didn't fall for any of his charms because he definitely wasn't running after God like she was.

"I bumped into Christos the other day in town," He stood up and she could see his shoulders tense when he mentioned his name. "Why him Saff?!"

"Look Dante, what I did while you were in prison is nothing to do with you. I'm sorry but after the way you ghosted me on that visit, I wasn't really thinking about you anymore."

"He's with that girl Amy or something."

"Amelia" Saff corrected him.

"Does she know that you and him got rid of a baby?"

Saff was taken aback, "What?! Dante, who told you that?"

"Might get him in a bit of trouble with his missus eh?"

folding his arms across his chest and straightening his back.

"Dante, that is not something to just throw about!" Her heart suddenly dropped as it dawned on her that she knew who had told him because few people knew.

"Let me guess, Amy, eh?" She could feel her heart beating fast. He didn't respond to that comment.

"I thought we were gonna have babies one day Saff" he almost sounded sad as he said that.

"Is there a point to this Dante? I've got things to do, and I don't really wanna be talking about this. I can't even believe she told you that stuff, it's private. And YOU need to remember that we are over" She walked back into the house and closed the door behind her.

Saff was fuming, she picked up the phone to ring Amy as she heard Dante roaring off in his car. The line just rang and rang. Surprise, surprise. That was low. Telling him about her personal business, business that she was still trying to deal with. The betrayal cut deep. Saff felt a real sense of loss and grief for the friendship they had, because she knew the friendship was over. Right now she felt like driving to her house and having it out with her. She could never trust her again. She could never trust anyone again.

Amy shoved her phone in her bag to ignore the calls from

Saff, couldn't she get the message that she didn't want to speak to her right now? She was busy anyway; her name had just been called for her waxing appointment. She had a night out ahead of her and having just booked a hotel for the night she wanted to make it worth his time, it was last time.

Saff was looking at her diary in her Filofax, she loved seeing everything laid out in black and white rather than using an online calendar. Pen and paper were much more her style. She was trying to distract herself from how she was feeling and the horrible thoughts running through her mind. Mondays were spent at the discipleship course in Bolton which Saff still loved. On Wednesday and Friday, she managed a shift in the church coffee shop. Friday nights was the youth Bible study group where they had a core group of around five teenagers coming. Saturdays she worked at the local sports centre, this was purely to bring in some money and it was a fairly easy job. Sundays were for church. Sienna was in nursery in the week, so this enabled her to fit these things in around her pickups, and still gave her free time to do what she needed to in the house. She even managed to get to the gym. She was finally feeling a real sense of purpose and fulfilment.

Now seemed the perfect time for her to meet someone. To meet that man running after God and get married. She was confused why it kept popping into her thoughts so much when nothing was happening in that area, apart from Dante and that was a no-go. The online dating was turning into a disaster, if she had one more conversation with a guy who hadn't realised she had children she might scream! What was wrong with her? Could men not see past this issue or think she was worth it? She had been single for almost five years now, the longest since she had begun to be interested in boys around fifteen years old. There was nothing wrong with being single and she had enjoyed this period much more than she could have ever imagined, but if singleness was what God wanted for her, then she prayed that he would make that clear.

"God, if the plan isn't for me to get married, please take this desire away. It's beginning to hurt and feel very frustrating. Am I not good enough? I thought you had made me a new creation so why did men not see that when they looked at her?" she was beginning to cry as she prayed. All of a sudden, she got the flash of someone's face in her mind. It stopped her in her tracks. It was of a guy she had met once at an event at The Message Trust in Manchester, he worked for them. But it was strange because she didn't even know his name. Why would she have suddenly thought of him? She picked up her phone to send a text.

Thea, remember that event we went at The Message the

other month, and that guy that was with Danny? What was

his name?? xx

Thea's reply came shortly after.

The rapper guy? I think it was Romario xx

Yes, that was it, Romario. Saff opened up Facebook on her phone and put her investigating skills to work, she had used them many times in the past with Dante and she was sure she could give MI5 a run for their money. Well not quite, but she was good at finding out what she needed to know. Romario Gordan, 86 mutual friends on Facebook!

How had she never met him before she became a Christian, and why on earth had God given her his face? What did it mean? Her mind was reeling but she tried to focus. She had been praying about being single, asking God for guidance, for help. Telling God that she wanted to get married and then pop, there he was. It was so strange!

Would he think it was strange if she added him on Facebook? What did she have to lose? She clicked Add Friend. Eek!

Friends, that made her think of Amy. Could she even call her a friend anymore? She still hadn't been able to get a response from her and she had tried several times. Maybe Zoe had spoken to her, she sent her a text.

Hey Zoe, hope you're good. Have you heard from Amy? XX

You free to talk a minute? was Zoe's reply.

Saff's phone began to ring.

"Hey Saff, so Amy not been in touch with you recently mmhh?"

"Yeah, she's not replied to my last few messages and calls."

"Well Saff, the last time I saw her was out in town the other week. We were in Tiger Tiger. Dante and his boys were there. Amy seemed pretty cosy with Dante you know babes."

"Really?!" A shiver ran down Saff's spine and she felt her skin prickle.

"Yeah, I'm sorry but there's been a few rumours that she's been chilling with him a bit since then."

"You know, Dante was a bit shady when I asked him the other week if he had seen her. Makes sense"

Saff let out a sigh, she wasn't with Dante and had no intentions of being with him but wasn't there this unspoken rule that we don't go out with each other's exes? It felt disloyal and if Amy had felt ok about it then why hadn't she told her? Saff felt betrayed.

"Na, it's not right Saff. We don't do that to each other whether you are with him or not. And to be honest, she knows how he cheated on you loads of times. So, I don't know what she expects" Zoe kissed her teeth.

"I'm not with him, but I didn't expect her to cross that

line. But saying that, I know she has told Dante some pretty personal stuff about me, and I didn't expect her to do that either! Thanks for letting me know anyway Zoe. How's your mum doing?"

They continued chatting for a while longer, Zoe updating Saff with her mum's health and that she was doing much better since she had finally agreed to move in with her. She was happy and enjoying looking after her, her two businesses were going well, and she felt in a good place. Saff was pleased and they agreed to meet up soon.

Saff felt a little deflated after the news of Amy and Dante, things had been going so well on this new path, but her old life was biting at her heels. She had already taken herself physically out of the life she had by moving away, but now she was learning to emotionally and mentally take herself out. As a Christian she was beginning to learn more about forgiveness, they had been discussing it on Monday at the discipleship course and how hard it was. The Bible said *"Let all bitterness and wrath and anger and clamour and slander be put away from you, along with all malice. Be kind to one another, tender-hearted, forgiving one another, as God in Christ forgave you."* *(Ephesians 4:31)*

If Christ had forgiven her for all the things she had done and said, then she needed to try her hardest to forgive others. But that was easier said than done, she felt hurt and angry by what she had found out, again! Could she forgive Amy for what she had done? Right now she felt the anger and pain in her body she still wanted to have it out with her, verbally and physically! Forgiveness was important, but did that mean letting people walk all over you? Let people take you for an idiot? Her fleshly nature was anger, she wanted to ring Amy and tell her how she felt, she wanted to cry, she wanted to lash out and tell Amy what she thought of her betrayal. But with Amy not answering her calls or messages, and Saff realising that she had even blocked her on all the socials she was unable to have that conversation.

She scrunched her eyes shut, feeling the tears stinging and prayed.

Please help me, God. I feel angry, hurt, betrayed, and I don't know how to handle these situations now. I want to fight, to scream! This hurts too much.

She felt the tears flow from her eyes, and she sensed a feeling of letting go. She knew she was going to have to let go of so much on this journey, but she hadn't realised how much it would hurt. It felt similar to the grief process, feeling angry but also grieving the loss of a friendship, the loss of a person in your life.

It was much easier to walk away completely, and it seemed

like God was cutting these ties severely so she wouldn't go back. Her phone pinged through a notification, she wiped her tears from her face and sighing she took a look. She didn't know if she could take anything else bad right now, but it was a notification to tell her that Romario had accepted her friend request.

That brought a smile to her face.

17

Letting Go

There had been several messages passing between Saff and Romario via Facebook. It was a nice distraction from thinking about Amy, because that scenario was annoyingly playing over and over in her mind, and she was still angry and hurt. Thinking about Romario was a nice change. He had sent her the links to listen to his music, which she had listened to and that had blown her away. He was an evangelist, which meant he shared his Christian faith, and he did this through his music. Listening to his music there was no denying the transformation that had taken place in his life, growing up filled with anger and not sure how to deal with it, resulted in him using violence, now he was working for a Christian Charity going into schools and prisons to share his faith with those dealing with similar issues. He was clearly running after God. She couldn't wait to update Thea when she saw her next, she understood where Saff was on her journey and still listened without judgement.

"The crazy thing is, that he is a guy I would have been

interested in before I became a Christian! That's exciting. You know, I thought God was going to make me settle on someone who loved God, but I wouldn't actually be attracted to them physically. But meeting and getting to know Romario has changed that. He's still not agreed to meet up for a coffee but there's something in me that wants to pursue him. Does that sound stupid Thea?"

"It sounds so flipping exciting! I'm so pleased for you, and God will never make us settle. His plans are perfect for us and as long as you keep seeking him and running after him, you will walk in those plans. I'm definitely praying for you Saff."

Saff was so grateful for her friendship and regular contact with Thea. It was life-giving. Becoming a Christian was becoming a new creation, and that meant things and people from her old life were being chipped away and new things were growing in their place. In church on Sunday, the vicar had spoken about a pruning process. *"Every branch in me that does not bear fruit he takes away, and every branch that does bear fruit he prunes, that it may bear more fruit." (John 15:2).* This process of pruning felt hard and painful for Saff, but she felt that new and exciting things were replacing those old things and that it was in her best interests that this was happening.

Romario was one of those exciting new things replacing the old. It had been three months since they had begun messaging and talking to each other, and he had FINALLY agreed to go for a coffee after being busy and away doing missional work. Saff wanted to be straight up; she had already made it clear that she had kids and was definitely not going to be tiptoeing around the fact that she had lived a colourful life. She felt God had led her to Romario, not that she was going to tell him that right now because that would probably sound very weird, but she felt a desire to pursue this. The desire felt different from how she felt about men in the past, it was more than a physical attraction, it wasn't even about sex anymore. It was something she had not experienced before.

They were meeting at Costa Coffee in the Trafford Centre during the daytime. A safe, public space with no alcohol involved. Sienna was in nursery, *thank God for free nursery places* she thought, and Levi was in school. She had nervously arrived early, finding a table, and pulling her book out of her bag. She always carried a book with her, hating feeling like time was being wasted sat waiting. She also pulled a little mirror out of her bag and checked her face and hair for what felt like the millionth time, she had tried to dress as casually and modestly as she could while also feeling that she looked pretty.

Romario arrived, a little later than the agreed time, which

had made Saff think he wasn't coming after all. But he offered to buy her a drink which was nice and made up for being late.

Saff stayed at the table while he got the drinks. She was nervous now he had arrived. He was very attractive, more than she had remembered and his green eyes drew her in. She tried to relax as he sat down with the drinks, putting her coconut milk latte down in front of her. He clearly wasn't nervous or shy, he could talk so the conversation flowed nicely.

"Christian dating is weird!" Romario said as they chatted, "You only have to speak to a girl, and she thinks you want to marry her" he joked.

"Oh really?" Saff grimaced, hoping he wasn't making that reference to her, "I've been single for over five years now and it's weird trying to figure it all out, having come from the world and a totally different way of doing things!" Saff replied.

It was nice getting to speak to him in person. They chatted a lot and there didn't seem to be any awkward silences. As their time together was coming to an end, Saff felt like she was just going to be completely honest and lay her cards on the table, well not absolutely honest and tell him everything just yet!

"Look, I like you and would like to do this again, get to know you more."

"That's cool" he replied, "I'm not promising you anything will happen though you know. I'm just tryna focus on what

God's called me too."

There it was, he was running after God. That made her like him even more!

"Soooooo, how did it go with Romario?" asked Thea later on the phone.

"Ahhh Thea, it was so nice. We get on really well and we come from pretty similar backgrounds. That makes me feel so much more comfortable. I'm meeting him for another coffee next week. And you wouldn't believe what happened. As we were walking out of the Trafford Centre back to the car park, we were walking up to where this lady was kind of bent over, she seemed to be struggling with her bags and looked like she was in pain. Romario stopped next to her and asked if she was ok. She began telling us that she was waiting for surgery for her back and was in a lot of pain. Romario told her he was a Christian and believed in prayer and if she didn't mind he would like to pray for her. And then he literally prayed for her right there and then. I mean, wow. I've never met anyone like him before."

"Oh, I'm so pleased. I will be praying for you. And what a guy! Anything happening on the job front?"

Saff sighed, "I honestly don't really know what is going on, but it feels like God doesn't want me to get a job right now. If that's even possible! I have put so much time and effort into applying for all these jobs, and nothing has come through. I'm going to have to leave it in God's hands because I don't know what to do anymore."

Over the next few months, Saff enjoyed getting to know Romario and they were spending more and more time together. It turned out that they had grown up in pretty similar environments and knew a lot of the same people, liked similar music, had been to the same clubs and events, had been a Christian for a similar amount of time, and had even been baptised around the same time. Things were going well; it couldn't be that they were going too well, could it?

They were shopping in Cheshire Oaks one day, when Saff saw Leon, one of the guys she had dated when she was younger. She felt her heart drop and knew her face must have a blush to it, before she had even decided if she was going to say hello or try to avoid contact, Romario let on to him.

"Easy Leon, you good?" said Romario.

Leon nodded and stopped to talk "Yes Romario," he said and touched his fist to Romario's. "I didn't know you two knew each other. Long time Saff."

Saff smiled awkwardly, nodded, and looked down at the floor. She hoped the conversation would be over quickly and was grateful when Leon walked off.

"I didn't realise you knew Leon," said Romario as Leon walked away. Did she tell him how she knew him? What was the right thing to do?

"Yeah I've known him for years" she replied hoping that was enough.

But then came the dreaded question – "Oh cool, how do you know him?"

Saff wanted to be honest and start things off on the right foot. She took a deep breath and told him she had dated him when she was much younger.

Romario seemed to be a little quiet for the rest of their time together and there was a tension hanging in the air.

Saff had tentatively asked Romario if he wanted to go to the cinema a few days later, he agreed so that was good, bumping into Leon hadn't put him off. But she was still a little unsure how he was feeling after that had happened. She tried to be cool and casual, keeping the conversation as light as she could and just hoping the Leon situation could be forgotten. Standing in the queue to pay for their tickets to *Spiderman: Homecoming* Saff was telling Romario a story about Sienna and her drawing on the living room door, and then tried to blame it on Levi. Romario was looking at her as she spoke, smiling in all the right places and being amused at the story when something caught his eye. His head flicked up and he waved and said hi to someone behind Saff. Saff glanced over her shoulder to see who it was and felt her stomach lurch as she saw Freya.

Freya was one of the girls that Dante had been seeing. Freya awkwardly nodded at her, and Saff turned back to Romario.

"Oh, do you know Freya too?"

"Erm yeah kind of," Saff said sheepishly.

"You've not got beef with her, have you?"

Did she tell him? It didn't go that well last time, but she wanted to be honest and be able to share her past with him.

"I don't really know her like that, but I know Dante."

"Oh, you didn't date him as well did ya?" he laughed but stopped quickly when he saw her face, "oh ok."

"Is that a problem Romario?" she quietly asked.

"Erm, na it's cool. I mean it is what it is." A cashier became available, and he walked over to pay. They enjoyed the rest of the evening, but Saff couldn't help feeling uneasy. Again.

Thea sat down after emptying the snack bag she had brought over on to the sofa. They were all placed nicely between Thea and Saff as they decided on a film to watch on Netflix.

"Why does my past seem to be constantly popping up trying to mess things up, Thea?" Saff moaned as she took another bite of her chocolate bar. "Look at me sat here stuffing my face, comfort eating. What am I going to do?!"

"Aww Saff, I'm sure if he really likes you, then none of that stuff will get in the way. He's praying about you, isn't he?" opening a big packet of Sweet Chilli Sensations crisps.

Saff nodded, "Yes, we are both praying and have actually prayed together. It's not just seeing Leon and Freya; we've had conversations about a few other guys too. Soooooo awkward. I don't want to lie, but I just don't know how to navigate this. All the online dating was horrible, and I found the guys pretty judgemental for being Jesus followers! Romario is different, but you know I do have a past, AND I have two kids. It's not easy to take all that on," taking a handful of the crisps as Thea handed the bag towards her.

"Saff don't think like that, you are amazing, and any man would be blessed to have you and your wonderful children. I think you are being too hard on yourself."

"Thanks, Thea, I hope you're right. I want to believe it but so far, it's not been my experience. Let's decide on this film before we end up talking all night" Saff hoped this time was different. That Romario could see her how God did.

As things progressed with Romario, Saff realised there were still some things that she needed to deal with. She still hadn't been able to forgive herself for the two terminations. It was still difficult to talk about, and despite her having shared her story many times, *that* was still a topic she didn't feel she had been released to share. A group of women Saff had met through Thea were hosting a conference for mums in Salford called Captivated. Thea encouraged Saff to go.

"It is important to find time as a mum, you're always so busy with everything you do. Go along and enjoy it" she had told Saff.

And how glad she was that she went. It was a refreshing day listening to other mums share their stories, and deliver teaching, there were book stalls and refreshments including free coffee and doughnuts! And she was learning so many new things and seeing things in a different light. One lady had shared that she had recently been watching the film Aladdin with her children and the song *A Whole New World* sung by Aladdin and Princess Jasmine had suddenly become alive as a reflection of what it's like to come to know God and be a Christian. Saff had loved that link and wrote it down in the journal she had taken with her.

During the final session of the conference, the mums were encouraged to spend some time in prayer, and it was during that prayer session that Saff felt God revealed something to her. As she was praying she felt very emotional and began to see a picture form in her mind. It was a picture of a field, and in the field walking away from her she saw a figure that she understood to be God. God was holding the hands of a small child on each side. Saff understood that those two children were her babies. She was overwhelmed with how much peace and forgiveness she felt there and then. She understood now that God had forgiven her and was telling her that her babies were with Him. It was a very freeing moment. It had been five years since she had said that prayer asking God to come into her life and change her heart, and so much had happened over that time but this, this was a big moment in her journey.

The traffic was awful as Saff drove over to Katy's in Whalley Range. The drive wasn't helped by the weather as the rain was coming down hard. Saff finally arrived, kicking herself that she didn't have an umbrella in the car. Zoe was meeting her there and Saff felt angry that Amy was still being evasive, even at a time like this when Katy needed them.

As she pulled her coat on and put the hood up, she thought back to when she had last seen Katy, it had been a while as she had been so busy, but Katy had just been through a horrible situation. Her boyfriend Jack had taken his own life. Saff hadn't been able to believe what Katy was telling her when she had rung her two days ago, and she agreed to come over as soon as they could. What do you say to someone whose partner has just taken their own life? There were no words that could make Katy feel better right now. Katy had said he had been drinking heavily lately and taking drugs but had moved on to taking some harder stuff – heroin. He had been in prison a few times for petty crimes, and Katy thought he was sick of the cycle but didn't see a way out. He had taken an overdose and Katy had found him. Saff had been praying as she had driven over because too many young men that she had known had taken their own life and it broke her heart.

As Saff was getting back in her car from that very emotional time with Zoe and Katy she checked her phone. Romario had sent a text asking if they could talk. Well, that was all she needed now as it was probably to tell her it was over. She started creating these scenarios in her head of the different ways he was going to tell her that she was too much to take on, he wasn't ready, etc.

These last few days she had felt such a lightness since the conference, then the heaviness of finding out about Jack and trying to offer comfort to Katy she just decided she would be ok with whatever he had to say. It wasn't what she wanted but with God she had everything she needed and if Romario couldn't see past her old life then she couldn't force him to. Life was too short she thought as she thought about Jack.

The light streamed in through the curtain windows and Amy squinted her eyes to block it out. Her mouth was dry, and she felt sick. What time was it? She picked up her phone to check, 1pm. She cursed, she had missed her shift at the tattoo shop, this was the third time it had happened, and she was sure she would have lost the job by now. *Oh well, easy come, easy go* she thought as she swung her legs down to the floor. She tried to stand up but felt lightheaded and fell back down on to the bed. She would give herself a minute, so she picked up her phone and looked at all the missed calls and text messages that had come through.

Yep, there was the text to confirm that she was fired, she clicked DELETE. Why did Saff keep trying to call her? She might have to think about blocking her number. Text messages from Zoe, who was again acting like an annoying big sister trying to tell her what to do including going to Katy's today. She would see Katy when she was ready not when everyone else was telling her to.

Amy tried to stand up again, taking her time this time, and walked over to her en suite bathroom, one good thing about living with her parents. She turned the shower on and ran it while she went back and checked her handbag, she could do with a few lines to take the edge off.

Cursing under her breath again when she found the little plastic bag empty, knowing she had taken it all last night. She rubbed her hand over her face, who could she call? Dante was probably the best shout, and she had driven him about last week while he was working and he seemed to like that, giving her an endless supply throughout the time she was with him. She would jump in the shower and make herself look decent so she could make the offer to him again.

Sitting down on the sofa in Romario's flat, Saff steeled herself for what he was about to say. She didn't even take her coat off as she thought it would be short and sweet and she could leave as soon as possible, grateful that the rain had stopped, and a beautiful rainbow had appeared in the sky. Maybe that was God telling her that she would be ok?

"I'm not gonna lie Saff, it's been different for me. Dating you I mean" he said quietly and slowly.

"It's ok to say it Romario, I know it's been hard, so if you want to walk away now, I understand." Saff noticed he was wringing his hands and not making eye contact with her.

"Saff let me finish what I'm trying to say. I want to put our pasts behind us and make this work. I've been praying and I believe that's what we should be doing. No one said it was going to be easy but I'm willing to put the work in if you are.

Before I met you, I was in a place where I was just focused on ministry and what God was calling me to. I wasn't interested in looking for a relationship, but I did tell God that if that was what he wanted for me, then whoever it was would need to do something different, something that made me take notice. You have done that; you've pursued me in a way that no one has before, and not in a weird way. It was unexpected, but it made me take notice."

Saff stared at him in disbelief. Well, it wasn't what she was expecting but she was pleased and relieved, to say the least. She felt her heart do a little leap and suddenly had to remind herself to breathe again. It finally made sense to her, why she had felt that urge to pursue him, it must have been God using her to show him something different.

"Well, I should tell you that I felt that God led me to you, and that's what gave me the energy to do that. It felt weird and I couldn't fully understand why I felt this need to pursue you, and I didn't want to tell you what I felt God had said to me because it might have sounded weird, or I could have got it wrong but that makes complete sense now. It's a relief because I really thought you were going to say it wasn't working out. I had prepared myself for that. I do feel God has brought us together and I appreciate the prayer and thought you've put into this. Are you putting the kettle on then?" she said as she took her coat off and felt more relaxed hoping she could share with Romario about the sad news of Jack's death.

Over the next six months, Saff continued to look for work, but no doors were opening. She had decided to offer a cleaning service to tide her over, but it wasn't what she wanted to be doing long term. She had to laugh at herself because a cleaning job was something she had told herself she never wanted to do.

A friend sent her a job offer for an Office and Events Manager for a Christian charity. Saff had met the guy who set the charity up when he came to her church to speak. She had been sitting listening to his story, about his life in Hulme as a drug addict, in the madness. As she was listening, the story felt so similar to how she had been brought up at that time that she began thinking that she had been there during that same time as a child.

At the end of the service, she went to speak to him and tell him what she thought. It turned out she was right, and he knew her mum and her mum's boyfriend at that time, Johnny! What a small world.

Now there was a job working for him, what did she have to lose?

"I got the job Romario! For months I have been looking for something and this just feels so right. I can work the hours around the kids and school, it just seems perfect."

"Well done Saff. The charity will be blessed to have you working for them."

18

I do!

Saff felt like she hadn't had a catch-up with her sister Jasmine for ages, so it was lovely to have her over for dinner. Jasmine had been telling her all about university and Saff felt proud of her.

"I'm proud of you too girl," Jasmine said as they ate dinner, "You've moved to a new church, got yourself an amazing new job that sounds like it was made for you and mum told me that you've paid off all of your debts!" she turned to Levi to give him a celebratory high five, but he just looked at her blankly. She turned to Sienna, "Don't leave me hanging like your bro did!"

Sienna giggled and put her little hand out to high-five, while Levi tutted and carried on eating his food.

"Aww, thanks. It has been a lot of changes, but good changes for us both eh? And one thing mum won't have told you, because I haven't told her yet, is that now I am working this job I have applied to buy this house under the Right to Buy scheme. Now I'm debt-free and working in a secure job I have been able to get a mortgage."

Jasmine put her hand up to high-five Saff this time, Saff laughed and responded with her hand.

"That really is amazing! You've been in debt for what, 18 years? How did you clear them all? You didn't win the lottery on the sly did you?"

"Jas, I think you would know about it if I had won the lottery, Levi wouldn't be sat there with a screwed-up face for one thing."

Levi snorted and mumbled something under his breath, he was going through his teenage years.

"So no it wasn't the lottery, it was actually a charity called CAP or Christians Against Poverty. They've been helping me pay my debts off and I finally got the news that they are all paid!"

"Really? And did you have to pay them to help you do that?"

"Nope. They do it for free you know, and my church is a CAP debt centre, so I've got the links" Saff laughed.

"That is so good! And of course, how are things with Romario? Do you think he will propose?" She asked, raising her eyebrows, and winking at Levi. He pretended to gag and stood up "Mum, I've finished and I'm going before you all start making me feel sick."

Saff shook her head as he left the room.

"I'm not sure; I hope so and believe me I have spoken about marriage A LOT! He knows that's what I want, I don't want to date if that isn't the plan. Things have changed for me in that area, but I keep getting those thoughts that I'm not good enough, you know, that he will decide I'm not wifey material. You know stuff that I've been through in my past, and we've dealt with a LOT of our past issues. I keep having this recurring dream, well it plays out in different ways, but the main theme of the dream is that he is going to leave me or cheat on me. All my old fears and experiences resurfacing."

"Saff I can't imagine what all that feels like, but it must be hard. You've been through some hard things and been treated very badly by some absolute idiots. I hope this time will be different for you, Romario shares the same faith as you so I believe he will treat you differently."

"Thanks, Jas. I didn't think I would meet anyone who shares my faith but still gets where I've come from you know. It was important to find someone who understood the culture of how we grew up, the music, the people, the language. I didn't want to have to keep explaining my life all the time and it's not like that with him because he gets it."

"That's really good! You deserve it and it is hard trying

to explain to people where you've come from because it can sound crazy for people who have never lived that life and to be honest it is kinda crazy but it's just our norm" Jasmine shrugged her shoulders.

"It is our norm, but I don't want that for my kids and I'm sure you don't either, that's why you are working so hard on your life now. I just want normality, and stability, I want to be a Sunday dinner kind of family which sounds so simple to some people, but it's not been our experience. I know that Romario values family too, he's really close to his but I know he won't rush anything. Like with marriage, he has to be sure, which is good. I do feel like he is finally seeing me as the new creation I am and I'm praying that it will be this year because I am getting older, and time is not on my side."

The dream Saff had mentioned to Jasmine was happening more and more. She was waking in a state of anxiety, worrying what it might mean. It was always a different dream but the same theme – Romario cheating or leaving her. He would leave her for a friend or cheat on her with people she knew.

All her past relationships had been toxic in some way and ultimately made her feel worse about herself. Dante was still texting her, and asking if he could see her despite her telling him that she was seeing someone. She knew she could get back with Dante if she wanted to, and sometimes she wondered about that phrase "better the devil you know." She knew what she was getting with Dante, would that be a better choice? But she felt that God had led her to Romario, there had to be a reason for that, and she wanted someone running after God, she really did.

Could she let go of her past and move forward?

There was a real chill in the air as Zoe walked quickly to her front door, enjoying the hot blast of heat that welcomed her as she walked in. She shrugged her coat off, dropped her gym bag, and swapped her trainers for her fluffy slippers. Hearing voices she made her way into the living room where she found her mum and Jane, Amy's mum.

"Oh, hi Zoe, Jane popped over for a catch-up. She brought us some of that nice bread and olives from Barbakan Deli in Chorlton."

Zoe walked over to hug Jane, "Lovely to see you, Aunty Jane. How's uncle doing?" Zoe realised that when she hugged Jane, she could feel her bones through her skin, and she noticed she was looking thin and drawn.

Jane returned the hug and settled back down in her chair, "Oh he's doing fine. I've left him pottering in his shed. Zoe, you look great" Turning to Zoe's mum, "Elizabeth, you must be so proud of your girl and how she is doing. I really wish I could say the same for Amy" Jane let out a sob and quickly lifted the crumpled tissue she was holding up to her mouth. "Oh I'm sorry, I don't want to get upset again."

Elizabeth reached her hand and placed it on Jane's knee, "You can get as upset as you need to be. Amy is really misbehaving at the moment. Zoe can't you talk some sense into her."

Zoe sat down on the floor near the fire, looking up at Jane "I can try but she doesn't listen to me as much as she used to." She wanted to ask more of what had been going on but didn't want to pry.

"Mmmm, she did used to look up to you like a big sister didn't she?" said Elizabeth, "when was the last time you spoke to her because she's going to end up making her mum and dad ill at this rate" nodding towards Zoe, "Jane, please tell her what she's been up to."

Jane stiffened her shoulders and jutted her chin out like she wanted to try to save some dignity as she updated Zoe with all of Amy's recent behaviour including the drug taking, using their house like a hotel, going missing for days, and recently having drug dealers knocking on the front door. "Even our neighbours are beginning to notice, we live in a quiet neighbourhood, and we really don't get much trouble, but these dealers have been pulling into our street at all hours in their cars playing loud music. Oh, and you should see the state of her, she's lost so much weight that even though she spends so much time on her appearance all of her clothes are hanging off her and I am sure she's lost a tooth, but she hides it from us."

Zoe felt sick, how had things gotten this bad? It sounded like she had become addicted to the drugs if she were using them that much it was visibly noticeable but what could she do? She wanted to help but Amy had become like a ghost, not answering calls, or returning messages and none of their friendship circle had seen her either. Zoe was trying to rack her brains as to what she could do or even say, "I take it she's not working anymore because without money that would make getting hold of drugs difficult."

Jane tutted, "That girl wouldn't know a hard day's work if it smacked her in the face. The number of jobs she has lost due to her sheer laziness I couldn't even count them. We have always given her an allowance, but Robert said that we must stop doing that now as we are part of the problem, so she hasn't had any money from us for weeks now."

"Well that should help," said Elizabeth.

"You would think it would," Zoe noticed Jane's shoulders dip slightly, "but things have been going missing from around the house and we know it must be Amy as no one else has access."

Zoe felt angry, she was stealing from her mum and dad now. Her parents had given her everything and out of everyone Zoe knew, Amy had the best home set up. Both her parents were still together, they lived in a beautiful house in Hale and Amy had never had to want for anything but here she was wanting a lifestyle that most of them were fighting to get out of.

"We don't know if it was the right decision to let her come home after she moved out the last time, but we don't want to see her suffer or be out on the streets" Jane's eyes filled with tears again, "I just want my little girl back."

They carried on talking for some time trying to figure out what they could do, and Zoe promised to try her hardest to help where she could. Jane and Elizabeth asked how Saff was doing, and Zoe was pleased to be able to talk about a more positive situation, letting them know how well she was doing and that going to church and finding God seemed to be the thing that had turned it all around. Zoe began thinking that maybe there was more to that than she had given credit to, and could that be the thing to help Amy?

Christmas was over, all the wrapping paper was in the bin and the presents were put away. For Saff Christmas hadn't always been a nice time, when she was growing up Christmas Day would usually end with just her and her mum left alone as her brothers and sister went off to see their dads and their families. The day usually ended feeling lonely, and this had continued with her children as Sienna would spend the rest of Christmas Day with her dad so it would be her and Levi who would be left alone. In the last few years, Saff had begun to appreciate and understand the real meaning of Christmas, the birth of Christ which had been predicted many times in the Bible and was an important part of the story because without him being born, He couldn't die for our sins and rise again, defeating death. Celebrating that was now at the centre of their festivities and having been able to celebrate with Romario and his family too meant even more to her, her heart was full. But despite all this, she still felt some frustration that Romario had not proposed yet, they had spoken at length about the desire to marry before the eyes of God, and although they had made the decision for Saff to join Romario at his church, taking a step towards that commitment, a proposal had not yet happened. Saff knew she was impatient and tried hard not to think about it, but her mind was always running wild with thoughts. The year was coming to an end, and there seemed to be no proposal in sight.

As the week between Christmas and New Year came to an end, they made their way over to their church for the New Year's Eve Celebrations. Romario would be performing during the event, and Saff couldn't hide her deflation that the year was ending like this.

"Saff, aren't you going to cheer up?" asked Romario as he drove the car over to the church, "I need to focus for this performance, and if I can guess what your frustration is about, then that kind of pressure isn't going to help me."

Saff turned to look out of the window, feeling tears prickling her eyes and silently kicking herself because she didn't want to be feeling like this. Why did she have to be so emotional and why did her emotions have to show themselves on her face so much? She had to give herself a talking to, and she prayed in her head asking God to help her, to help her take her thoughts captive and bring them in line with God's word and promises for her life. It didn't matter when it happened, and she needed to relax.

The atmosphere in church was electric, the building was full of people who at this time of the year would have normally been out clubbing and drinking and taking drugs, and here they were in a church building and the only high they had was the Most High God. It was truly incredible to be part of. The worship band played upbeat songs and encouraged people in their faith from the front, and then it was time for Romario's performance. The bass was thumping as his music poured out of the speakers and he danced around the stage rapping his lyrics as the people around Saff jumped and danced.

Saff knew his set was coming to an end as he was only performing three songs. He was taking a minute to have a sip of his water and wipe his forehead.

"Before I leave the stage tonight, I've just got something to do. I've checked it with our pastor, so don't worry, I'm not hijacking the night" he laughed. "I would just like to ask a question."

Saffs heart was beating fast, he hadn't mentioned this to her when he had told her about his performance, what was he about to ask? Her hand suddenly went up to her mouth as she let out a gasp as Romario had dropped down on to one knee and had a ring box in his hand. This was not what she had expected and as much as she wasn't a fan of surprises, it made her feel much safer to know what was coming, she was ok with this. She was more than ok with this.

The next few days felt like Saff was floating on a cloud and she was still berating herself for getting in a sulk earlier on that New Year's Eve. She was having so much fun telling her family and friends who were not at church that night and was looking forward to planning a wedding but not paying for it. Getting engaged was one thing, but getting married, well that looked expensive, and they really didn't have the money. Was that the thing that would delay everything?

"I just don't know how we will afford it; everything costs so much." Saff was sharing her worries with a friend from church later in the week.

"Saff, honestly God will provide. We felt the same when we got married but God provided everything we needed, including the money to pay" Courtney reassured her.

Saff appreciated the chat, but would God do that for her? Did God really provide all the money for Courtney? How did that even work? She needed to talk to Romario.

Saff and Romario agreed to keep the wedding talk to only once a week. They sat down on a Friday afternoon at a Costa Coffee local to Saff's house, and Saff pulled her notepad and pen out of her bag ready to get started.

"I've got a list of things to look at today....." Saff started.

"Let's get something to drink first and I'm kinda hungry," said Romario looking up at the menu on the wall, "I've not eaten since lunch and could do with something soon."

Saff wanted to get started, they had agreed to keep wedding talk to a once-a-week meeting as Romario had found it was all Saff could talk about and he had told her that it was becoming overwhelming. She tapped her foot impatiently as she wanted to get started.

Once their drinks had been ordered and brought to the table,

Saff looked at Romario expectantly. He laughed, "Right I know you've got stuff to say so let's get on with it."

Saff looked at her list and excitedly began working her way through it while sipping her coconut latte.

"I know it's not the same for you, but I have been thinking and dreaming about this day since I was a little girl just like many other little girls. I know some might not be bothered but I am, and even more so now I understand what marriage is before God." She looked over at the millionaire's shortbread on Romario's plate which was waiting for him once he had eaten the toastie he had bought.

He pulled the plate nearer to him, "No Sapphire. I asked you if you wanted a cake and you said no."

Saff put her fingers together to indicate that she only wanted a little bit and smiled softly at him. He laughed and said "Just a bit ok" pushing the plate back toward her. "And our marriage before God is what's important to me, it's just all this other stuff that you are clearly bothered about that I'm not really fussed about. But I'm here and I want to help."

"I would love that big white wedding, like the ones you see on TV, lovely dress, all the flowers" She looked dreamily while the small bit of the millionaire shortbread melted in her mouth, making her want more. "But" almost snapping out of her dream, "the movies on TV don't show you weddings with families like ours. We don't have your typical mum and dad on each side. I won't have my dad there so who will walk me down the aisle? Then there's the top table. Who will sit where?" Saff felt herself getting a little teary and a lump forming in her throat.

Romario reached across to put his hand on hers "I know that stuff really matters to you, but we just have to do things differently. Do it the way we want it to be done and not the way everyone else has done it. This is real life, it's our real life and not a movie."

Saff appreciated how he grounded her and reassured her. They chatted a bit more about how God had already done a lot of healing for Saff in the father area, God had become a perfect father who loved her unconditionally. She decided to ask her son, Levi, to walk her down the aisle and hand her over to Romario. Levi had been the man in her life for years and she decided that he was the only man, now 20 years old, that she wanted to give her away. They made the decision that the top table would be Saff and Romario. Their respective families would be sat across several tables nearby with Levi and Sienna as close as they could be. They continued to work their way through the list.

"It's really good that we've been able to pray together about all of this Romario, and we need to keep doing it to really commit this wedding to God and if He wants it to happen, then He will need to provide because I don't know how else it will happen," Saff told him, hoping to share the burden that she was beginning to feel. "I've also been enjoying the pre-marital stuff; we've been doing with Jimmy and Mandy. I know we've only done two sessions with them but that has been eye-opening so thanks for committing to that too."

Saff chewed the end of her pen as she looked over the list and the notes she had been making, and ticking things off when she felt they were a job done. "I can't believe I've got my dress already! For your sister to have a dress available that is my size, and she will let me use it for free, is amazing and she will be using her amazing dress-making skills to make our bridesmaids dresses. We can't underestimate how much of a gift that is to us from her."

Romario finished the last bit of the shortbread and wiped his hands and mouth on a napkin. "People have been really kind and generous, more than I ever expected them to. Money has been appearing everywhere it seems. We've had a number of people asking for our bank details so they can send us a financial gift. There was that money from the event last week where someone came up and put money in your back pocket. And I can't believe that money I found the other day. I was literally sitting waiting for the traffic lights to change and saw something on the side of the road. There were no other cars around, so I jumped out to be sure and it was a £10 note!! I really feel like God was showing me, and us that He is going to provide for us, but we need to steward it well and not go overboard." Romario sounded so encouraged and Saff was just pleased that he was taking it seriously too. He may not get as excited as her about picking flowers and chairs, but he was committed to this marriage and wedding and that was what encouraged her.

"How excited are you?" Thea exclaimed as she helped Saff prepare to leave the hotel room and get across to the church, "Wow, you look incredible Saff." They had all stayed at The Holiday Inn in Salford as the church was right next door, so Romario couldn't be late, as he typically was.

"Thea, I just can't believe we are at this point, it feels like a dream. It almost feels like something is going to happen to ruin it, but I am praying that won't happen. God has been so good, despite how stressful it's all been. Everything has been paid for and all of that finance has been covered by other people. I am still in absolute shock of that. The only thing we don't have is the money for a honeymoon, but we are hoping and praying that will come to us soon." Saff beamed, and she believed with all of her heart that God would provide for them.

Even though the hotel was next to the church, the car still arrived to pick her and the kids up. She got herself and her dress in the car, and Sienna climbed in next to her and Levi sat in the front. They drove around the block a few times and pulled into the church car park. They were early. Typical for Saff she was always early! But they were too early and had to drive round the block a few more times to wait for a few key guests to arrive. As they drove around, the driver chatted a bit too much. Levi kept catching Saff's eye in the mirror and making facial expressions to indicate that he thought he was chatting a bit too much too. Saff just couldn't wait to get into the church and marry her man and say her vows before God. They had already been to the registry office early in the morning and done the legal bit but this bit in church, this was the bit that they wanted, this was the most important.

The day was perfect. Saff and Romario were married in front of their family and friends. There were tears, including from Romario who did not cry, especially in front of people but the presence of God was strong in the church. There was a real sense of God moving them forward. As they drove from the church to Marie Louise Gardens in Disbury for photos. They sat in the back of the car together and wanted to take a moment to take in what had happened in church, and that they were officially married.

"And now me and the missus aren't together, she's got legal custody of the kids so I'm going back and forth trying to sort that out" the driver was saying. He had not stopped talking since they had got in the car. "So getting this car and starting this new business, hopefully, it will show the judge that I'm settled now and ready to have the kids with me."

Saff stared wide-eyed at Romario and in her mind willed the driver to stop speaking. They were driving down Princess Parkway, through Fallowfield, where Saff had previously lived many years ago.

"Did you see who that was Saff?" Romario suddenly said, and Saff whipped her head round just catching the back of Gabe's head as they drove past him.

"No way" Saff sat back, "imagine seeing him today of all days."

"Well, he is behind us now, literally" Romario laughed, "And ain't no way he will ever cause you any pain ever again" as he squeezed her hand.

Saff felt protected and she prayed a silent prayer of thanks to God, as he had given her His best with Romario, and this was just the start of this next season.

As the evening wedding celebrations took place, Saff looked around at all of her friends and family and her heart felt full, this was a day that she had longed for but as the years had passed by she was not sure would ever happen. But God had intervened and changed everything. She was so happy to see people laughing, dancing, and talking. She also felt a pang of sadness at those who were not there, her grandma who had passed away from cancer a few years back, Jack wasn't by Katy's side and even Amy, it was a day they had spoken about over the years. Saff had hugged Katy tight and thanked her so much for being able to come, it hadn't been that long since Jack's funeral and that had been a hard day for them all but here was Katy, taking those baby steps to move forward and Saff was grateful that she was in a position to pray for her. At the end of their spectacular day, they took all their gifts and cards to the hotel room where they spent their first night together as a married couple. Their friends and family had been so generous, and they had more than enough to book a honeymoon with some spending money. God had provided for them. What a start to their married life!

19

Lockdown

The news was on the TV "with the public ordered to stay at home and only leave for essential purposes. From this evening I must give the British people a very simple instruction - you must stay at home. Because the critical thing we must do is stop the disease spreading between households......The people of this country will rise to that challenge. And we will come through it stronger than ever. We will beat the coronavirus and we will beat it together. And therefore, I urge you at this moment of national emergency to stay at home, protect our NHS, and save lives." Boris Johnson's speech continued. The news of the coronavirus was all anyone could talk about, and everyone had been waiting to hear the government updates. Today's updates meant a lot of changes for everyone. They were approaching the end of March 2020 and Saff and Romario were six months into married life. Talk about being thrown into the deep end, there was no hiding from anything now they were entering an unknown period of lockdown.

"I've already been and picked up all my office stuff last week when we were asked to work from home if we could. If I set up my workspace in the kitchen, maybe you can set yours up in the spare room Romario? Sienna will probably have to do her online schoolwork in the kitchen with me."

They hadn't even unpacked all of Romario's things since he had moved in but now they had to make their workspaces comfortable as they hadn't been told how long things would be like this for.

"It will be nice not having to go out and drive to work, rushing around. We can even wear our slippers while we work" laughed Romario.

"Can I wear my slippers for school too?" asked Sienna.

Three weeks later, the government televised update told them that the lockdown would be extended by a further three weeks.

"I feel like it's actually helped us mesh together because we have had to really work together! We are both working from home and Sienna has her school lessons via remote learning. But it's strangely been nice" Saff shared with Thea during a Zoom video call. This had become the way everyone was communicating as they were not allowed legally to meet up with anyone outside of their own household. "And the weather has been beautiful, it makes you so grateful for things like having a garden. We take all our breaks out there and have been able to spend so much time together as a family. Are you missing church?"

"Yes! Online services are just not the same are they?" complained Thea.

"They aren't but it's so interesting to see how everyone is adapting so quickly. It's refreshing to see what's important in life because life as we know it seems to have disappeared."

"I agree, I almost feel healthier. The daily exercise that we are allowed to do has become a breath of fresh air. I've been trying to go out for a run or at least a walk and this sunshine just makes it so much nicer."

"Thea, we've been doing the same. Sienna has been getting on her bike and we've been running together, oh and we've been doing P.E with Joe Wicks every morning. Anyway, I better get on as we have a prayer zoom with church at 7pm and my eyes need a little break from all this screen time."

Saff sat back and rubbed her eyes. The screen time was becoming a lot, as they had zooms for work, church, online school, with family, with friends and Saff was still one of the facilitators on the Bolton Discipleship Course, which was also now online. Some weeks they had around thirty zooms a week, but Saff knew people all around the world were all experiencing the same thing, and she was grateful they still had ways to keep in touch.

They were trying to watch the daily government update on TV every day to know where they were up to with work and school. Saff was watching for other reasons.

"Ro, I can't believe that we decided to wait six months before we tried for a baby and just enjoy time together, and now this stupid lockdown means I can't get the contraceptive implant removed from my arm. The first time in both of our lives that we are in a loving marriage, and we can't even try. I'm waiting for Boris to tell us we can start going for appointments for this stuff again."

"I can't believe you were literally sat in the room with the nurse to get it out and the news came in that meant they wouldn't do it. You were right there; it wouldn't have taken them long to get it out would it?" Saff felt a little bit of comfort that Romario felt her frustration.

"No, it wouldn't!" Saff was exasperated as they remembered that morning. The nurse had called her into the room and then had been suddenly called out. When she returned she told Saff that she was no longer allowed to perform anymore procedures or tests etc. Now here they were two months later, and services had not yet started again. Saff could feel her biological clock ticking, knowing she was turning forty next year.

The daily government updates brought the daily death toll and the news of how the virus was spreading and mutating, it instilled a sense of fear into you if you let it. Saff often thought about her family and friends, and how they were coping. She knew her mum had housemates so she wasn't alone, Yasmine lived with her boyfriend, Zoe's mum had moved in with her so they wouldn't be alone, and she was sure Dante wasn't feeling any fear or letting lockdown rules stop him from doing what he wanted to which was flitting around here, there, and everywhere. Katy had moved over to Dubai just before lockdown had hit the UK, she was desperate to start a new life after losing Jack. And then there was Amy, Saff often thought of her even though it still brought so much pain to think about, but she had been back with her parents for years now so surely she was ok but maybe she would ask Zoe about her next time they spoke.

It was another five months before Saff was able to find a health service to remove the implant from her arm and she had got to a desperate point of even considering removing it herself.

"It feels like my past is just holding us back and getting in the way again. The only reason I had the implant was because of what I had been through and to be sure it never happened again and now it's preventing us from moving on. Both times

I've had a baby it's been as a single parent and it's been tough, I feel so much more ready now. Older, wiser, more prepared, and now this! It's not fair on you either" as she reached for Romario's hand.

Romario took her hand and squeezed it, "Saff, it's not your fault. It's been completely out of our hands, who was meant to know that we would get locked down like this? No one! But you have an appointment now, so let's see what happens once you've had it removed. We can't keep thinking the worse, as much as this lockdown has been a time of reset and realising what's important, we can't let it control us or stop us from moving forward in the way God wants."

By June lockdown restrictions seemed to be easing, you were now allowed to meet with groups of six from other households but still maintaining social distancing, even the Premier League Football had started back after a 100-day absence much to Romario's delight. The rules seemed quite confusing at times and as Saff was now actively trying for a baby, they tried not to mix outside of seeing family and the odd friend. They wanted a baby, and they didn't fancy catching COVID while doing that and with the rules changing so much, Boris Johnson not explaining them very clearly, they didn't rush back out into the world.

Zoe had let Saff know that Amy wasn't in a good way, she had been buying cocaine regularly from Dante. She thought it was a way she could keep seeing him, and Dante had even tried sending one of his boys instead of going himself, but she would buy drugs so much that he often had to go. Zoe had said she was sure she was addicted; she was using it during the day just to cope with the lockdown restrictions. This had made Saff sad, and she knew she had to pray for her.

It was a relief once school finished in July, supporting Sienna with her online school activities while both trying to work was a juggling challenge. Saff understood the need for a change and wanted to keep Sienna safe, but she knew she was not a teacher, and she appreciated the provision of school so much more, longing for the days when Sienna could be back with her friends. Hopefully, things could start feeling fairly normal for her now as it was so uncertain the effect all of this was going to have on our children.

Romario had just got back from the barbers, grateful that they had opened back up in July. "Oooo it looks nice and sharp," said Saff when he got back. She knew he had been dying for a haircut and hadn't touched his hair himself since lockdown. "I could have always tried to do it for you."

Romario looked at her, "Nope. My barber is the surgeon when it comes to my hair and only he can touch it. It's him or no one."

"I know, I know. I was only messing with you. Anyway, I've got something to show you" as she took Romario by the hand into the living room.

Romario looked down at the table, to the pregnancy test lying on a couple of sheets of kitchen roll. He looked down, and then back up at Saff,

"Is it positive?" Romario asked,

"Yes, it is," Saff replied planting a big kiss on his face, "finally."

They were both happy and excited. Romario had been a great stepfather to Sienna and Levi, but this would be Romario's first biological child and the first time Saff was having a baby with someone she felt love and stability. Having a loving family home with two parents was something Saff had craved since she was a child, and now she was going to bring a baby into that home. Finally.

The pregnancy was exciting, and they told Sienna first. She had been through many changes with her mum getting married and Romario moving into their home, they wanted her to feel included, so she was the first to know.

"This week the baby is the size of a blueberry" Saff shared as she read from her pregnancy app that was helping her track the pregnancy. Morning sickness was creeping in, and she was struggling with energy levels already.

"I am really feeling it this time round. It's got to be my age. When I had Levi, I was seventeen years old, with Sienna almost thirty and now I am almost forty and I can feel it" she laughed, "I have struggled with nausea in those pregnancy's, but I feel achier and more tired this time round."

They had their first scan booked for the day before their first wedding anniversary. This would be at twelve weeks gestation.

"How amazing is that? I can't wait to be able to share with everyone once we've reached that first scan," they had told family and some close friends but had decided to wait before announcing anything to everyone else.

Just over a week before the scan Saff had an uncomfortable day. Her back was aching, and she had been trying to reduce the pain by using a hot water bottle when she was sat down.

"Is it something to worry about?" asked Romario.

"I don't know, it just feels weird, but I've got a hot water bottle and will see how I get on."

After dinner Saff went to sit on the sofa, as she did, she felt a gush of water and ran up to the bathroom.

"No, no, no," she said to herself but once she saw the blood she knew. "Romario" she shouted, "quickly please!" How could this be happening? Had she done something wrong?

God, please help me, don't let me lose this baby.

The bleeding didn't stop and neither did the tears. The out-of-hours GP had recommended going to the hospital but there were so many rules around lockdown and what they were allowed to do and not do. Even amid all the pain and fear, Saff's mind reeled with thoughts around lockdown and rules, not wanting to get in trouble - *if we go to the hospital, who will look after Sienna? Were we allowed to have anyone to come round? What were the rules and why were they so confusing? Why did they need to add an extra layer of fear into an already horrible situation?*

Her head hurt and she knew she needed to get to the hospital. "Ro, ring Jasmine, please. Ask her to come and stay with Sienna."

Jasmine had come straight over to look after Sienna so they could get to the hospital. As they sat in the waiting area Saff thought how horrible it was going through all of this while wearing these stupid masks, she could hardly breathe, and the tears were soaking right through it. Our faces expressed so much, but you couldn't see enough to know what the nurse's faces were expressing. *Did they think I was worrying over nothing? Did they think I shouldn't have come while we are living through a pandemic? Did they know my baby was gone already?* Saff searched their eyes as they examined her, but it was hard to know what they were thinking from just looking at their eyes.

After the examination, the nurse said that Saff just needed to go home and come back the next day for a scan, in the meantime there was nothing they could do but just see what happened. Saff was in so much pain all night, the painkillers seemed to do nothing, and the bleeding continued. She felt so out of control knowing her body was going through this but there was nothing at all that she could do. There was so much blood, Saff may as well have slept in the bathroom the amount of times she had to keep getting up and going there. It was a horrible night for them both and neither got much sleep.

The scan the next day confirmed that they had lost their baby. Time seemed to stand still. Neither Saff nor Romario knew how to deal with this. They had been praying for this baby every day, for its growth, and its health. Why had this happened? No one had an answer other than *"these things happen."*

Physically Saff's body was still in pain although the nausea had stopped. She couldn't understand why this had happened. People had babies every day, she had never had a problem with getting pregnant before. Was she too old? Was it her fault? Oh my gosh, was this punishment for what she had done in her past? She had thought God had forgiven her but was He now punishing her? This was all too much for her and she was struggling. There was a heaviness on her, she struggled to get out of bed and the tears wouldn't stop. As the days passed by Saff would sit on their bed and look out of the bedroom window watching people walk and drive by, wondering how they could just go about their lives while hers had come crashing down. Did they not know that their baby had just died?!

This was the first time she had questioned her faith, questioned God. She had asked questions before but now she was questioning everything she believed, was it even real? She had been unable to pray or read her Bible, her time with God had been limited to her expressing her anger and asking why, over, and over while the silence rang loud in her ears.

Almost two weeks had passed, and they were approaching the day of their first wedding anniversary. A day she should have been looking forward to celebrating but what did she have to celebrate now? This day was meant to be a double celebration, and now it was a day she didn't even want to think about.

"Saff, some friends from church have rallied around and want to pay for us to have a night away somewhere. Let's go. Have a change of scenery."

He was right, and she knew it. Without Romario, she would stay in bed as long as she could. Romario booked them into The Grand in York, a beautiful 5-star hotel with a spa.

"I've made us a dinner reservation for 6pm, so there's no rush".

Something Saff appreciated because she didn't feel good about herself so getting ready was a challenge, but she made herself up as best as she could, and they enjoyed a lovely meal and had some mocktails. They were in bed before 10pm and ready for a comfy night's sleep in the huge hotel bed.

York was a beautiful city steeped in history - the city walls, York Minster, little cobbled streets with cute little shops. The next day they took their time, exploring, taking photos, and enjoying being together. Sitting on one of the benches along the wall, they took a moment to sit and chat.

"I'm really glad we came you know Ro, just being with you and celebrating our first year of marriage has brought me back to the moment. It felt like everything paused after we lost Baby J, and it has only been two weeks."

They had given the baby this name so they could always remember them.

"But I am ready to get going again, and I know that will be hard. I know I have really wrestled with God over what's happening, but I believe God is a good God, I believe his plans are to prosper us as we seek him. I'm not going to lie; I fell off and I didn't know what was going to happen, but I don't want to deny God in my life because of one tragedy. I honestly feel like I had a crisis of faith and I've never had that before. I'm so sick of hearing "everything happens for a reason." What possible reason could there be for our baby to die? I don't actually believe everything happens for a reason, but I do believe the Bible verse *"that for those who love God all things work together for good."* I love God and I want to look forward. I think we should try again as soon as the doctor feels it's ok." She reached for Romario's hand.

"I've really struggled to Saff, I just can't get my head around it, but I have been praying, for us both so it's good to hear that. I don't think I've processed what's happened properly, I feel angry too but moving forward is good. Let's do that together." Squeezing her hand in return.

20

Broken Heart

There was still so much fear everywhere, the news on the television, the newspapers, and social media. Everywhere they looked there were signs of the pandemic – masks, signs, news, rules. Life had to go on, and both Saff and Romario had jobs to return to. Sienna was still in school, bills had to be paid, and food had to be cooked. Dealing with baby loss was traumatic, and new territory for them. The COVID restrictions had added an extra challenge as most of the ways friends and family would usually support you during a time like this were off-limits. There was to be no mixing of households. The fear around spreading or catching this dreaded virus, the rules given by the government about who could meet and when and how were not easy to navigate when your mind was ok but when you were already struggling mentally and emotionally, Saff didn't know if she was coming or going. They had coped pretty well with the new routine at the start of the lockdowns, it had even been fun, but since losing Baby J anxiety and worry were crippling her. It was a relief when things began to ease.

Saff was so grateful when the COVID restrictions changed around being able to meet with friends, she had arranged to meet up with Chris and Sarah Rowling with their kids in a local park to go for a walk. She pulled into the car park and saw them getting out of the car, waving she found a space near them and reversed in. They decided to get a coffee from the van parked nearby before going for a walk.

"It's so nice to see you guys, I've really missed being able to meet up with friends."

"Us too," said Chris, "this has been tough for us extroverts" he laughed.

"It really has though! But not so much for you eh Romario, being an introvert, I think you've enjoyed it much more than me" She poked Romario in the side with her elbow as they walked through the park. Sienna had run on ahead with the Rowling kids who had also brought their dog.

"How are you guys doing with everything that's gone on?" asked Sarah. She had such a gentle voice and always made Saff feel cared for when she spoke, her pale green eyes searched Saffs and Romario's faces as she waited for their answer.

"I've found it hard trying to process it all because of the restrictions. I like talking and sharing, and not just over the phone or a Zoom video call. We are both still working from home, as the government are advising us, but that has it's pro's and con's. The pro's not being at risk of catching anything, but also not having to see other people's pregnancies. I'm sorry if that sounds bad but some days it's really hard to hear those announcements or see pregnant ladies. I don't think it's jealousy, because I'm happy for people but just that pang of sadness that stings and those constant questions hang in the air why us?" Saff took a sip of her coffee and felt that pang inside her. It was like an ache in her heart and in her stomach, but it also felt good to talk about it with her friends.

Romario took her free hand as they walked, she was grateful to feel the warmth of him so close, reassuring her that they were in this together. "But we are going to try again, aren't we?" he smiled at her, as she nodded back. "That initial excitement doesn't feel like it's there, it feels like it's been replaced by anxiety, but we are placing it back into God's hands and asking for His will to be done. And hopefully we will be able to let you guys know that we will be having a baby sometime soon. Right now, I think we should try to catch up to the kids as they seem to have picked up their pace" he indicated with his head as they all looked up the path to see the kids had broken out into a jog with the dog trotting behind them.

As soon as Saff found out she was pregnant again they

told their close family and friends straight away, knowing that whatever happened they would need their support rather than trying to cope with this on their own. They didn't want to forget Baby J and had been able to go to a service at the local crematorium for people who had lost their babies. It was the first time they had been inside a church or chapel since lockdown had started. The lockdown had been lifted and a second lockdown had come into force in November, just before the memorial service. The service was nice. There were three other couples there and Saff and Romario stayed sitting there for a while longer once it was finished and the other couples had left. It was peaceful to sit in there, quietly praying and hoping their baby was now with God, with her two other babies. They were always on her mind.

Saff suffered from the worst sickness she had ever had with this pregnancy. In the past, it had been the feeling of nausea but this time around, she was sick, and it was not confined to the mornings. Why on earth was it called morning sickness when it plagued her all day long? The evenings were the worst, and no matter what she tried it only got worse. It meant she spent a lot of time in bed, physically not able to get out and do anything.

One morning Saff had dragged herself to the bathroom. Blood. There was blood in the toilet. She burst into tears, and it took her right back to the moment she had lost Baby J. She gripped the sink to steady herself as she felt she couldn't take it, the fear that she was losing this baby now was too much. With Romario by her side, she called a nurse at the hospital who said the best thing she could do was to rest and see how she got on. Bleeding in early pregnancy did happen. This was not what Saff wanted to hear, how could they just leave her without checking on her baby? It was hard to think about anything else and she was grateful that she worked part time so she could take that time to rest. Her head was reeling, why did they not want to see her at the hospital? What if she lost this baby? Fortunately, the bleeding seemed to have been a one-off, but it didn't do anything to reduce the fear they both felt.

Romario was different in this pregnancy, he avoided conversations about baby plans or names. With Baby J he had been speaking to her tummy all the time, this time round he barely even looked at it. It felt like their lives were on hold and they couldn't move forward until they knew this baby was ok. It wasn't enough now to get to the twelve-week scan, they wanted to get to the twenty-week scan before they were able to relax and know things would be ok. This meant they didn't buy anything and were unable to let people know what they needed. It was too much to have baby stuff around them if they were not going to be able to keep this one.

The twenty-week scan date appointment came, and it

was the day after Saff's 40th birthday. Why did her scan appointments always fall around important dates for them? She really hoped and prayed that this time round they could celebrate the pregnancy and her birthday together. Romario had made some plans for her birthday, which hadn't been easy as there were some lockdown restrictions in place. He had also booked them into a little retreat place for the weekend, they would drive there after the scan. They had both agreed that after this scan they would be able to relax about the pregnancy and hopefully begin to enjoy it.

Saff lay on the bed in the scan room and Romario sat on a nearby chair. The sonographer kept asking Saff to move into different positions, and the scan seemed to take a long time. The sonographer finally placed the wand back on its stand and handed Saff some blue paper towel to wipe the gel off her tummy. She sat back in her chair and spoke to them both.

"I've not been able to get the views on babies heart today. It could be the position baby is in, but we would like to refer you to be seen again."

Saffs eyes darted to Romario's. What did this mean? Saff had never experienced anything like this during the scans for her other babies, they were always straightforward. This scan was meant to be the time they told them their baby was fine and they could celebrate. Now they were told there may be an issue, but they wouldn't know until they were seen by another specialist which may not be until next week. They made their way to their car once their appointment was over, their stuff for their weekend away was already in place and they started the drive over to Stoke. Romario was trying to be positive and talking about the best-case scenario, that she could have got it wrong, and it was just the way the baby was lying, he was saying we needed to pray. Saff was listening but she couldn't find any words to respond and nodded in agreement from time to time. Her phone suddenly rang making her jump and snapping her out of her thoughts. It was an unknown number.

"Hiya, it's Julie one of the nurses from the hospital. The sonographer today made a referral for you to come to Wigan for another scan, but we actually want to send you straight to St Mary's in Manchester to be scanned by a cardiologist. We would only be referring you there anyway if there were any issues so I would rather speed up the process and cut out the middleman if you like."

Wow, they both sensed there was something serious going on here. They needed to find their prayer warriors and also let the family know. The place they were going to was in a remote place with limited phone reception, so they made a few calls in the car to update their parents and family members who had all been excitedly waiting for news from the scan, asking if we had found out the sex of the baby. The sex of the baby had completely gone out of their mind. A boy, they were having a boy! This news had overshadowed it, and it almost didn't matter to them anymore. You often heard parents saying that they didn't mind what gender the baby was as long as it was healthy. Well, what happens when you find out your baby might not be healthy?

"We need to spend this weekend praying and seeking God Saff" And that is what they did. They put on worship music and prayed. They prayed together, they prayed on their own, they prayed out loud and they prayed silently. The cottage had a lovely little garden with views over fields and the sun shone. It was so peaceful and felt like the best place to prepare them for whatever was going to come at the appointment they had been given on Tuesday in Manchester. It had certainly changed the purpose of their time away. They were going to stand firm on their faith and cry out to God to give them the strength to get through this. They also decided on a list of people they would be personally asking to pray to.

The following Tuesday, they drove to St Mary's for their appointment in the Foetal Medicine Unit. A department neither of them had ever heard of nor been to. The walk to get there took them through the normal scan department. Saff couldn't bear to look at all the happy expectant mothers with their partners sitting there waiting, she kept her eyes down as they hurriedly made their way through the Foetal Medicine Unit door.

The cardiologist Dr. Gladman, came out to greet them. He was a tall man, with grey hair and smiley eyes. He led them into the room and asked Saff to lie down so he could begin the scan. The room felt hot, and as they were still required to wear masks due to the COVID guidelines, Saff began to feel faint and uncomfortable, it was almost suffocating. The silence in the room was painful and the scan seemed to take forever with Saff being asked to move to different positions again. Saff and Romario spent the time silently praying and looking into each other's eyes from time to time. Once it was over, they were asked to go into one of the side rooms where the doctor would come and speak to them.

The room had a red sofa and some comfy chairs. There were paintings on the walls and a small vase on a table with some fake flowers in it all tying in with the red colour theme. Dr. Gladman and one of the nurses joined them in the room. He began talking and explaining what he could see on the scan of their baby boy's heart. Saff felt like she was underwater, his voice was muffled. Why was he saying this stuff to them? She was holding Romario's hand but could feel that she was digging her fingers into his palm. She wanted to scream; she wanted the doctor to just stop talking. Just shut up! The doctor had drawn a picture. On one side there was a normal heart and how the blood flowed through it and on the other was their son's heart. He would require surgery at birth, at nine months old, and before he was five years old.

"There are three options before you. One, you carry on with the pregnancy and the baby will need to have those surgeries. Two, you have an Amniocentesis test to check if the baby has any genetic or chromosomal conditions such as Down syndrome. Three, you don't carry on with the pregnancy."

Saff sat up straight, her back stiffening. "I don't think three is an option for us, we are Christians, and we don't want that. Our baby is here now, and he deserves a chance. I don't see the point in two because the results wouldn't make us change our minds and there are risks with that, so we will go away and talk but I believe our decision will be to continue with the pregnancy."

She didn't even know how she had found the strength to speak those words but that was what she wanted. She looked to Romario, who nodded and agreed.

They had to walk back through the normal scan department to get back to their car. Saff looked down at the floor, her eyes were red from crying, and she didn't want to make eye contact with any of these parents to be, all full of hope and excitement. Once in the car they just sat and stared, Saff still crying. This hadn't been the news they had wanted. They had wanted to relax and shout from the rooftops that they were having a boy! But we don't always get what we want, do we?

How were they going to tell their family the news? They hadn't properly processed it themselves.

"Ro, can we go to our pastor's house, please? I need them to pray with us."

Romario rang their pastor and his wife who said of course they could come over. Sitting with them in their garden, feeling the sun on her face and drinking the cold water they had given her, she felt more relaxed as they showed them the diagram the doctor had drawn and shared everything he had told them. It was good to sit with them, they listened and empathised. They offered words of comfort and prayed for them, and they told them they would be there for them throughout this.

Saff was thinking about her old life, and how she would have handled this situation. Would she have been able to have the baby? Would she have found the strength to fight this? She wasn't sure. She was trying to keep herself busy, as busy as she could while feeling exhausted and being sick. She was still working from home but on reduced hours. Romario had a new job working for a mental health charity with young people. He was finally being recognised for all his experience and skills.

She turned to him one night as they lay in bed, "Most days I feel ok. I can almost forget it's happening but then I remember, and it floors me. I will end up sitting on the floor crying. But once it's out and I've given it back to God in prayer, I can usually pick myself back up and get on with things. I just can't even imagine dealing with this without knowing God. I've been through some stuff, some very hard stuff but this blows my mind. Prayer and faith are carrying me. There's a strength inside me that I know has to be from God. How are you finding your new job and coping with it all?"

Romario had his eyes closed and his hands folded across his chest "It's hard to focus with everything that's going on if I'm honest Saff. But I'm going to give it my all because it's a good job, and it's good to support the family."

"That's good and I know you will be great babe. I've been thinking about the baby and the pregnancy. I think we've both had a few weeks to get our head round things and I want to start enjoying the pregnancy. I want to celebrate our baby. He deserves that and we have been holding back for so long. What do you think?"

Romario rubbed his face with his hands, he looked tired. "You're right Saff. He's our baby boy and I have been holding back for fear of losing this baby too. Now we are facing this."

"I felt the same Romario, I really did. And you know that my faith was shaken after losing Baby J, but this time I feel a determination to fight this in prayer. Our baby can't fight for himself, so we have to fight for him, and I won't give up on that. Whatever is trying to come against us, against our baby I will do my best to fight it. I'm grateful for this God-given strength because I have crumbled at less in the past. What does that Bible verse say? *In my weakness, He is made strong.* I don't think it's possible for me to be any weaker now."

They made the decision to make their pregnancy more public, sharing it on their social media accounts. They wanted to celebrate their little boy as they normally would have if they hadn't lost Baby J or if they hadn't been given this news.

It was a relief to be able to tell their wider circle of family and friends that they were pregnant, but they had decided to keep the news of his congenital heart defect to those who already knew, they were not ready to keep going over things with people.

Saff's care was transferred to St Mary's Manchester, and she had been scheduled for extra scans and appointments to continue to check babies' growth. This definitely increased their faith levels. They trusted God and were praying and believing for healing. As the months passed, and they continued to pray for healing, they would ask at each scan "Has anything changed?"

The sonographer or the cardiologist would look at them strangely and say "No." But Saff and Romario continued to give it back to God and asked their prayer group to keep praying. During one particular scan with the cardiologist Dr Gladman, they asked their usual question "Has anything changed?" And surprisingly he said "There has been one change. A small one. The aortic arch, which had been half the size of the other arch, had grown. I had initially thought it might wither away completely but it has grown. I know you were hoping for a miracle, but we don't see many of them."

Saff and Romario smiled at each other, a look passing between them that said, "you don't know my God." And for them right there, the growth of that aortic arch was a miracle.

Another miracle was that every growth scan showed that the baby was growing fine, there seemed to be no other concerns that can so often come with babies with a congenital heart defect. Saff was having an internal battle in that she was exhausted and sick, there was a desire for the pregnancy to reach its end. She wanted to meet her baby. But while he was inside of her, he was safe. The moment he enters the world and needs to breathe oxygen, that's when his problems would begin. The plan was for Saff to be induced around one to two weeks before the baby's due date. She had found it incredibly hard to prepare for a baby that would need to go straight to the Neonatal Intensive Care Unit.

"Ro, I don't even know what he will need. Does he need clothes? Blankets? They've said I will probably not be able to breastfeed, but do we need to buy bottles and a steriliser? I just don't know. I actually hate this feeling of things being out of my control. I've been asked a few times if we have a baby wish list, but I can't even think. I feel like I am on pause, but time is ticking."

"Well if you don't know the answers to those questions, I definitely don't" laughed Romario, "this is my first baby but the hospital stuff I have no idea about. Can't we ask someone?"

Saff had met up with Zoe for a coffee in a lovely coffee shop near to home. Grabbing a seat by the window where the sun was shining, she lowered herself and her bump into the chair. It was getting harder and harder to do simple things. Zoe brought over two cups of coffee for them,

"Decaf for you Saff," she said as she put them on the table "And the slice of cake you asked for" she grinned.

"Thanks, Zoe, it's so good to see you. The last time was our wedding, wasn't it?" looking at the delicious slice of chocolate cake in front of her.

"Yeah, it was such a beautiful day Saff, and such an honour to be there. And we've had a few lockdowns to deal with in between. So, you've got a date to be induced now?" looking up as she stirred her coffee with a spoon.

"Yep. I've never been induced before, and I am really hoping I don't need to have a C-section. I understand they need to induce me so they can plan to look after the baby, but both other times I've gone into labour naturally. I just don't know what to expect you know." Using her fork to scoop some cake into her mouth.

"Have they said you will need a C-section?"

Saff shook her head while she swallowed the cake in her mouth "No, the doctor said they want to keep everything as natural as possible, apart from being induced of course."

"Well Saff, focus on that and try not to worry about what could happen. I know that ain't easy. I don't want to pry or upset you so please tell me it's none of my business, but I guess I'm just trying to understand. Do they know why the baby's heart is like this?"

"Zoe, it's fine honestly. We've known each other for a long time, so don't worry. To be honest, it just seems that these things happen. It's actually really common and affects one in every hundred babies. I've tried to get my head round it, I've prayed about it, I've asked God why, but it just seems that this happens."

"Why do you think God let it happen? You know if you believe in Him and you're going to church, doesn't he protect you from that stuff now?"

"Ah Zoe, if only it was that easy. One thing I have come to realise after asking why us? for a little while, is why not us? Why someone else? I believe God protects me and there is a blessing as I seek Him. But what is a blessing? We have decided what it looks like to be successful in the world and to be honest, there have been so many blessings in my life. I'm married, I've changed in so many ways, I've got my house but even more than that I've been forgiven, I have been transformed from the inside out, I have hope, and nothing in the world could give me those things. And all of that was given to me by Jesus who was God's son. Years ago he was sent into the world by God, and the plan was for him to be a sacrifice for our sins which is why he had to die on the cross. But the thing is, he rose from the dead three days later and because of what he did I can have all those things that I've just mentioned. Does that make sense Zo?" she looked into her eyes, hoping it did.

"Yeah, you just give me goosebumps saying all that. It's so true, we want the money, the house, and the car but from what you've said, it's so much more than that. I might even start coming to church myself" she chuckled, "I could do with some of that in my life."

"You are more than welcome anytime! I've battled this in my mind, and I think I was really shaken after losing Baby J, by the time we found out about this baby's heart, I knew I just needed to fight for him. I feel strong but don't get me wrong, this is hard. But I trust God and I trust that he will get me through whatever comes. A big part of my faith is trusting God, especially in times when you can't see what's ahead. It's easy to trust when you know what's coming but how much harder when you don't know. You know me, and you know in the past this would have broken me. I don't even know if I could have continued with the pregnancy if I am honest, but with God everything is different. It's strengthened me and Ro, it's increased our faith, it's shown us how much our church family supports us, it's shown us who is there from family and friends, even though it is so frustrating hearing people say those cliches like *"stay strong"* or *"trust God."* It feels so dismissive of what we are going through, and I feel like replying *"Don't you think we are already doing that?"* All we can do is trust God and try to be strong but it's not a flippant thing. We have stepped into a new season and it's scary, but I would not want to do this without my faith."

"With you saying all that, and sounding like you are in

a good place, I need to tell you something." Zoe suddenly looked very uncomfortable. "Amy is pregnant, and she says it's Dante's."

"Oh," Saff sat back in her chair and shifted into a more comfortable position. She was unsure how she felt and took a minute before she responded, "Is everything ok with her, and the baby? I know she hasn't been in a good place for a long time, and she still refuses to speak to me like I was the one that did her wrong."

"As far as I know, yeah but I do know that she's still using drugs. I tried to tell her the last time I saw her that she needs to pack it in, for the baby's sake. It made me so angry and even now hearing you talk and all you are going through; I just don't get it" Zoe was visibly upset.

Saff had to take another minute to think, to silently pray before she gathered her thoughts to say anything. Hearing someone was pregnant was hard, her initial feeling was happiness for them but sadness that her journey was that of loss and now a heart defect.

"Are you ok Saff?" Zoe asked cautiously.

Saff sighed, "Yes and no. I will be praying for Amy, I really hope she begins to see what a blessing she is carrying in her body and begins to make changes. I'm sad for her, and to be honest I don't get it either. The way God works, the way things like this work, like why some people are given a healthy baby and pregnancy even when they aren't taking care of either. I think I have learnt that my feelings and emotions don't get to change their path or change my path. I'm grateful that you still get to see her and hopefully, she will hear what you're saying sooner rather than later."

Zoe found herself crying on her drive home. Things were so hard for Saff and her heart broke for her and her baby. Zoe couldn't understand why she was so forgiving towards Amy when she felt angry with her. She reached into her handbag to find a tissue while she was sitting at the lights, she needed to sort her head out so she could continue driving home. Wiping her tears from her face, she was overcome with anger, and anger at God. She began to speak out as she drove "God, hello it's me, Zoe. Why are you letting this happen to my friend and her baby? Why are you letting her baby suffer when she has actually decided to become a follower of yours? It's really not fair. What's the point of becoming a Christian if you aren't even going to protect her?" Zoe was on a roll; she could feel all her frustrations and anger rising up and she was going to stick it all on God today. "Why are you letting Amy continue to ruin her life and use drugs? Why can't you stop her? Saff says you can do anything so surely you could stop her from killing herself like this. Why have you allowed a baby to grow inside her when she's toxic right now, literally toxic with drugs?" She was beginning to feel a little better, maybe this prayer stuff was good, it seemed therapeutic, and she might give it another go the next time she felt such anger and hurt.

Amy opened her eyes and strained to see where she was. The room wasn't familiar to her, she looked around. The window was covered by a sheet held up with drawing pins, there was the mattress she was lying on, and she could see blankets and rubbish strewn across the floor. She groaned as she sat up, licking her dry lips looking for something to drink. There was a can of Red Stripe on the floor near where she lay, reaching for it she was pleased it still had something inside and she took a big gulp, wiping her mouth with the back of her hand.

"Mawning" a voice called from across the room, Amy's eyes came into focus as she noticed the woman sat on a blanket on the floor for the first time. "You was havin' a proper snore last night. Had a good mind to give you a kick but I couldn't be bothered getting up" the woman cackled before she took a long pull on the cigarette she held in her hand.

Amy sat up and checked her clothing, pleased that she was still fully dressed. She wasn't hundred percent sure what had

taken place last night, she grabbed her handbag and rooted
through it for her phone.

The woman cackled again, "You lookin' for your phone
ain't ya? Well, ya won't find it because Ged took it off ya as
payment for the drugs." The woman looked right into her eyes,
"Ya don't remember, do ya?"

Amy shook her head and felt tears stinging her eyes, but
she pushed them back and jutted her chin out, "Yeah, I do
remember and it's fine. I wasn't looking for it anyway" she
replied defiantly but silently kicking herself for having made
that decision at some point last night. "This Ged, when will he
be back?"

"Oh, you won't see him for a couple of days, he will be
off doing his rounds, collecting his money." The woman eyed
her again, "If you need to earn some money, I can help ya
out with that. You're a pretty girl and the punters don't even
mind you've got a belly." She said flippantly as she waved her
cigarette in the direction of Amy's pregnant belly.

Amy's hands went protectively to her belly and covered it.
"No thank you. I can get my own money and right now I need
to leave." She got up and made her way out of the house as
quickly as she could. Once she was outside the light hurt her
eyes, she put her hand over them so she could try to get her
bearings. The night was beginning to come back to her, Dante

had refused to sell her any more drugs and banned all his boys from answering her calls or doing any more drops to her. So, she had needed to find a way to get them from somewhere else. She walked fast up the road in the direction she hoped would lead to the main road. Hyde Road, she let out a sigh of relief as she recognised the road name and knew she would be able to get a bus back into Manchester. She stopped and searched her handbag for change, there were a couple of coins loose at the bottom and she could see a few pound coins so that should be enough to get home. She pulled out a flyer for a nightclub in Manchester and remembered that's where she had gone to see if she could find someone to buy drugs from. Yes, she clicked her fingers as she remembered that's where she had met Ged and he had promised her some drugs back at his. And there was his number written on the flyer, she would be keeping that safe as it may come in handy if she got desperate.

Stopping at a bus stop she checked the timetable, there should be a 201 bus along soon from Gorton to Manchester. She plonked herself down on the ledge the council had the cheek to call a bench and had another root in her bag to make sure she had her house keys. There was another flyer crumpled at the bottom of her bag and she pulled that one out ugh she shuddered; it was a flyer for an event at a church. Her thoughts went back to the group who had been standing outside the

Printworks trying to talk to people as they were just trying to enjoy themselves. She had taken a flyer as it was handed to her but only to be polite. *Why couldn't they just leave people to have fun?* She ripped that flyer up and dropped it back into her bag, that would be one event she would be avoiding.

She stuffed her hands in her coat pocket, feeling a chill in the air and willing the bus to hurry. She needed to get home but wasn't looking forward to the lecture from her parents about staying out and now needing a new phone. Her hands came to feel her belly and she rubbed it. Her piece of happiness, her piece of Dante, this baby would keep them together forever, no matter what he said now, she would always be in his life once their baby was here. Her positive thoughts towards the bus must have worked as she could see it coming up the road towards her. Who needed God when she had her own mind? She chuckled to herself.

Saff's induction date soon came around. The prayer team were in full force covering them all in prayer. Their lives were about to change, and they were about to meet their baby boy for the first time. Elisha was born weighing a healthy 7lbs & 7ounces. The labour itself was quick and Saff was able to give birth naturally.

"Oh Ro, look at his little squished-up face, and look at his hair!"

"He's beautiful Saff, and well done, you did great. I'm proud of you."

"Do you guys want to have a quick hold, take some photos and then baby will need to go with the nurses to NICU?" asked a midwife.

Saff looked round the room, as if seeing it properly for the first time and suddenly noticed the number of midwives and nurses in the room, and then the incubator to take their little man away. It was four hours before they saw him again. Saff was wheeled into the NICU in a wheelchair just after 4am. The lights were dimmed and there were the noises of monitors beeping all over the room giving an eerie chill across the room. There were eight incubators in the room, all with a tiny baby inside, some had blue lights shining on them illuminating their incubators. They were taken over to see their baby, Saff felt tears sting her eyes and took a sharp intake of breath seeing her baby like that. She felt Romario squeeze her shoulder as he stood behind her, thankful that he was there too.

Romario wheeled Saff next to the incubator. Elisha lay there asleep, all he had on was a nappy, a hat and some woollen booties on his feet. There were so many wires and monitors around him and the nurse who was attending to him explained what they all were. He had a monitor on his foot to monitor his oxygen saturation levels, little stickers on his chest to monitor his heart, an NG feeding tube down his nose and taped onto his cheek which was how he would be having his milk, a blood pressure monitor on one hand, a canular in the other hand and another canular in one of his feet. To say it was overwhelming was an understatement. They sat by his incubator just staring at him for a while.

"Would you like to hold him?" the nurse suddenly said. They didn't need to be asked twice, of course, they did! The nurse had to carefully place him in their arms with the tangle of wires and leads attached to him. And to their joy, he opened his eyes and began taking a good look at them. It was surreal to sit there, having just given birth, staring into their son's eyes while all the machines and monitors beeped around them, and nurses continued to move between babies. It didn't feel like it was the early hours of the morning, it felt like a room that didn't sleep. They stayed as long as they could until they couldn't keep their eyes open any longer and Saff needed to get back to the post-natal ward to get some painkillers, she had almost forgotten she had only just given birth until she felt the twangs of pain sharply in her body.

"I will see you back here in the morning. I'm going to go to the NICU as soon as I wake up" she told Romario.

"Yeah Saff, I will be back here as soon as I can be. I've

got to drive home first and try to get some sleep, so I am safe driving back. Do you need me to bring anything?"

"No, just get some sleep and get back here safely."

The next few days continued like that, Saff was able to stay in the post-natal ward, which was a short walk from the NICU, and Romario had to go home each night. They spent their days sat next to Elisha's incubator, trying to take in what was happening, listening to the doctors, the nurses, asking questions and trying to spend as much time as they could with their son. They sat and prayed together while they were there, not only for Elisha but for the other babies. It became a place where you got to know the other parents and their babies. It felt like a privilege to be able to pray for their needs too, and this was something Romario would do often, with the parents' permission of course.

Elisha was receiving a medication called Prostin which was in effect keeping the hole in his heart open until he was able to have surgery. Every day was getting harder, it was hard to be away from Romario and Sienna, and Levi no longer lived at home. It was hard not being with Elisha every night, and it was even harder to see him there in the NICU.

The NICU was a hard place to be generally, it was like a mini hospital inside the hospital. Some days they would turn up to see Elisha, but they were unable to enter the room due to an emergency with another baby, or they would have to leave the room while they did an x-ray of another baby. Each day the doctors did their ward rounds they waited nervously to hear their updates. They felt very out of control, like strangers in the house of someone else, not even sure if they could just pick their baby up without asking one of the nurses. They actually felt really blessed that they could even pick Elisha up because some of the other parents in the room were not able to do that with their babies. Some could only touch them through holes in the side of the incubator.

To look at Elisha, he didn't look like he was poorly or in need of surgery. Of course, he had all the wires and leads attached to him, but they were able to put clothes on him, pick him up, cuddle him and feed him through the feeding tube. One of the nurses said, "Elisha is one of the babies in the room that almost babysits himself as he doesn't require us to attend to him as much." To Saff and Romario, that was where they saw God, in those encouraging words, in those moments that Elisha was doing well. That feeling of running away kept rising inside Saff, if only they could all run away from this situation, to pick Elisha up and run far away with him to a safe place. But that wasn't going to change things, and right now this was the safest place for Elisha. Only God and prayer were going to get them through this. There was an expectation on them to trust the medical team implicitly but yet some people could not understand their trust in God. It was He that they had almost ten years of experience and knowledge of, seeing Him work in their lives, hearing His voice. That was what they were leaning on, and Saff wanted to stay right where she was in His presence.

21

Heart Surgery

Elisha had been in the Neonatal Intensive Care Unit at St Mary's Hospital in Manchester for six days when a bed became available at Alder Hey Children's Hospital in Liverpool. The nurses explained that this was where he would have his open-heart surgery and he would need to be transported in an ambulance with the blue lights flashing as he needed to get to the bed before an emergency was brought in.

"How you doing Romario?" Saff gently asked as he drove their car over to Alder Hey. He sighed and rubbed his face with one of his hands, the other tightly on the steering wheel.

"I just don't even know. This is hard, harder than I could have imagined. Seeing my little man like this just breaks my heart. I feel angry and confused. But we need to keep praying and supporting each other. How about you?" he glanced over to her.

"The same I guess, plus my body is still in pain and my ankles are super swollen. Have you seen the size of them?

They won't even fit into my trainers and my slippers need throwing in the bin I've worn them all over the hospital. But it was really good to see Sienna before, and Jasmine has been so good coming to see us so much. It's going to be weird being in Liverpool."

Arriving at Alder Hey Hospital they rushed to see Elisha up on the ward he had been taken to. They walked along the corridor and came to a room where the nurse directed them. There in the room was an incubator with their tiny little boy inside, swaddled tightly in a purple hospital blanket.

"He looks so tiny," said Saff, taking a deep intake of breath. Tears began to sting her eyes. "Will he be in here on his own?"

"The nurses monitor all of his machines from the nurse's station, over there" the nurse indicated, pointing to a station in the centre of the corridor. "I know that's probably different from where Elisha has just come from, having a nurse by his bed 24/7 but we are here 24/7 and we will be right here if he needs anything" the nurse walked over to the sofa in front of the window, "this becomes a bed by removing the back cushions so one of you can stay here. We have some fresh bedding over there in the cupboard and you can also pop clothes and bits in that cupboard too. The remote for the television on the wall is over on the windowsill and you guys have your own bathroom here with a shower. Let me show you how to close the blinds on the windows here that look into the corridor, and I will also show you how to use the lighting system. It can be dimmed and change colour which will hopefully create a nice relaxing atmosphere during the evenings and nighttime."

Saff sat in the tall, backed hospital armchair, next to the incubator, she reached down and rubbed her calves, her feet were aching as she tried to take in all the information the nurse was giving them.

"Someone will be up to show you across to The Ronald MacDonald House shortly. It is up to you guys if you both want to stay across there or one stay here. We know you are both tired and it will take a while to get your bearings but if you need anything else, we will be out here at the nurses' station" the nurse said before heading out of the room.

"I hope it's not too far to walk across the Ronald MacDonald House because I'm shattered, and my feet are killing me" Saff continued to rub her swollen feet. It was easy to forget about her own pains and that she had just given birth as all the focus was on Elisha, but sometimes it felt like the pains were reminding her that she needed to look after herself too.

Saff slid open the door to Elisha's room just a little after

9am one morning later in the week, Romario was still lying on the sofa bed. He opened his eyes as she closed the door behind her.

"Morning sleepy head," Saff said to him as she walked over to Elisha's incubator to see him sleeping. "How did you guys sleep?"

"Not well. I'm exhausted, to be honest. The machines just beeped all night, and I found it hard to stay asleep when the nurses came in to do his observations every three hours, and then of course there's feeding him every three hours. I'm glad we are taking it in turns staying here and in Mac House. I'm hoping I will be able to sleep tonight."

"Well I brought you a coffee and a pastry for breakfast and hopefully there will be time for you to have a nap at some point, I didn't sleep much as I kept waking up to express milk and then kept checking my phone to see if you had messaged" Saff put the coffee down on the floor next to Romario's head and handed him the bag with the pastries. "I feel like I've already spent a fortune this morning between these bits and putting some clothes on to wash over at Mac House. I was going to buy some bits from the restaurant, but it isn't cheap, and we should probably get something from there at lunchtime. I can't face doing any food shopping or cooking if I am honest."

Romario had got up off the sofa bed, "Let me just brush my teeth and get a wash, and we can figure out what we will eat for dinner later. It's probably going to take us some time to get used to the routine in this hospital, and then figuring out what we will eat and all that. Everything seems like it's a much bigger task than being at home where we just do things without thinking."

Elisha stirred in his incubator, and one of the monitors began beeping. Within a few seconds, a nurse opened the door.

"Morning guys. Let's see what little man is doing now eh?" she said brightly, striding over to Elisha. "Oh, I see, let me just reattach that right there for you" as she adjusted the monitor on his foot.

"I'm Ruth and I will be on with little Elisha today and tomorrow," the nurse said as she turned to Saff. The nurses changed on each shift and often each day, so much of the day was spent getting to know the new nurse and answering a lot of the same questions. "The doctors are already doing their ward rounds, so they will get to you soon and update you on their plans. If you guys need anything today, just come and see me."

"Thanks, Ruth" replied Saff as she pulled her journal and pen out of her bag so she could read what she had written yesterday. There were so many different doctors, nurses, and consultants to get to know, and so much medical language to learn that she found it easier to write in a journal. Romario came back out of the bathroom and began turning the bed back into a sofa and putting the bedding away.

"All these COVID restrictions are making things harder, not being able to have visitors, no one able to meet Elisha or come and sit with him so we can sleep or eat. And these masks, I really hate them you know, they feel suffocating having to wear one so much."

"I know, and I wonder what Elisha thinks of all these faces looking at him half covered up. It is a strange time to be alive" Saff responded, "Zoe rang me last night; Amy has had her baby. They are all ok, which is good, but she told me Dante is back inside. He's been locked up for a couple of weeks now."

"Oh really? Well, looks like nothing's changed there then, and a shame he will miss all those first with the baby. How do you feel?"

"It's so hard because it's an amazing miracle, a baby has been born, and it's healthy. But there is always that part of me that feels sad. Sad that that wasn't something we got to experience. Of course, I am happy for Amy, and Dante no matter what has happened, but my mind always goes back to why. Why is it ok for them but not for us? And thinking about the way Amy was living, it breaks my heart."

Romario came over and hugged her, "I understand, well

I don't but when I say that I mean I understand how you are feeling not why these things happen."

"But Zoe did have some other news, she said that with all that she sees us going through and the way we have still held on to her faith, she wants to know more. She's signed up for an Alpha course at a church near her!"

The door opened before Romario had a chance to respond; the doctors had arrived on their ward round. The doctors went over all the tests and scans they needed to keep doing. Elisha had to have his blood taken via heel prick every three hours which meant his poor little feet were covered in the pricks. He needed regular echocardiograms, or "echo", which is a scan used to look at the heart and nearby blood vessels, a type of ultrasound scan done on a machine that the doctors wheeled round the ward.

"We will also need to do a CT scan" explained cardiologist Dr Jones, "this will require Elisha to be put under General Anaesthetic as we need to keep him really still. We will get the anaesthetist to come and speak with you, and they will bring the consent form for you to sign and go over the risks that come with a GA."

Saff was writing down as much as she could, and Romario was asking questions. He wanted to understand why things were being done and if they were always necessary because it seemed like poor Elisha was being prodded and poked all day long. After the doctors had finished with them, they both sat on the sofa. Romario was yawning and rubbing his eyes, "I have never felt this tired in my whole life. It's not just a physical tiredness, there's a mental exhaustion alongside it. I just don't even know how we are going to get through surgery."

"I don't know either. The level of tiredness is unreal. I feel like I am on a Holiday Camp, but it's the worst holiday I've ever had, and I don't know when it's going to end" Saff was serious, "It's like we are living in The Matrix. This world that exists inside this hospital, disconnected from the outside world. We see the same people every day, walking around in their pyjamas and slippers. Going to get breakfast from the restaurant like it's the hotel buffet."

"Aww don't Saff, it's mad ain't it? I can't even focus on anything going on outside of the hospital. My head hurts just trying to understand what's going on here."

"I know but the rubbish thing is that we still do have to think about what was going on outside the hospital though. Sienna needs to be looked after and she's starting high school. We need to make sure things are ticking over at the house, bills are being paid, and all that. You've not long started your new job and you're still trying to sort your paternity leave out. I know the family have been doing as much as they can, bringing food, washing our clothes, looking after Sienna. It was so nice of Jasmine to bring Sienna, Levi, and my mum out to see us, and that they even got to peek through the window into our little room to get a glimpse of Elisha. I wish they could come in and see him, but I guess it was better than nothing."

Romario's eyes were closing, Saff got up to get one of the blankets and put it over him. "Get a little nap, it's fine" she whispered to him.

Saff sat in the hard-backed chair and watched Elisha as he slept. How she yearned to be at home with her family. That time when you just bring a baby home, and family and friends come over and visit. Bringing you gifts or offering to do little jobs in the house, the peacefulness of everyone being quiet while the baby sleeps, trying to catch a nap here and there, those things didn't exist in the hospital. Doctors and nurses were in and out of the room all day and night whether the baby was sleeping or not, or the parents! There was no quietness, just the hustle and bustle of the hospital. *A place that doesn't sleep,* thought Saff. She closed her eyes and prayed silently, *"God, I can feel this pressure building, it feels like we are in a pressure cooker and all the pain, frustration, lack of sleep, lack of control and understanding, are all bubbling away. I don't want it to explode. It is only by your grace that we have got this far. Please, please help us. We need you. Amen."*

In the run-up to the day of surgery, Romario and Saff were trying to prepare themselves for it. They had been praying for healing from God and had been hoping he wouldn't need the surgery at all but understood that God could heal through surgery too. The wonders of modern medicine had to be miraculous.

"The last few nights Elisha's oxygen saturations have been dipping below their accepted levels and the machine was beeping almost all last night. I don't think I slept at all." Just as Romario had finished speaking, the machines began beeping and suddenly several nurses rushed into the room. Saff and Romario stood back to let the nurses get around the incubator, their eyes moving from Elisha to the nurses searching their faces to see if they could work out how serious this was. Saff began silently praying but all she could do was say *God please help* over and over again.

Ruth was on shift today, "Elisha's heart rate is very fast at the moment and it's what we call Tachycardia. We have two choices, we can give him some medication to bring him out of it or we can dip him in cold water to shock him out of it, either way, it's very dangerous to leave him like this."

Saff looked at Elisha, he was fast asleep and seemed to be completely unaware and unfazed by all the commotion taking place around his bed.

"I really don't like the idea of cold water, he's a newborn baby, it doesn't seem nice," Saff said worriedly and looked to Romario. He looked pale and she suddenly noticed how tired he was looking.

All of a sudden, Elisha coughed, and the beeping stopped.

Ruth laughed, "Well it looks like he's brought himself out of it, and he's still asleep!! Panic over guys."

Saff reached for Romario's hand and squeezed it, hoping and praying this nightmare would end soon.

The surgery was planned for a couple of days later. Elisha was thirteen days old. The nurses had given them a little surgical gown. It was blue with little stars all over it and it was tiny.

"I didn't even know they made them this small" Saff exclaimed as she prepared to put Elisha in it. Tears were welling in her eyes, again.

They walked behind the incubator as the orderly pushed the bed Elisha had been placed in. The nurse on shift with them today was Georgia, she was chatting away to the orderly as they walked down the long white corridors. The words of the surgeon the day before were swirling around Saff's head *the surgery would take six to eight hours, many risks including a*

10% chance of mortality, it was all too much to take in, but she knew that the risks of him not having the surgery outweighed the risks of him having it.

"You guys can give him a little kiss once he is under the anaesthetic" said Georgia as they turned to push the bed into a room to the left of the corridor, "and then I will walk you back up to the ward."

Leaving Elisha there, they walked back up to the ward behind Georgia. Neither of them could speak and Saff was sobbing as softly as she could.

"Will you go back to Mac House and try to get some rest?" asked Georgia as they entered the door back onto the ward.

"We had wanted to go to a church up the road, they are opening their doors today to pray for Elisha, but of course, we aren't able to leave the hospital, are we?" said Romario.

Georgia nodded and smiled sympathetically.

"So, I think we will go to the hospital chapel for a while and then yes, back to Mac House to try to get some rest."

Saff and Romario were lay in the single beds in their room at Ronald Macdonald when the phone in the room rang. Even though they were expecting and waiting for the call, it made them jump. It was the surgeon; Romario held the receiver and Saff leaned over to she could have her ear as close as she could. Elisha was being settled in the Paediatric Intensive Care Unit (PICU) and the surgery had been a success. Saff silently thanked God.

Walking down the corridors to the PICU, Saff felt herself picking up her speed to keep up with Romario. She felt like she was walking around some kind of spaceship. The walls were huge, and the corridors were long with brightly coloured doors appearing now and then. Romario stopped; this was the unit where Elisha was. Saff grabbed his hand and took a deep breath as he pushed open the door. The room was huge with about five or six babies in total, all surrounded by so many machines, each allocated their own nurse as the care was one-to-one and hooked up to a lot of medication. Beside each bed were two chairs so parents could sit next to their baby. They walked over to the bed, their pace slowing, Saff felt the tears prickle her eyes, and she took a sharp intake of breath. His beautiful little face was all puffy due to fluid, his chest was still open so they could check on his heart, but it was covered with gauze, there were so many wires, and so many machines and he was intubated as he was heavily sedated, so they needed to breathe for him.

They sat down and just held hands for a moment before a nurse approached them. She introduced herself but Saff immediately forgot her name as she began listening to her explain that Elisha was on some very strong painkillers and sedatives which he would need to be weaned off as the days went by. The nurse told them they could sit for as long as they needed and the only time the ward would be closed to visitors was during shift handovers each morning and evening unless there was an emergency. She also encouraged them to get some sleep back at Mac House while he was there, she pointed to the whiteboard behind the bed to show them that they had all their contact details there should they need to contact us. They left the unit feeling relieved that the surgery was successful, but the journey was far from over.

Epilogue

Sinking down onto the sofa in her new comfy pyjamas, Saff picked up her cup of coffee in her own mug that she enjoyed drinking from and snuggled under a blanket.

"I actually can't believe we are finally home Romario. I think I may have lost my mind if we had stayed much longer, five weeks has felt like forever. I mean I nearly lost it last week when I had to come back and help Sienna getting her things together for school. I feel like I have had so much taken away from me as a mother, and missed so many firsts that I probably took for granted last time. And seeing that nurse put my baby in a pram for the first time and I wasn't there, for some reason that was like the straw that broke the camel's back. Out of all things, that was the thing that pushed me over the edge."

Saff and Romario recalled that particular incident, and how Saff had felt unable to go back to the hospital and spent the night at home alone, in bed crying. She had wanted to give up. She didn't even feel like she was a mum, everything had been taken away from her, the nurses were doing her job, what did they need her for? Those familiar feelings of not wanting to live any more were strong at that time. How was she meant to bond with her baby with everything that had been going on? She had felt like a stranger to her son, just another person in the room. What difference would it have made if she had not been there?

"Saff, you've done great. You really have and you're a great mum. Elisha needs you and so do I. We've overcome a massive hurdle and now we have to get through the next season we are in. We can do this. You can do this. We've got God on our side, and He has brought us through this because without him, I don't know if I would be standing today, and I'm sure you would say the same. I am so glad to have us all back at home and to start having some normality back. As much as we can anyway. There's a plan in place with the community nurses' weekly visits, the health visitor, the dietician, and all the guys at Alder Hey. We just have to take it one day at a time. I don't know why we have had to go through this, why it had to be our little boy that this happened to. I hear of so many others that we know having babies with no issues and I would never wish this on anyone, but I always think, why was it us? It's like our road will never be easy and we know this journey isn't over as we have another surgery to face, but I know we will always overcome because we have Jesus, and he has already overcome."

Saff leaned forward to check on Elisha who was fast asleep in his Moses basket in between them. He was still sleeping soundly, his little chest rising and falling which brought Saff so much peace.

She sat back in her seat, "I know it's been hard, and I've really been thinking about the scripture in John, *"I have told you these things, so that in me you may have peace. In this world, you will have trouble. But take heart! I have overcome the world."* *(John 16:33)* God tells us that we will have trouble, not that we might but that we will. He knew what was coming and He will carry us through. We know that by others hearing our story, they will be encouraged, and I pray that they will be encouraged even more to know that God was at the centre throughout. I hope it's ok for Zoe to come over and visit, I'm dying to let her meet Elisha. She told me that Amy's mum and dad are helping her with the baby and Amy has agreed to go to rehab which is great. She also tells me that she's got some good news that she wants to tell me in person, and I am really hoping she is one of those who have been encouraged by our journey and can see God has been our strength."

Authors Note

Whatever you think you have done bad in your life, God still loves you and you can receive forgiveness. You are never too far gone. Saff came to God broken and an absolute mess. Come to God as you are, with all your faults and failures. Once Saff realised that she needed a saviour and understood what Jesus did for her and you on that cross, she was able to fully surrender her life. To be able to surrender that control that she had felt she needed to hold on to so tightly after everything she had been through, that's when she was changed. She no longer wanted to run away from herself.

I love the Bible verse below; I feel it describes the transformation Saff experienced. The things that fell away from her, the things she had to work harder to stay away from, and the new self she found herself putting on every day.

3 For you died, and your life is now hidden with Christ in God. 4 When Christ, who is your life, appears, then you also will appear with him in glory. 5 Put to death, therefore, whatever belongs to your earthly nature: sexual immorality, impurity, lust, evil desires, and greed, which is idolatry. [6] Because of these, the wrath of God is coming. [7] You used to walk in these ways, in the life you once lived. [8] But now you must also rid yourselves of all such things as these: anger, rage, malice, slander, and filthy language from your lips. [9] Do not lie to each other, since you have taken off your old self with its practices [10] and have put on the new self, which is being renewed in knowledge in the image of its Creator. Colossians 3:3-10

Through Saffs story, I wanted to show that becoming a Christian isn't waving a magic wand and then you live a life free from trouble. Jesus tells us in the Bible *"I have told you these things, so that in me you may have peace. In this world, you will have trouble. But take heart! I have overcome the world." John 16:33*

This verse shows us that we will have trouble, but Jesus tells us to take heart because he has overcome the world. The burden becomes lighter as Jesus walks through it with you; giving you hope and peace at times when chaos and pain are present in our lives.

I pray that this story has inspired you, encouraged you and if you are going through a difficult situation, I pray it gives you

hope. Hope in Jesus. There is no other hope like it, and I urge
you to seek him. You too can have a new life, a new start. You
can receive that change, the love and the forgiveness you have
been longing for.

If you would like that, there is a simple prayer below
that you can read out loud. The prayer isn't what saves you,
Romans 10:9-10 says that *"if you declare with your mouth,
"Jesus is Lord," and believe in your heart that God raised him
from the dead, you will be saved. For it is with your heart that
you believe and are justified, and it is with your mouth that you
profess your faith and are saved."*

**"Dear God, I know I'm a sinner, and I ask for your
forgiveness. I believe Jesus Christ is Your Son. I believe that
He died for my sin and that you raised Him to life. I want to
trust Him as my Saviour and follow Him as Lord, from this
day forward. Guide my life and help me to do your will. I pray
this in the name of Jesus. Amen."**

If you prayed this prayer, please tell another Christian. If
you don't know any, feel free to connect with me via social
media and I can see if I can connect you with a local church.
I pray that you will know the transforming power of Jesus
Christ.

<u>Running from Myself - You Version Bible Study</u>

Have you ever felt like you wanted to run away from a situation, a place, a person, or even yourself? Have you tried everything and don't know where to turn? Maybe you've been told that you will never be able to change. This plan will look at how we can move from desiring change to being dramatically changed and staying changed.

https://www.bible.com/reading-plans/45973-running-from-myself

About the Author

Amber Gilbert is a Christian speaker and author who loves reading, drinking coffee and eating chocolate – not in any particular order! Originally from Manchester, she turned to Christianity in 2012 after growing tired of her party lifestyle and making bad choices. She is now passionate about sharing her faith to inspire and encourage others to overcome life's challenges.

Running from Myself is Amber's debut novel. Her writing reflects her faith and is inspired by personal experiences.

Amber now lives in Cheshire with her husband Marvin, a rapper and evangelist, and together they are raising three children. One of their children has a congenital heart defect, which has led them down an unexpected path. You can find out more on Instagram @azariahthechampion

Connect with her on Facebook, Instagram and Tik Tok by searching for @itsafaiththing, visit www.itsafaiththing.com to subscribe to Amber's blog posts.

Acknowledgements

My biggest thanks go to God for bringing me out of the darkness, for the sacrifice He made with His son Jesus so I can live forgiven and redeemed, and for inspiring this story and giving me the gift of being able to write it.

I want to thank my amazing husband, Marvin for being my biggest cheerleader, encouraging me along the way, and believing in me even when I didn't believe in myself. Knowing you are fighting in my corner keeps me going. To my beautiful daughter Diaz, you are amazing and your voice matters, don't ever forget that! There is so much more to come for you. Azariah the Champion, my strong boy full of character who puts a smile on my face every day, I cannot wait to see all the amazing things you will do in life. Kyro, my first-born son, keep going. I love you and will keep cheering you on.

Thank you to my family who read early drafts of my book, my mum Ava, my sister Jade, and my Mother-in-law Maria. I appreciate that you were comfortable with the story, particularly those bits inspired by my life.

Thank you to the rest of the family of which there are too many to name. I love seeing you all going from strength to strength.

Thank you to my boss Barry Woodward, for encouraging me and offering advice on this journey, and for creating opportunities where you could.

Thank you to friends who read drafts and encouraged me along the way; Emma Nicholson, Xiayah, and Rod Williams. Thank you to the lovely Louise Coop for being one of the first to review my book and I look forward to the review being published on your Instagram and TikTok.

Big thank you to Laura Murray at Peanut Designs for walking alongside me, patiently, through the self-publishing route, for my beautiful book cover, and for all of your encouragement and help.

Thank you to Fiona Myles for reading my book and inviting me to join the Write That Book Challenge with Michael Heppell, which kickstarted my writing. Thank you for all the teaching you shared Michael, and to the guys in the How to Be Brilliant Facebook group for being brilliant! Thank you to the Association of Christian Writers, Tyldesley 'Saturday Sentence' Writing Group and the Kingdom Story Writers, for all the new friendships made around a shared love of writing.

Thank you to those who offered me writing advice, including my aunt, Mandasue Heller, and Tarnya at TC Publishing. Every bit, no matter how small or big has been helpful.

I want to thank Mark and Rachel Cowling for training me on the New Wine Discipleship Course all those years ago and becoming great friends, thank you for being so supportive and reading my book. Thank you to Rosie for being there from the start and being part of unveiling a whole new world to me. Thank you to Alison for being courageous in sharing your faith with me in the workplace and pointing me toward our local church Christ Church Pennington. Thank you to Matt and Jude for being my youth work buddies all those years ago, I am sure I learned as much as the young people through our Impact youth group sessions.

Thank you to my pastors Paul and Vicky Lloyd, and those at Victory Outreach Manchester, for your spiritual covering and prayers. I also want to acknowledge and thank those at Christ Church Pennington and Sports Village Church who were part of my early faith walk.

A big thank you to all those at Alder Hey Hospital for their care and treatment of Azariah, particularly our surgeon Dr. Ram who performed both his open-heart surgeries.

And of course to our prayer warriors who covered us and encouraged us throughout Azariah's journey.

My final thank you goes to you for reading this book. Thank you for taking your time and money to buy it, I cannot thank you enough. If you have enjoyed it, please do share it with someone who needs to know they are loved and that there is hope for them! Thank you.

ENDORSEMENTS

Amber is the real deal, and this book carries the weight of her experiences as she's walked with Jesus. Reading it will enrich your life and add some real value to you as you journey with Christ.

- Rev. Paul Lloyd, Lead Pastor at Victory Outreach Manchester and author of Leading Broken People.

I love how Amber weaves part of her journey into this narrative. I recommend this great read!

- Barry Woodward, Author of Once an Addict.

Running from myself is an unfiltered glimpse into the raw and real world of a life looking for love and acceptance. Saff's (the main character) journey is portrayed with such authenticity that you not only feel every moment of her pain but also the joy and hope she found in her darkest hours. Can't recommend this enough.

– Rodric Williams, Author of The Real Deal.

I have known Amber for a few years now as a member of our church. In this book, she shares the testimony of her life using a wonderful story. Amber is the real deal living out her faith in Jesus Christ through real-life circumstances. My husband and I are those pastors she sat with and told the worst news she'd ever received about her son. I've seen her cling to her faith in God, and I've seen the miraculous ways He has met Amber and her family. I recommend this book to you whether you've experienced domestic violence, or addiction or are a single parent pressing through life and those unexpected roadblocks that we face even as Christians. This book is raw, real, and, most importantly, it's inspired by truth.

- **Vicky Lloyd - Pastor at Victory Outreach Manchester, UK & Germany and Author of The Bionic Woman.**

I love this story! Amber shows us how God hovers over us in the darkest valley and the highest mountain moments of our lives. The Bible tells us people can overcome all the powers of death and shame in this world through God's saving work and the power of our testimonies. I'm certain this story will help many triumph as overcomers.

- **Mark Cowling, Church and Community Leader**

References:

Worship Songs:

Great is the Lord - Steve McEwan *© Copyright 1985 Body Songs

Lord I lift your name on High – Rick Founds Copyright © 1989

Maranatha Praise, Inc

Bible references:

Therefore if anyone is in Christ, he is a new creature; the old things passed away; behold, new things have come. 2 Corinthians 5:17 ESV

Do not be unequally yoked with unbelievers. 2 Corinthians 6:14 ESV

Let all bitterness and wrath and anger and clamour and slander be put away from you, along with all malice. Be kind to one another, tender-hearted, forgiving one another, as God in Christ forgave you. Ephesians 4:31 ESV

Every branch in me that does not bear fruit he takes away, and every branch that does bear fruit he prunes, that it may bear more fruit. John 15:2 ESV

For those who love God all things work together for good. Romans 8:28 ESV

In my weakness He is made strong (paraphrase) 2 Corinthians 12:9-11 ESV

I have told you these things, so that in me you may have peace. In this world you will have trouble. But take heart! I have overcome the world John 16:33 ESV

For you died, and your life is now hidden with Christ in God. When

Christ, who is your[a] life, appears, then you also will appear with him in glory. Put to death, therefore, whatever belongs to your earthly nature: sexual immorality, impurity, lust, evil desires, and greed, which is idolatry. Because of these, the wrath of God is coming. You used to walk in these ways, in the life you once lived. But now you must also rid yourselves of all such things as these: anger, rage, malice, slander, and filthy language from your lips. Do not lie to each other, since you have taken off your old self with its practices and have put on the new self, which is being renewed in knowledge in the image of its Creator. Colossians 3:3-10 ESV

If you declare with your mouth, "Jesus is Lord," and believe in your heart that God raised him from the dead, you will be saved. For it is with your heart that you believe and are justified, and it is with your mouth that you profess your faith and are saved. Romans 10:9-10 ESV

Music references:

Honey by Mariah Carey, 1997

Shake it Off by Mariah Carey, 2005

The Emancipation by Mimi by Mariah Carey, 2005

A Whole New World, music by Alan Menken and lyrics by Tim Rice Aladdin 1992

Crazy, Sexy, Cool by TLC 1994

Misc:

Prime Minister Boris Johnsons televised speech on 23rd March 2020

Printed in Great Britain
by Amazon